THE DIARY OF DORCAS GOOD
CHILD WITCH OF SALEM

THE DIARY OF
Dorcas Good
CHILD WITCH OF SALEM

by

Rose Earhart

ℙB

Pendleton
Books

Published by Pendleton Books
666 Fifth Avenue Suite 365
New York, NY 10103

Printed in the United States of America

Library of Congress Catalog Card Number: 98-88603

Earhart, Rose/The Diary of Dorcas Good, Child Witch of Salem

ISBN 1-893221-00-8

FIRST EDITION

CONTENTS

FOR MY HUSBAND, JIM,

AND

MY BROTHER, DAVID.

ACKNOWLEDGMENTS

I would like to thank the Peabody-Essex Museum, the Salem Athenaeum, the Salem Public Library, the Witch Museum, the New England Pirate Museum, the Witch House, the Wax Museum and the Witch Dungeon, all of Salem, Massachusetts. I would also like to thank the Peabody Library of Danvers, Massachusetts, that stands near many of the sites of the original happenings in this book. In addition, there are four authors to whom I am deeply indebted; Richard Trask, Francis Hill, Anne Llewellyn Barstow, and Shirley Jackson. Thanks also to Laura Bjorklund of Higginson Books and to Frank Sweetser for all their help. Most of all I would like to thank my husband, Jim, who has been a constant source of encouragement.

All Photographs were taken by James H. Kilroy of Salem, MA.

THE DIARY OF DORCAS GOOD
CHILD WITCH OF SALEM

PROLOGUE

Hannibelle Black to Mercy Phillips:

January 21st, 1711

Friend Goodwife Phillips,

Young Dorcas and I are leaving Salem Village at dawn. That should give us time enough to make our way to Gallows Hill and finish our great task. If not for the wolves and Indians that roam the woods we would have departed sooner and tried to find our way by the light of the moon, but it would do no good to be captured by savages or torn apart by wild beasts. I know that the snow is deep, and the cold will be harsh upon us, but to stay any longer would truly be the end of all we have fought for. Even you, my saintly friend, must realize what will occur if we remain one more moment under the roof of that devil, William Good. We have suffered greatly at his hands, hiding the marks upon our bodies and sheltering the wounds upon our souls. There has been only you, our dearest Mercy, to turn to for a kind word or a loving caress.

I have held Dorcas' sobbing body for hours now and there is no stilling of her tears. All she can do is cry "Mama", over and over again. We both know that Mama will never come, save as a loving spirit. Poor Sarah Good's bones lie rotting under the rocks where she was placed many years ago.

Even now, William Good, Dorcas' fiend of a father, sits at his table at Ingersoll's gleefully telling of the thirty pounds of silver he has received for his foul deed. It is indeed fitting that he was first in line to gather his 'due' from the general court. I myself heard him say he put to paper the mark that has made him a comfortable man. And what did rich William grant

1

to us for our evening meal? Nothing but bloody wounds and the usual thin broth with a bit of green rye bread. A curse upon William, gorging himself upon fine victuals and rum at Ingersoll's Tavern.

Never will we forget that it was William Good who spoke the foul words that put the noose around Sarah's neck. He said, "Sarah is an enemy to all good, and is either a witch now or will be one very quickly." His words against Sarah still swirl in my mind and fill me with a madness that is rage itself. Such a man surely deserves heaven's righteous judgment here on earth. I know that if I remain under his eye another day my hand will find a way to still William Good forever.

You see now why we must flee. I will not do the devil's work for him, and I cannot leave young Dorcas behind. She would be left to suffer tenfold for my desertion and that I could not bear. It would be far better for us to perish in the wind and snow of cruel New England than to suffer any longer.

So here we sit, waiting in the dark until old William stumbles through the door to untie us and then lay upon his cot in a rum soaked stupor. Pray God he sleeps like the dead. Do not grieve for us, dearest friend. I send this message to you in our secret way and leave behind the hidden diary Dorcas gave us. Guard it well and wait. When the time is right, use it as an instrument of vengeance upon all those who say there was no harm done to Dorcas Good, child witch of Salem.

Forever Yours,
Mistress H. Black

PART ONE

MOTHER AND CHILD

FIRST ENTRY

Dear Little Book,

My name is Dorcas Good and I am a child of Salem Village. I have two best friends who are much older than I and will not leave me in peace until I speak to your pages, Little Book. These friends are Goody Mercy Phillips who listens, and loves me beyond compare, and Mistress Hannibelle Black, who is so gifted that she tells us we must hide her light from the elders less they punish her for being an 'improper woman'.

It is because of my two friends that you exist at all, Little Book. Hannibelle said "that it was time for me to speak my thoughts to you". She said, in a firm Hannibelle voice, that she was "tired of seeing me mope about watching the birds fly overhead and speaking only in my mind". I would have run from her then and there had not Goody Phillips echoed her words in a more kindly manner. She placed her sweet arms about my neck and whispered into my ear, "let Hannibelle have her way darling, what harm could it do?"

What harm indeed! We all know that if I give in and let Mistress Hannibelle put down the words that Goody Mercy draws from my soul, Father may have us whipped, or worse. Well we know it is a crime for a woman from Salem Village to be anything but a loyal and loving servant, ignorant of all fine knowledge and higher ambitions. But that is not Hannibelle's way. She can read and write. In many ways she is as learned as any master from Harvard College. Why, I'll warrant that Cotton Mather himself is not so skilled with a pen as our Hannibelle Black. No one would ever believe that Hannibelle is self taught, gleaning her knowledge on the sly. There are those that would say her brilliant skills were a gift from the devil. And now she has rounded upon me and wishes to hear my tale from first to last. I cried to Mercy that a child's tale could not possibly be of interest to any but the child. That was when Goody Mercy Phillips held me tight and hugged me until the tears ran down my cheeks. "You are wrong, my dearest one," she said, calming me with her motherly manner, "yours is a tale beyond believing and must be told if you are ever to free the woman within you. Until all is said you will remain but a small child imprisoned by stone and chain".

It was then that I knew my friends spoke the truth. I was indeed imprisoned, not in body, but in spirit. Bless their courage and their love. It will be the hangman for us all if the elders discover you, Little Book.

SECOND ENTRY

The people of the village say that Mama was always mean and contentious, but that is not true! She was the warmth of the sun to me. How she would make me chuckle and then laugh outright at her imitations of the fine folk who lived in Salem Town nearby. I will never forget how she used to clear her throat, stick her thumbs in her imaginary pantaloons, and grumble out a sermon full of damnation and silliness, just like the esteemed Reverend John Higginson. Then there was her mocking of wealthy Philip English and his beautiful wife Mary. We all knew that they loved each other more that was proper, and Mama took full advantage of their infatuation. She would play first the man and then the woman, swooning in her own arms until overcome with an unseemly passion that was absolutely ridiculous in its pantings and groanings. "So much for fine folks and good manners", she would say to me with a wink. "Why, Mama herself came from such and you can see where riches can lead."

It was true. Mama had grown up in comfort. She often spoke of her blissful days in Wenham where she was treated with the respect due the daughter of a well-to-do innkeeper. Mama told the story over and over again about how her happiness had ended the day her beloved father went mad and drowned himself. Mama was only a girl when her world was transformed from one of happiness to one of evil injustice. It was her own mother who turned upon her, betraying young Sarah Good in a cruel manner. My grandmother Solart remarried, and her new husband cheated Mama out of every bit of her inheritance. So there was Mama, nineteen and alone. She was ripe for any comfort offered her. It came quickly in the form of Daniel Poole, Mama's first husband. He was a poor indentured servant who saw Mama's inheritance as a way out of his wretched condition. Mama said Goodman Poole was a spendthrift who often left her alone with only a shift to wear and nothing to eat. She said he was deeply disappointed because he married her for her money and found, out only after it was too late, that Sarah's new step-father intended to keep every penny of her inheritance. Mama said that Daniel would leave her to cry on the earthen floor while he went about running up debts that he couldn't pay. When he died, Mama was cursed with the load of Daniel's debts as well as her own poverty. There was nothing left to do but remarry quickly or starve.

Salvation came in the form of my father, God curse him. Goodman William Good still hoped that there was some way of recovering Mama's money. How disappointed he must have been to find himself saddled with Daniel Poole's debts as well as his own. His greed turned to bitterness and hate for Mama. Mama said if it hadn't been for me she would have gone mad and thrown herself in the lake like Grandfather Solart.

I was born during the first blizzard of the season in 1688. Mama says that as far as she can remember it was the middle of November. I was a blessing to her, no matter what Father said about us all starving if Mama could not get on her feet and beg for food. Mama had lost four babies before me and I was her dearest companion. She called me her miracle child.

Father threw us out into the bitter weather as soon as he could. We were forced to go from house to house begging for our bread and butter. William Good stayed at home sitting at his loom with idle fingers until Mama became sick. It was only when she took to her bed with fever that he offered himself out as a laborer to the villagers. But he hated any who tried to hire him and he brought his hate home to us. My first memory of William Good is his hand across my face, shaking loose my new teeth. I know the baby Jesus says that it is wrong to hate, but I hated Father, not for what he did to me, but for his cruelty to Mama. He would whip and beat her until the blood ran down her arms, and her dear face was swollen into shapes like the ones she would make up in jest. I am still ashamed that I couldn't stop him. I remember pounding upon him with my small fists until he threw me against a wall. Mama cradled me in her arms and told me never to fight Father again, no matter what he did. She told me I must live, because I was her precious Dorcas and she would die if anything were to happen to me.

It's funny, but even now I believe I am precious and still Dorcas. Mama taught me that.

Note from Goodwife Phillips: Here Dorcas begins to tell her tale as if she were living it once again. Hannibelle and I believe her healing started at this moment.

THIRD ENTRY

"Can we stop now," I pleaded as I held onto Mama's chilblained fingers with my small soft ones.

"Not yet, darling. We haven't begged nearly enough for supper. You wouldn't want your father to go hungry," said Mama, smiling down at me. "It's amazing how one so small can bring such comfort," she said as she gave me a hug.

"But my feet are cold and I can see my breath in the air," I argued as I bent down to rub my little red toes.

"Perhaps the next home will grant some covering for those sweet little feet," muttered Mama as she pushed me in front of her. If she had been able to, Mama would have carried me, but I know now that she was heavily pregnant and sick with worry.

I cheerfully hurried after Mama, excited by her words. Perhaps if there was a pair of shoes for me than there would be ones for Mama too! Even at my young age I knew it was too late in the season to be barefoot. My fourth birthday had just passed, and Mama had given me her own stockings, cut down to cover my legs, as a gift. It was to her sorrow that she discovered I had outgrown the little shoes she had begged for me but a month before. As a result we were both walking around bare legged and barefooted in the cold November weather, while the hard won stockings went abandoned in a drawer until Mama found a pair of shoes for me.

"Look Mama!" I cried, "there is a fine house now. And see, there are girls running about. They seem so much older than me, Mama. Maybe their mother would have some used shoes for the asking."

"Oh child," said Mama, "that is not a place we should stop. 'Tis the house of Goodman Zachariah Herrick and his family. Don't you remember that we stopped there once asking for shelter? How cruelly they turned us away. They said it was because poor old Mama was smoking her pipe and they were in fear of her, but the truth of it was they wanted none of us. We were not even good enough to seek shelter in the barn that held their animals."

With those words Mama began to chuckle and then to laugh outright. "I'll never forget, daughter, how that pimply faced son of Herrick's, Henry I think his name was, followed us out of the yard. Remember how we lingered by the barn as long as we could? It was a pleasure seeing that fat young man shiver in the cold. How afraid he was that elder Herrick would beat him if we so as much as huddled against the barn door for shelter from the snow."

"Why I do remember, Mama!" I said joining in her laughter. How funny fat Henry had looked as he tried to stare Mama down. His face was so red! "It was so clever of you to pretend to curse him Mama! I remember that your exact words were, 'it would cost Zachariah Herrick one or two of his best cows if you weren't given shelter'."

"And it did too, didn't it lovey," said Mama hugging me tight. "It was not long after that young Jonathan Batchelor, Herrick's grandson, came bleating around our house looking for two young calves that had been spirited away. 'Twas not Mama who took them, but I can tell you daughter that I was rightly glad the Almighty had seen in his wisdom to punish the meanness of the Herrick clan."

"Why are people always so mean to us, Mama?" I asked snuggling into her thin skirt.

"Why darling," sighed Mama," I suppose it is because they hate our poverty. You see Mama was once like they are and now she has fallen low. If it could happen to Sarah Good it could happen to any one of them."

"Ann Putnam's mama was left with nothing and Ann says that her father was cheated out his portion by his bad brother Joseph. Why doesn't Ann have to beg like I do Mama?"

"Because you are a Good, not a Putnam, Dorcas," said Mama grimly. "The Putnam family must own everything they can set their eyes upon. They are like a group of greedy children who own a great pile of gold. They can't bear to think of anyone else, no matter the need, taking anything away from them. If a person so much as stole one farthing from the great Putnam gold pile, the Putnams would spend the whole stinking pile

10

of gold hounding that person to justice rather than giving those who need it some charity. They must have it all. Dogs in a manger is what they are and that's a fact. Ah well, at least we know that their covetness will be punished by the Almighty. They are great sinners Dorcas, for all their righteous ways."

"How can that be, Mama? They sit right up front on meeting days and fill half the seats with their family. Why, Ann says that her father really owns the church and Reverend Parris is only there because he is nice to Master Putnam and does whatever he wants. The Putnams must be good if Reverend Parris likes them so much."

"The Reverend has a family to feed, Dorcas. Never forget what I tell you now. When a man's stomach is at stake he will do anything."

"Anything, Mama?"

"Yes, my love, anything including murder. It would be a good thing for you if you stayed far away from such folk."

"I don't understand, Mama. They always give us what we ask for."

"That is because Mama knows Reverend Parris' slave Tituba, sweetheart. The Putnams, for all their holy ways, are afraid of hags who mutter and curse. Mistress Putnam would rather give me the whole of her cellar than to run afoul of my evil eye. They are just making sure that they aren't cursed by the devil's handmaiden 'tis all," said Mama cackling as she relit her pipe and hurried me along.

"Come now daughter, I see the Reverend's house straight ahead. If we are fortunate Tituba will be baking corn bread and heating cider!"

FOURTH ENTRY

As we approached Reverend Parris' house I could smell something sweet and wonderful.

"What is it, Mama? It smells like heaven!"

"Why 'tis gingerbread, my little love," said Mama as a beautiful smile lit her face. "Hurry now and pray that luck is with us."

"Isn't praying for luck a bad thing, Mama?"

"Not if your names are Sarah and Dorcas Good," shouted Mama yelling above the howling wind.

As we approached the sturdily built wooden structure, the door flew open revealing a woman who was as brown as the door she held open against the wind.

"Hurry now," she cried as the wind tried its best to drown out her voice. "I see a storm cloud gaining on you and it would be your end if you were to be caught standing in the snow, such as you are."

Mama and I ran towards the voice and just managed to get inside the house before the storm struck. Reverend Parris' house was one of the largest in the village. How unlike our small one room cabin it appeared to me. I often thought that good Queen Mary and King William must have lived in just such a place. But Mama said their home was a castle, which is a house even grander that a Reverend's house.

The Parris house had four rooms, two on each floor, and a small room behind it that Tituba said her husband John Indian had to sleep in when he was drunk. It was a joy to stand upon the large wooden planks that served as the floor. How much warmer it was than our own cold earthen floor. In the main room was an enormous fireplace that filled the room with heat. The caldrons, hanging from hooks attached to the bricks, held savory stew and soup. There was even some spicy bread baking in the wall oven on one side. To me, the Parris house was heaven itself on that cold November day.

"Oh my", laughed the beautifully sumptuous brown woman wearing a turban of gold and red, "weather like this makes me wish I had never been born."

"Don't say that, Tituba," I said hugging the woman's knees with all my might, "you are the beat story teller I ever heard. How sad I would be without you. Mama says that your stories about Barbados make us forget all about the cold New England weather. Is it true it never snows in Barbados?"

"Very true, Mistress Dorcas," said Tituba with her eyes twinkling down at me, "and if I had listened to my brothers I would have stayed there rather than following worthless John Indian to this lonely place. My brothers would have helped me run away if I had been willing, but I thought I was in love. That is why I stayed with John and found myself here. It is so far from my beautiful green blue sea."

"But the sea isn't ever green," I said, thinking that Tituba was telling me ia story.

"It is where I come from, Dorcas. Ask the Reverend Parris if you don't believe me. We all know he would rather be roasted on yon spit rather than tell a lie."

"And what a fine scene that would be, eh Tituba," laughed Mama as she headed towards the great fireplace.

"Yes, and I'd be glad to turn the spit until my arms ached if it were ever to come to pass," I heard Tituba grumble as she followed Mama over to the fireplace.

The room was a marvel of wonderful sights and spells. Try as Reverend Parris might, there was no erasing the peculiarly fascinating style of his Caribbean slave. Here and there in the room lay touches of color that the Reverend must have thought of as evil, but he was often to busy to take the time to stop Tituba. Even if he had destroyed the bit or ribbon here, or the artfully arranged leaves and dried flowers there, she would have quickly replaced them with something more exotic. How she must have yearned for her home and family.

"I hear your mistress is still sick," said Mama leaning towards the fire and breathing in the heady aromas.

"Yes," said Tituba. "Mistress Elizabeth never got over having baby Susannah five years ago. She ails all the time and runs me ragged with her spells and fevers. It's a shame too. The children won't listen to me the same they would to their mother."

"But I hear nine year old Betty is an angel," said Mama, boldly taking a bit of cloth from beside the fire and opening the door of the bread oven.

"Aye she is, Goody Good," said Tituba, "but that devil of an Abigail encourages even little Betty to mock me and be naughty. Abigail Williams seems to forget she's only an orphaned niece with not a penny to her name. She should be helping me, rather than running about the village with her pack of friends. If not for the Parris' kindness she would have found herself starving in the snow. She sees fit to pay them back by bedeviling me with her tricks and using up my time begging for dolls and spells. Why she's even taken to bringing others here so I can amuse them too! Just think how Reverend Parris would beat me if he knew. That is why I keep on. Abigail threatens to tell him if I don't do what she and her friends want. It was an evil day when I first told them about the magic of my land. It shames me to think that just yesterday poor little Susannah went without dinner because I was kept too busy dropping eggs into a cup trying to satisfy Ann Putnam's curiosity about her future sweethearts."

"Tituba, my friend," said Mama, so alarmed that she put down the pan of gingerbread she was cutting, "you must stop! There is no telling what Reverend Parris will do to you if he finds you've been teaching the girls magic!"

"Tisn't magic at all," laughed Tituba, breaking off a piece of the wondrous bread and handing it to me, "Tis just a few tricks to keep them quiet."

"But many have been burned for such tricks," said Mama looking about the room with alarmed eyes.

FIFTH ENTRY

It was at that moment the door flew open and several young girls tumbled through. They were laughing and brushing the snow from their capes. Even bundled up as they were, I recognized little Betty Parris with her eleven year old cousin Abigail Williams. The other two girls who were giggling at some joke told by twelve year old Ann Putnam were strangers to me. They gave us a disdainful glance and boldly brushed past, heading for the bedroom that was to the right. Ann spied the gingerbread clutched in my small fingers and swooped down upon me. She deftly snatched it from my hand.

I must have cried out because she said, "hush now Dorcas Good, you know that stale bread is fine enough for poor girls." With those cruel words she followed her friends into the bedroom beyond and slammed the door behind her. I stood there stunned at first, and then burst into tears.

"Never you mind little one," said Tituba gathering me into her strong arms as I cried uncontrollably, "Tituba will find you another piece of gingerbread, even bigger than the one that selfish miss stole from you. Can't you manage a sweet smile for me?"

I looked up at the kindly Caribbean woman and tried to smile, but the tears would have their way. There was no stopping the sadness that clutched my heart.

"But Ann is right, Tituba," I sobbed as I clutched her wool gown tightly, "I am poor and all I deserve is stale bread. Everyone knows it. God punished me for trying to be finer than I should be."

"What nonsense is that, Dorcas Good," stormed my mother she as grabbed me from Tituba's arms and set me on my feet in front of her.

"It's not nonsense Mama," I said, the shock of her anger stopping my tears. "Wherever we go they call us poor and useless and say that if Father were less idle others wouldn't have to pay for his family's keep. Father is idle and we do live off of other people's charity. Don't be mad Mama, I promise I'll never ask for gingerbread again."

"Oh my darling," said Mama quietly as she looked at me with sadness. "If it were up to Mama I would clothe you in nothing but velvet and silks and see that you ate fare fine enough for King William's table. Such a sweet child deserves nothing less. 'Tis not your fault, Dorcas, that we are poor, and 'tis none of Mama's either. Nothing but fate has brought us low and it is up to us to love each other even when those around us hand us charity with one hand and beat us with the other. Life can be long, my Dorcas, and things could one day turn in your favor if you think yourself worthy. You are the prettiest, brightest and kindest child in Salem Village. Don't you ever forget that Mama told you so, do you hear me?"

"Yes Mama," I said, strangely comforted by her words. Let Ann Putnam take the gingerbread from my hand. I knew I was more fortunate that Ann would ever be. I had a mama who loved me while Ann Putnam's mother was so busy with the affairs of the town she never had a word for her poor daughter except to tell her to mind her younger brothers and sisters.

"Now then," said Mama drawing me over to the fire and putting another piece of gingerbread in my hand. "It's time to tell you Mama's special secret."

"A secret Mama? Oh I love secrets! What is it? What is it!" I said bouncing into her lap as she sat down on a sturdy caned backed chair.

"It's a secret that means you will have to bounce on Mama less and help her more Dorcas, are you willing to do that?"

"Oh yes Mama, I promise," I said wrapping my small arms about her.

"Well," said Mama, "in the early spring you won't be the only little one with the name of Good. Mama is going to have a baby, someone for you to hold when he is little and to play with when he gets older."

"Mama," I said trying not to sound selfish, "do you think you could have a girl. I'd much rather have a little sister. Girls are much nicer."

"We'll have whatever the good Lord wants " said Mama, drawing me close and hugging me tightly.

"I can tell you what the baby will be, little mistress," said Tituba as she leaned over the fire and arranged the embers in a strange pattern.

"Oh how? How!" I cried, bouncing again on Mama's lap, completely forgetting that I had to be careful.

"By reading your Mama's future in the fire," said Tituba, squinting into the glowing embers.

"There will be none of that, Tituba," said Mama quite alarmed by the Indian woman's motions. "If Reverend Parris were to catch you he'd punish us all"

"All Reverend Parris would see is my giving help to folks in need and tending the fire," said Tituba with a laugh. "Old Tituba knows what she's doing. Ask John Indian if you doubt me. He remembers when I told of my own son's death three years ago.

"You had a son, Tituba?" said Mama as she looked at the slave.

"Yes, I had a son named Fortitude," said Tituba. "That is what the Master bid me call him. Fortitude had grown from the seed of a man as black as these cinders. How it grieved me when I saw that he was to die of a fever before he became a man."

"How sad for you Tituba," said Mama. To Mama, Tituba was a woman just as Mama was, not a slave to be despised and mistreated. She had often said to me we were all God's creatures, equal in his eyes, despite anything the village elders might say.

"I thought my heart would break when we left Fortitude's body buried in far away Barbados," said the slave, "but the master said I should stop crying because my son was now in a better place."

"What place is that?" I asked, sad for Tituba and her dead son Fortitude.

"Why heaven of course," said Mama. "That is where all good people go when they die."

"The Master said that because Fortitude had lived and died a slave he was assured of a place in heaven, right next to Jesus himself," said Tituba with a strange smile. "So you see, Dorcas, the more you suffer on earth the greater your reward is in heaven."

"How wonderful," I said clapping my small hands together. "Oh Mama, let's die now so we can go there. I don't think the baby Jesus is ever cold, do you? They might even have shoes, mightn't they?"

"Don't talk so, Dorcas Good," cried Mama, "to ask for death is to invite it into your house. You must live long and well. We'll find you shoes here on this earth, I swear."

"All right Mama," I said, disappointed that we couldn't go to heaven today. It sounded far more pleasant than trying to walk home in the snow with no shoes.

"Now then Tituba," said Mama, "what is this talk I hear about John Indian and the master's rum?"

SIXTH ENTRY

I quickly grew bored listening to Mama and Tituba gossip by the fire. The heat of the embers along with the drone of their voices were dull fare for curious child of four. From behind the door on the right I could hear the shrieks and giggles of the big girls. It ebbed and flowed with a rhythm of it's own. I glanced from Mama to Tituba, realizing to my delight that they had forgotten I was there. They thought me asleep, so I quietly moved toward the forbidden door that housed the delights of the big girls.

Ann Putnam, Betty Parris and the rest held all the enchantment that there was in this world for me. I thought the girls in the room beyond lived like princesses. I suppose they did when you compare their lot to mine. If only I had known their true circumstances I might not have admired them as much. It was only later that Mercy Phillips told me of each girl's true plight and how jealousy can poison the soul.

Ann Putnam was the oldest of seven children with a mother who was half mad with grief and envy. As a twelve year old she was much put upon, and if I had looked and listened to her more closely I might have realized she was on the verge of hysteria all the time. Nine year old Betty Parris was the much beloved elder daughter of Reverend Parris, but she was also of a delicate nature. It was sad her father filled her so full of warnings about the devil and sin. It was the talk of the town that she would often awake from some evil dream or night terror. For all my poverty, I slept soundly in my mother's arms every night. Betty's cousin, Abigail Williams, was the same age as Ann Putnam, and the one that I envied the most. She was a lovely girl with flashing eyes and perfect teeth. How was I to know that Reverend Parris treated his orphaned niece more like a servant than one of the family.

Then there were Mary Walcott and Elizabeth Hubbard. Seventeen year old Mary was the step-daughter of Ann Putnam's aunt, Deliverance. She seemed to have an easy lot, but the strange light that glowed in her eyes

21

when she witnessed the misfortunes of others always shook my soul and made me wonder if she even had one. Elizabeth was also seventeen, but she, like Abigail Williams, had been made a virtual servant by her own family. Elizabeth was made, by her aunt's marriage, the great niece of Dr. Griggs, the village physician. She had been taken in by the elderly couple to cook and clean for them. How rare and wonderful must that moment of laughter and secrets behind closed doors felt to these girls who were beleaguered with adult chores and sinful terrors.

I carefully stepped into the shadows by the side of the door, hoping against hope that I would hear something that might delight me as much as the girls within. I knew I was being naughty as I pressed my ear against the wooden planks, but I felt that they deserved a little eavesdropping after what Ann had done to me. Mama had said I was just as good as an Ann Putnam or a Betty Parris, so why shouldn't I share in their laughter and jokes? I glanced back at Mama and Tituba and saw to my delight that they had no notion I had wandered away, so I cautiously held my breath and waited to hear the first words dropping from the girl's enchanted lips.

"Abigail," said the voice of Ann Putnam, "you have to make sure Betty doesn't tell what we've been doing. You know that your uncle, Reverend Parris, would have us all beaten."

"He wouldn't beat Betty, she's his favorite and he loves her more than he should," said Abigail smugly.

"But if he finds that the rest of us have drawn her into witchcraft and fortune telling he'll have us denounced at meeting and shamed before everyone. Not even Betty could stop that," said Ann frantically.

"But I won't tell. I promise!" sobbed little Betty, making sounds like a kitten."

"Even if you don't," snapped Ann, "what's to keep Tituba from opening her mouth and getting us all into trouble. We've gone too far and Betty's bad dreams have already started talk. I think the only thing for us to do is blame Tituba before she blames us."

"But that's not fair," cried Betty softly, "you made her show you her spells and dolls. She didn't even want to until you threatened that you would have her whipped. Tituba loves me and has always been kind to all of us."

"Tituba is a slave," said Ann, "not a human. Why, blaming her would be no worse than blaming a dog for stealing food from your plate. Don't worry. No harm will come to her. They can't hang someone who's not human."

"That's right," said Abigail in a kindly voice. "Tituba's safe, Betty, I promise you. Stop your crying now before Uncle Samuel comes home."

With those words I heard the girls heading towards the door, but it was too late. I backed off quickly just as Ann Putnam came striding out, but it was obvious to her that I had been standing there. The look in Ann Putnam's eyes as she glared at me and then exchanged glances with Mary Walcott let me know that I was in trouble.

"What are you doing there you little sneak?" said Ann as she pushed me roughly against the door.

"Why nothing," I stammered as I fought to regain the breath that had been knocked from my body.

"Mistress Ann!" cried Tituba rising quickly from her chair and hurrying over to where I lay cringing. "You stop that this minute! Dorcas is only a little girl, I'm sure she meant you no harm."

By that time Mama had reached me and was holding me in her arms. The fury glowed from Mama's eyes and I could feel her body trembling with anger.

"If I ever see you near my child again, Ann Putnam, I'll make you pay," screamed my mother in a voice beyond reason. "Do you hear me, you spoiled brat? We've taken more than enough from you and your kind and I'm through being silent about it. My daughter is a freewoman, same as you, and you've no right to touch her. Watch your ways young mistress or you'll be finding Sheriff Corwin at your door."

It was then that I looked up at Ann Putnam from the safety of my mother's arms. What I saw filled me with fear. It was not the angry look on Ann' Putnam's face that frightened me, but the strange smile that spread across her cousin's face. Mary Walcott leered at me with a demon's grin and then softly touched Ann's arm.

"Come along now, Ann," she said as smooth as silk. "Goody Good is quite right. You had no right to touch the child. Apologize and be done with it before she thinks us ill-bred."

Ann looked at Mary in puzzlement and then she nodded her head in agreement.

"You are right as usual, Mary. I'm sorry Goodwife Good if what I did harmed the little one," she said patting my curls and smiling at me fondly. "Twas a fit of temper I had and there's no excuse I can offer except tiredness and worry. You see, I've not been feeling well and I'm afraid I let it get the better of me. Please forgive me my rude ways and send us on our way with your blessings."

"Well then," said Mama, rather astounded by the sudden change of mood in the sharp tongued Ann, "I forgive you, and so does Dorcas, don't you darling," said Mama looking at me for an answer.

"Yes Mama," I said looking once again behind Ann at Mary Walcott, who was avoiding all eyes by helping Elizabeth Hubbard put on her boots.

"There you see?" said Tituba breathing a sigh of relief, "all's well that ends well."

"Yes indeed," said Mary as she turned toward the front door. "Come along, Ann. Elizabeth and I have chores, and I know your mother must be looking for you."

"Coming Mary," said Ann as she hurried after her friends and ran out the door and right into Reverend Samuel Parris.

"Why, what's this?" said the tall man with small brown eyes and long chestnut hair. "Such haste could cause an accident, Mistress Ann."

"I'm sorry, Reverend," called Ann as she fled towards her friends and away from the gathering storm behind her.

SEVENTH ENTRY

"Tituba," said the Reverend as he firmly shut the door behind him. "How many times have I warned you about letting the village girls idle your day away? They are neglecting their duties and causing you and Abigail to do the same. The next time I catch you stealing time from your master to stare into the fire will mean the whip for you, do you understand?"

"Yes, Master," said the slave lowering her eyes so that Samuel Parris could not see the murderous hate in them.

"Now then, where is my supper!" said Reverend Parris, going to the fire and staring into the stew and soup pots that were steaming above the warmth.

"Right away, Master," said Tituba as she hurried to set plates and cups on the long wooden table that stood in the center of the room.

"Father," said little Betty, coming over to Samuel and taking his hand. "This is Goodwife Good and her daughter Dorcas. They have been visiting, too." With that she led her father over to the corner where Mama was straightening her skirts and attempting to make me presentable.

"Welcome, Goodwife," said Samuel Parris in a tired voice, "I suppose you are here to beg some bread from our table so that your man can go on sleeping his days away in sloth."

"No sir," said Mama proudly, stung by the man's cruel words. "We were caught in the storm and sought shelter within your walls until the wind grew less fierce. Now that it has, we will be on our way." With that, Mama bobbed a curtsy to the Reverend and headed towards the door.

"But Father," cried Betty, "they can't go out into the snow with no shoes. We must give them some."

"No need to worry about us, little one," said Mama looking at Betty with a kindly smile. "We've walked this way before and we can again."

25

"My daughter is right," said Samuel Parris. "I am ashamed for my thoughtless words a moment ago. Let me offer some shoes for you and your child. 'Tis only the Christian thing to do."

"I'll not take charity when handed to me with a closed fist," said Mama dragging me towards the door. "You should be ashamed to call yourself Reverend, sir!"

"Now then," said Reverend Parris, truly stung by Mama's words. "I am ashamed and see the truth in your words, Sarah Good. Abigail! Betty! Fetch some old shoes quickly. And while you are at it, find some good wool stockings to go with them. I'll not have it said about the village that I sent a woman and child into the snow bare legged."

"But Uncle Samuel," said Abigail, "the only other shoes I have are my new ones that I planned to wear to meeting on Wednesday. Surely you don't mean for me to give those to that slattern."

"I most certainly do, Niece," roared Samuel Parris, "and I would think about your own conduct before you go about calling others slattern. There is no extra wood by the fire, and by the looks of it, your sewing basket is overflowing with mending. I think it would be well for you to think upon your own folly and look upon the loss of your shoes as a just punishment for your lazy ways."

Abigail turned and ran up the stairs, but not before she looked at Mama and me with eyes full of hate. She returned a moment later with some sturdy brown leather shoes. They were just Mama's size.

"Oh look Mama," I said clapping my hands together with delight, "now you won't be cold anymore."

"And neither shall you Dorcas," said Mama, as Betty Parris handed me a lovely little pair of shiny black shoes.

"There now. I wish you both well and will expect you at meeting on Wednesday, Goody Good," said Samuel Parris as he stroked my hair.

"Oh thank you, Reverend," I said as I smiled up at the man with tears in my eyes. "You don't know what it means to Mama and me to be warm. I'll never forget your kindness." With those words, I felt myself overcome with emotion, and impulsively hugged the Reverend around the knees.

"Get away from my Uncle, you little bastard!" cried Abigail as she pushed me away from the Reverend and caused me to fall and scrape my knee. "'Tis unseemly that you should touch him in such a way."

"I was just saying thank you," I said rubbing my sore knee. It was at that moment that an unusual fury filled my soul. Something within me had broken and the pain began to flow from my lips. "I hate you Abigail Williams. I do, I do! And I hate your friends too! Don't any of you ever touch me again. You can keep your stupid shoes, and I hope you freeze to death in them. You're mean and evil and nothing but a selfish pig!"

"Hush now Dorcas," said Mama trying to grab me before I rushed towards Abigail. Unfortunately she was too late.

"You and your friends think you are so fine, sitting by the fire and telling fortunes and making magic dolls. But I know better," I screamed for all the world to hear. "I know what your mean plans are and I'm going to tell. I'm going to tell!"

"Tell what?" asked the Reverend, alarmed by the words that I had spoken.

"They are nothing but a bunch of evil girls and they want to hurt Tituba, I heard them say so!" I cried, almost beyond reason.

"Dorcas Good," said Mama as she approached me and quickly swept me into her arms. "How many times have I told you not to make up stories. Come now and be grateful for the Reverend's gifts. Reverend Parris," said Mama turning towards the man, "I can't tell you how sorry I am for the child's outburst. The cold and hunger have gone to her head 'tis all. Please forgive her foolish words and take our thanks for your gifts."

With that Mama bobbed a curtsy and fled out the front door, carrying me and the shoes in her slender arms. It was not until we reached the fence at the edge of Reverend Parris' property that she stopped for breath, dropping me and the shoes into the snow.

"But Mama," I whimpered as she firmly tied my new shoes on my feet. "I'm not crazy, you know I'm not."

"I know that darling, but think for a moment. What if you had told the Reverend about Tituba and her little tricks. He might have beaten her, or worse."

"But Ann Putnam and Mary Walcott are going to tell on her anyway. I heard them say so Mama."

"Heard them say what?" said a voice behind us.

"Nothing Mistress Williams," said Mama firmly clasping her hand over my mouth.

"It had better be nothing, you little imp," said Abigail towering over me as she flung two pairs of woolen stockings at me. "If you so much as breath another word, I'll see to it that you suffer."

"Don't you threaten my daughter!" said Mama standing toe to toe with Abigail.

"I'll do what I like, Sarah Good," said Abigail roughly pushing away the hand Mama had laid on her arm. "It seems to me that there may be more than one who could be called a witch in this village. Stay out of my way and keep your mouth shut if you know what's good for you. Go now before I tell Uncle that your mad mutterings come from the devil."

"Tis my psalms I say as I walk and you know it Abigail Williams," said Mama backing away from the furious girl. I could feel her hands tremble as she held me tight.

"Then you better say them twice as loud, Goody Good," said Abigail Williams with an evil glint in her eye. "Sounds like a witch's curse to me," she yelled at us as she made her way back through the snow to the warmth of the Parris homestead.

"What did she mean, Mama?"

"Nothing dearest, nothing," said Mama as she grasped my hand and pulled me towards home. "Just say your prayers and be a good girl like Mama told you. Nothing can harm you as long as I am here."

"Nothing, Mama?"

"Nothing, my love."

Note from Mistress Black: By now I feel it must be clear to any who have happened upon this diary, that the writing is not that of a child who is but four and a half years old. While our Dorcas has always been quite precocious for her age, with intelligence beyond measure, she is still but a child, with a child's speech upon her lips.

Goodwife Phillips read this first bit and has sternly chided me for not telling the reader that I have often translated the words of little Dorcas into an order that can be understood. 'Tis true, I have. It is my belief that the words of Dorcas Good must be spoken in the clearest way possible so that her message will ring true and not be lost in the vagaries of a child's wandering speech. I assure you, however, that all that is written has been said or implied by our dearest Dorcas and is either her very words or the essence of them. This I swear upon the holy book.

EIGHTH ENTRY

I am ashamed to admit it, but I was glad that the snow was too deep for us to go to meeting the following Wednesday. It is true that my shoes were wonderful and I enjoyed running about with no fear of cold toes, but the thought of seeing Abigail Williams' sour face so soon again filled me with dread. You cannot imagine my delight when Mama told me that we would have to stay home, safe from the blizzard's vicious winds and mounting snow drifts.

How cozy it was snuggling up to Mama and listening to her tell stories about our new baby. Mama loved to talk about how the baby would be a strong little boy or a beautiful little girl, just like me. I wanted a sister more than anything in the world. Just think! A little baby sister to hold and to love! Mama said that someday the baby would grow into a playmate. When Mama asked me what we should name the baby, I immediately said Dorcas. How wonderful it would be to have a namesake. Then she would really belong to me. I will never forget how angry I was when Mama told me she couldn't have two little girls with the same name.

"But Mama," I argued, "my real name is Dorothy, so we wouldn't really have the same name."

"There's no getting around this one no matter how hard you try, Dorcas," said Mama with a merry smile. "Dorothy and Dorcas are the same and you know it. Besides, we might have a little Thomas or William instead."

"No Mama," I said, suddenly sure that I would have a sister, "we will have a girl and you will name her Mercy."

It was then that a strange fear gripped my being. Why was I so sure of my words? It was as if a tiny voice within me was guiding me towards a dark tunnel with no light. I could hear my voice still speaking, but it sounded as if I were in another room.

"Her name will be Mercy, Mama, because she will never receive any on this earth. She will live in the dark and damp and always be very cold. But Mercy will be happy even in her misery, for she will be with you all her days and there to greet you when you enter heaven."

"What is this you are saying?" I heard Mama say as she shook me roughly. "Dorcas, come back to me. I like not the light that glows from your eyes."

I remember blinking furiously and feeling the hot tears that fell from my glazed eyes. What had happened? Had I been possessed by some strange spirit like the ones in Tituba's stories, or was there someone sharing the small body I called home?

"Mama," I cried as I flung myself against her, "make it go away!"

"Make what go away my darling?" said Mama taking me into her arms and holding me close.

"The thing behind my eyes Mama. It's in there and it won't come out. It scares me. Please make it go away."

"What is it like darling?" said Mama looking at me with alarm.

"It's big and cold, Mama," I said shuddering at the thought. "It wants me to go inside with it and never come out. It wants to tell me more things. I don't want to know what it wants to tell me Mama. It scares me. Oh Mama make it go away now!" I screamed grasping at her skirts. I felt that if I could hold her tight enough, the demons or angels or whatever it was that was causing me such pain would go away. I shall never forget the pain of that first time.

"Dorcas Good, look at me," said Mama as she gently raised my face to hers. "There is no evil spirit inside of you. 'Tis only a fantasy you've had, brought about by staying indoors over long, and too much hunger and worry. Mama promises you that there is nothing wrong. Speak not of such things around anyone else. They do not know you as Mama does and might take you away. Do you understand me, my little love?"

"Yes Mama," I said, quietly letting go of her skirt. As I looked up at my mother I was struck with horror. Surrounding her head was a halo as dark as night. A black cloud began to form behind her and envelop her. I watched steadily, trying not to let my feelings show. When it reached Mama's belly, the cloud stopped and began to be absorbed by the little sister that lay within. I watched, fascinated, as the cloud disappeared and the air became clear again.

"Now then, my darling," said Mama trying hard to look as if her small daughter's fears were the fantasies she wanted to believe they were, "Let's make some of that flour we begged into bread so that Father will have something to eat when he returns."

"Oh Mama, you know he won't be hungry," I said, smiling at her foolishness. "He never is when he spends the day at Ingersolls' tavern."

"Be that as it may my daughter, we will do our duty even if your father doesn't see fit to do his. Never let the misbehavior of others bring you low, Dorcas. You should always live your life in honor."

"Yes Mama," I said looking about our cold and drafty home. It seemed to me honor was a scant substitute for a warm body and a full stomach.

NINTH ENTRY

It was that night that I had my beautiful dream. I dreamed that I was in a faraway place where the sun was shining and there were large red and pink flowers. The bright yellow birds that circled overhead sang to me in unearthly tones. I had my little sister Mercy by the hand and we were running through sand as smooth as silk. The surf we were playing in was unlike any I had ever seen in this life. It was gentle and warm. The ocean beyond was a lyrical green-blue wonder.

How I loved my little dream sister. Her laughter and smiles filled my heart with a joy beyond compare. We were making a game out of splashing water on our naked bodies. The freedom of running in the fresh air with only our long hair to clothe us was delicious. Mercy had hair the color of a roan pony, while mine was a pure gold, much brighter than it is now.

In the distance I could see Mama beckoning us to come out of the water. She had laid a feast of apples, grapes and some long yellow fruit, quite unknown to me, on a brilliantly white cloth. As my sister and I ran towards Mama, she opened her arms to embrace us both. Mama laughed as we soiled her brightly colored dress with sand and salt water.

"What are these Mama?" I asked as I held up the yellow fruit.

"Bananas, my love," laughed Mama, looking at me as if I should have known the answer to my own question."

"Of course," I said, realizing suddenly I did know what bananas were. We always ate bananas under the sun after playing all morning. Mama would sit on the beach and make us beautiful hats out of long green leaves.

"Come now, my daughters," said Mama as we finished the last of the fruit. "It is time to sleep. Lay your heads upon my lap and rest quietly."

Suddenly I was afraid. I knew that if I slept my dream would disappear and I might never find my way back to this place again. But my weariness soon overcame me and I sank onto Mama's lap and slept as she stroked my golden curls.

When I woke, I found myself on the thin blankets that Mama laid on the floor to make a bed for me every night. Father had promised to make me a bed, but somehow he never seemed to get around to it. How I sobbed when I realized my bliss had been only a dream. If Mama could take us away to my dream place I knew everything would be better. I felt this in my heart. But how could I tell her that my dream was real? Mama always looked frightened and told me to hush when I would tell her about things that hadn't happened yet, or places I had never been but knew in my heart.

I did know that Mama was in great danger. The black halo I had seen swirling about her head had entered her body and been shared by my sister. If only I knew what it meant I could tell Mama. But she would just scoff if I told her what I had seen. She would tell me to hush and be quiet about it. I had to save Mama from the black fate that encircled her, but how?

TENTH ENTRY

"Dorcas Good, you lazy bitch, come help me with this wood!"

I jumped up quickly at the sound of my father's voice and tried with all my might to raise the rude wooden latch that held our door shut. It took me several times, but I finally managed to open the heavy door and let my father in.

"What took you so long," yelled my father as he dropped the wood. Before I could duck he raised his large heavy hand and slapped me hard on the side of my face. I stood very still, knowing that if I ran from him he would only catch me and beat me until I couldn't stand.

"I'm sorry Father," I said, knowing that these were the words he wanted to hear. No excuse was fine enough for William Good when he was drunk and angry. It mattered not that I was only four and couldn't reach the door. I must do what he said, impossible though it may be, or suffer the consequences.

"Then let's see how sorry you are, you useless piece of fodder. Pick up that wood and stack it by the fire. I swear you are almost as useless as you mother."

I trembled as I turned to the wood. The pieces were large and I knew that if I tried to drag them Father would hit me again. I took a great breath and managed to get the first log into my arms as my small body screamed with pain. But the pain in my body was nothing compared to the dred in my soul.

"Oh God," I whispered silently, "don't let him hurt Mama. She is not well and the baby is too small to be hit. I promise that if you keep Mama safe I'll be good and not cry when Father hits me."

"Where's my dinner, you slattern," I heard Father say to Mama.

"I'll get it Father," I said as I ran as fast as I could. I knew from experience that if I got my body between him and Mama he might hit me first.

"Lay down, Father, and I'll bring you some soup and bread right away," I said, putting my small hand upon his brown woolen sleeve and tugging him towards the bedroom.

"There's my girl," said Father smiling at me strangely. "you do just that and I'll let your mother be. She's no use to me as she is now anyway. You just bring me my victuals and I'll leave Mama alone."

"If you touch her I swear I'll kill you," cried Mama grabbing me suddenly and hiding me behind her skirt.

"I'll do as I wish in my own home or see you both whipped for insolence," said Father shoving Mama against a wall and holding his long knife to her throat. "If you want her to live through this night you'll keep your useless mouth shut and stay out of my way. It's time she earned her keep around here."

Somehow Mama managed to knock the knife from his hands and they began to struggle. "Father, Father, stop! I'll go with you. I'll be good, I promise!" I cried as my father threw Mama to the floor and began beating her head against the frozen earth.

"You had better be," growled my father as he picked me up and carried me into the bedroom. From over his shoulder I could see Mama lying on the floor not making a move.

ELEVENTH ENTRY

I will never forget the sound of my father's breathing as he latched the bedroom door. The hands that held me burned with a fever that I had never known before. I knew that it was useless to cry for Mama, because she was either dead or senseless. It was perhaps a mercy that my fear for her was so great that I had little terror left for myself.

"Rest easy little maiden," said my father as he gave a grunt and gently laid me on the bed. "What a pretty thing you are Dorcas Good, why you are as unlike your mother as a swan is to a crow. 'Tis a pity you have a temper to match hers. But never fear, daughter, there is still time to drain that from you before it causes you anymore harm."

"Yes Father" I said, strangely bemused by his gentle tones. This was not the William Good I knew. This was a man oddly kind and soothing of manner. Where had my real father gone? Who was this being who had taken over his body. It was strange, but at this moment I felt affection for my father such as I had never known before. Then I had a wonderful idea! What if Mama was only sleeping on the floor outside the door? What if I could persuade my father to be kinder to her and even help her bear her burdens? If I could do that then this time spent with him was well done. It was then that I prayed as Mama had taught me. "Oh God, help me find the right words and actions to bring about a miracle in my father's soul."

"Father," I said putting my chubby little arms around his neck, "I'm sorry I was a bad girl. I promise that I will try to do better."

"Do you now, my sweet," said Father as he placed his large, hot hand beneath my dress. "Do you really wish to make Father happy?"

"Oh yes, I do. I really do with all my heart."

"Then my little love, just lay back and do as Father says."

I held my breath as his hands slowly took my small woolen dress and slip from my body. What was this game we were playing? It was like none

I had ever known before. It was strange, but if that is what it took to free Mama than I was more than willing to lie naked before my father.

"Father?"

"Yes my sweet," said my father as he stroked my legs and rubbed my chest.

"If I'm very good, will you be nicer to Mama?"

"Why you little vixen," said my father with a jolly laugh, "already you know how to ask for favors before granting your pleasures. 'Tis a little woman you are Dorcas Good and as ripe as any for merriment."

"But will you Father?" I said holding my breath and waiting for the blows that I was sure would follow my boldness.

"Yes, my princess," said my father as he untied the piece of hemp cord that held up his pants. "I promise that your mother will not suffer my ill will as long as you are my true and loving daughter. Pleasure me well and we will have peace in this house such as you have never known."

"Oh thank you Father," I said gratefully, as he pulled the woolen leggings that served as underdrawers from his legs.

"Now then my lovey," said my father as he lay upon me, almost crushing me with his muscular body. "Not a word of this to your mother or our pact is broken, do you hear? No matter how much she questions you, you must say nothing to her or anyone else. If you do I shall beat Mama and the baby until they die. Do you understand Dorcas Good?"

"Yes Father," I said realizing that the sweet spoken stranger I had seen in my father was just a mask for the evil man I knew. The sound of his breathing as he stroked my nether regions was more than I could bear so I turned my face to the wall and stared at a small knothole. I tried to ignore the large burning stick of flesh that my father pressed against my tiny stomach, but there was no help for it.

"Don't forget your words, daughter. You vowed to make me happy. Now then, show Father how sweet you can be or I'll make you watch as your Mama dies."

"Yes Father," I whispered as he rose from my body and pressed his hot stick to my lips.

"Kiss Father and show him how much you love him. 'Tis not a hard task. Just put your hands about me and suck me as you would a sweet candy."

"Like this Father?" I asked, getting on my knees and wrapping my tiny hands about the strange heavy thing that hung between his legs.

"Yes daughter, just like that," said Father, giving a sigh as he shoved himself into my mouth and started to pump.

"Suck it, my little love," he said in a trembling voice as he held my head fast against his stomach. The thing in my mouth tasted strangely of salt and if it had not been for the largeness of it, I would have found my task far easier than some that my father had set before me. It was only when I began to choke that my father withdrew himself.

"There now little one," said my father as he lay me on my back again. 'Twill do no good to have you swooning the first time. Spread your legs so that Father can give you a present."

"Yes Father," I said, horror struck at the size of the swelling thing he was pressing towards me. What did he mean to do? What did he want of me?

"Remember, my little love, any cries from you will go hard on your Mama. You wouldn't want her to wake, now would you?"

"No Father," I said as a few traitorous tears fell from my eyes. All I wanted was my Mama.

"Relax now, love, as Father enters your pretty little grove."

With those words my father slid his hands beneath by buttocks and shoved his flaming fleshy stick into me. The pain that seared through my small body and tender parts burned into my soul. As he grunted and groaned on top of me, I heard a strangely familiar voice.

"Come and play with me Dorcas, I will keep you safe."

It was my own little dream sister, beckoning me to join her in the beautiful land of yellow birds and green-blue sea.

PART TWO

WONDERFUL WITCHES

TWELFTH ENTRY

It may sound hard to believe, but as cold November shrank into cruel December and endless January, things fell into an uneasy rhythm. Father was nicer to me than I could ever remember. The times we spent in his room began to take on a dreamlike state for me. Mistress Hannibelle has tried to explain to me how that could be, but I am still confused by it all. I knew Father's touches and brutalities were unspeakable and evil beyond belief, but I had been so numbed by past beatings that the peace of letting him have his own way was almost a blessed relief. Lord in heaven knows I knew how to take the pain and keep my mouth shut. I had been trained since birth to do that. It was to my delight and terror that when his touch threatened to became too much to bear, the angels sent my little dream sister to spirit me away to our land of sunny joy. It sounds like madness I know, but if it took being used as my father's whore to buy peace and health for my mother than I was more than happy to do it.

The worst part of the whole thing was Mama's eyes. How she would stare at me after one of Father's ruttings. He would always say that I must come into the bedroom to rub the aches and pains that he suffered after the day's labor, but Mama knew, oh how she knew. I could hear her quiet whimpers of agony from outside the closed door and yearn to comfort her, but what could I do? Both Mama and I knew that we had no choice. If we fled from Father's cruelties we knew we would perish in the cold of the icy New England winter. It had happened before in our small settlement. There would be no hand lifted to help us, not with Father standing ready and able to offer us food and shelter for the winter. Many a woman and child suffered as we did and bore their lot as they made their prayers to the Almighty while silently screaming for deliverance.

Little did Father know I was playing a waiting game. In his pride he made the same mistake that most adults make about small children. He thought that I was just a sweet innocent soul, ready to take his blows and caresses with no feelings or opinions of my own. Goody Mercy Phillips has said that he probably thought I was too young and would not remember most of what he did to me. How mistaken he was! To this day, and probably into eternity, I remember. I remember every touch, every pinch, every prod. It is my curse to always remember. I am one of those whose eyes opened upon the world the day I was born and may never close. Remember I must, and so I do now. If I am mad, than it is the madness of sanity.

The last day of February began as bright and as hard as a pirate's diamond. I remember trying not to shiver as I lay in my little blanketed heap on the frozen floor. How hard it was to hold myself still as Father stepped over me and out the door. The moment I heard the latch close I leapt to my feet in joy. He was gone and the day belonged to Mama and me. What a rare and wonderful treat. Maybe I could even coax her into leaving her bed. I will never forget my innocent joy as I ran towards her.

"Mama. Mama!" I cried bouncing upon her with four year old happiness, " it's time to get up!"

"Not today, my love," groaned Mama in a strange voice. "Today Mama has work to do. Today is the day the baby will be born. Oh Dorcas, 'tis an evil thing to be born on such a day."

"What do you mean, Mama?" I said alarmed at how weak Mama sounded.

"Tis February 29th, child. This day happens only once every four years and is known to bring bad fortune to all. Woe to any child born upon such a day."

"How silly Mama," I said trying to sound like a woman grown, not a child, "the Reverend Parris himself says that superstition is the devil's work. Why Mama, I warrant that our baby will be very special because she was born on such a special day. Just think of it, she will always be young if she only has a birthday every four years!"

"Why 'tis true, my wise little Dorcas," said Mama smiling and holding me tight. "How smart and brave you are, my girl. Now do you think you can be a bit braver and help Mama?"

"Of course Mama," I said, made proud by my mother's praise.

"Then run along to the Parris' house and fetch Tituba to me. Tell her the baby is coming and Father is nowhere to be found."

"But Father is at the Higginson's. He's repairing their barn, Mama."

"I know that darling," said Mama with a wink, "but let's not remember that for a while. 'Twill be easier on us all if we bring the baby without him."

"Yes Mama," I said pulling on my stockings and shoes.

"And Dorcas," said Mama as I wrapped myself in her tattered shawl and opened the door, "speak not to the village girls. They have been casting their evil eyes too much our way lately."

"Yes Mama," I cried as I closed the door behind me and turned my face into the bitter wind.

THIRTEENTH ENTRY

The cold gripped my body and left me all but breathless as I struggled towards the house of Reverend Parris. How sweet it would have been to lay down in the snow and close my eyes for a moment. I could feel a comforting exhaustion coming upon me, coaxing me to rest for just a moment. It was as if time had stopped and me along with it.

Suddenly, I saw a soft light in the snow before me. It was both warm and beckoning.

"Come Sister," came a voice from the light, "follow me."

It was to my amazement that a great warmth flooded my body and my feet began to battle through the snow with a renewed strength. It seemed but a moment later that my poor sun-blind eyes spied the glass panes of Reverend Parris' windows.

I stumbled towards the warmth of the house with a joyful heart. How I longed to feel Tituba's arms around me telling me not to worry. I knew that once she followed me home, Mama would have nothing left to fear. As I watched, the door opened and the West Indies slave came into view. But something was wrong! Her body was at a strange angle and there was a look of dread upon her face. Her hands had been cruelly tied behind her back and her brightly colored turban was listing crazily to one side. I stopped short and ducked behind the small shack that Reverend Parris used to store odds and ends.

"What is this you are doing to old Tituba," I heard the slave cry as I watched Constable Herrick take Tituba by the shoulders and roughly shove her into the back of his wagon.

"Quiet the witch!" came a voice from inside. "Quiet her now before she harms our Betty again. 'Tis a wonder the child still has breath within her body after the torture that evil Tituba has put her through!"

I recognized the voice as that of Elizabeth Parris, the seldom seen mother of little Betty Parris. What did she mean? Why was she calling Tituba a witch?

47

"Take her then, Joseph," said the Reverend Parris following the constable to the wagon. "And be sure to bind her tightly. Young Ann Putnam and my own niece Abigail says 'tis Tituba who has been torturing my daughter so. Along with you now and get her out of my sight until the morrow. I swear that if there is the devil's work hereabouts that I will soon discover it. The devil hath been raised in Salem Village and 'tis my duty to put him down."

"Yes sir, Reverend," said Joseph Herrick as he pulled a chain tightly against the sobbing Tituba's chest. "But don't forget 'twas yourself, sir, that bade me visit upon Goody Osburn and Goody Good this day as well. They too have been named as witches and must spend this night in my custody."

"Tis Tituba that has been most cried against and she who must be put away with all speed," said the Reverend. I know now that he secretly wanted Tituba out of sight before the whole town began talking about how the sainted Reverend Parris had hidden evil beneath his own roof. "Off with you quickly, my man. Tarry only long enough to find Osburn. It shouldn't take you overlong. I have heard that she is ill and lays upon her bed."

"Then what of Goody Good?" said the constable with an annoyed look upon his face. It was bad enough being dragged out of the warmth of Ingersolls' tavern so early on such a day. To not be allowed the freedom to carry out his duties properly was almost more than a man could stand. But Joseph Herrick knew his place and knew the Reverend must be heeded, no matter how foolish his notions seemed.

"Let her wait until the morrow," said Samuel Parris. "She's great with child and won't be running, even if that no good man of hers tells her of Tituba and Osburn. There's time enough tomorrow to gather up Good and take her to Ingersolls to be examined. Away with you now, man, and lock this devil's imp up tightly before my little one suffers unto death."

"Yes your Honor," said Constable Herrick as he tipped his hat to the Reverend with a respectful gesture that belied the scorn in his heart. High and mighty folk were always ordering such as Joseph Herrick about with no thought to his comfort. Little did Parris care that his wishes would result in another cold and unpleasant journey out to William Good's house early tomorrow. Hannibelle Black told me that she knows Joseph Herrick had secretly planned to slip into Ingersolls early and have a few pints before the fun began, but now the Reverend's orders had spoiled his plans. In anger, he whipped his horses forward, throwing poor Tituba to the floor of the wagon.

"Look out now, or I'll curse you as well," shouted Tituba as the wagon sped past the shack where I had taken shelter.

I watched from a crack between the old weathered boards as the wagon disappeared from sight.

"Oh God, help me save Mama," I prayed as I gathered her shawl around me and dashed for home.

FOURTEENTH ENTRY

By the time I reached home the sun was directly overhead. I shoved the heavy door open and rushed in. It was not until I heard Mama's groans that I remembered about the baby. What were we going to do? I knew that going to Father for help was useless. He'd shown me many times over the last few months that he didn't care if Mama lived or died. Besides, Mama couldn't go anywhere!

"Dorcas, Dorcas," came her weak voice from the next room.

"Coming Mama," I said as calmly as possible. Mama had told me never to panic when things looked impossible because that would only make everything worse. What I had to do now was keep my wits about me and face the task at hand. There would be no fleeing through the snow until my little sister was safely wrapped in something warm and snuggled in Mama's arms. I resolutely pushed the door open to let in as much light as possible. Mama was panting on the bed with the twisted coverlet stuffed in her mouth. Her face was pale with the strain of her pains.

"Oh thank the Lord you're back, my darling. Mama has never had an easy time and this promises to be the worst yet. Bring Tituba to me Dorcas, she'll know what to do."

The hopeful light that shone in Mama's eyes, despite her pains, was almost more than I could bear. How could I tell her that Tituba was not coming? It was then that I told Mama a lie. Many years later I still felt the guilt of it upon my heart.

"Oh Mama," I heard myself say in a strange voice, "Tituba said she would be right along. Mistress Parris is quite ill this morning and needs tending. Tituba promised to be here within the hour. Don't be afraid, Mama, I can help you until she arrives, I know I can."

"Well then we must make the best of it until she can be here, mustn't we," said Mama with a voice full of courage. "What would I do without you my daughter, you are such a comfort."

51

"Am I, Mama?" I said filled with guilt at the way I had just deceived her.

"Yes, my little love, you are. Now then, toss as much wood as you can on the fire and keep Mama warm. 'Twill do no good to see our breath freeze in front of our faces, now will it. And Dorcas....."

"Yes, Mama?"

"Get Father's other shirt from the cupboard. Mama will need something to wrap the baby in when he comes."

"She Mama, she," I said running into the other room laughing at the mischievous look on Mama's face. If Mama was well enough to tease me about the baby then there was hope indeed.

I will never know where I found the strength that day, but it was supplied to me in full measure. There was no time to think, only to help Mama. As I stood stoking the fire Mama gave a great cry."

"Hurry Dorcas, bring the shirt and the knife that lays by the fire, hurry!"

I dashed back into the bedroom, shirt in one hand, knife in the other, just in time to see Mama's body arch with inhuman effort. Her eyes met mine as the baby gushed out from between her legs. I will never forget the mixture of agony and triumph in Mama's beautiful brown eyes.

"Wipe the baby off and cut the cord while I press this against me," said Mama calmly binding the coverlet around her legs and thighs.

"You mean this, Mama?" I said reluctant to touch the strange fleshy object that connected the baby to my mother.

"Yes Dorcas," said Mama with a smile. "That is what gave the baby life while it was inside of Mama. Don't be afraid of it, 'tis a wondrous thing. But now it has served its purpose and must be cut if the baby is to live on its own."

"Yes Mama," I said biting my lip and grasping the cord in one hand and the knife in the other.

"Go ahead now Dorcas, you must do it for Mama and the baby."

"Yes Mama" I said again, closing my eyes and blindly stabbing at the cord. Miraculously the blade found its mark and separated the baby from Mama.

"There's my bright girl," said Mama gently. "Now give the baby a bit of a shake so that it can cry."

"But I don't want to make the baby cry, Mama!" I said in alarm.

"Go on now, Dorcas," said Mama sternly, "the baby must cry if it is to breath. 'Tis the way of it."

Chastened by Mama's words, I gently lifted the baby in my arms and shook it. How like one of Tituba's dolls it felt as it lay lifelessly against my body.

"Hurry Dorcas, hurry," said Mama frantically trying to raise herself from the bed.

In a panic, I forgot my fear and gave the baby a shake. Its little eyes popped open and the baby gave a small cry.

"There now, my sweet," I said pressing the baby tighter against my thin body, "all is well now. Big sister will take care of you." I grabbed the shirt and laid the baby gently upon it. It was then that my heart filled with an unspeakable joy.

"Mama, the baby is a girl. I told you the baby would be a girl!" I picked up the swaddled baby and began dancing wildly around the room.

"Careful now Dorcas, bring your little sister to me. Remember she's a baby, not a doll," laughed Mama as she reached for my little sister.

I looked down at the baby and then at Mama. It was then that I realized that where there had been two there were now three. Mama and I were no longer alone in our small world. This little stranger would change everything between us. I gently placed the baby in Mama's arms and backed away as she put my sister to her breast.

"What shall we name your sister," said Mama looking at me with a contentment I had never seen on her face before.

"She already has a name, Mama," I said, amazed that Mama did not know what I knew. "The baby's name has always been Mercy."

Note from Goodwife Mercy Phillips: I have always felt that there was a special tie between Dorcas and myself because of the happy accident that bestowed both me and her beloved sister with the same name. If not for that coincidence, Dorcas may never accepted my friendship.

FIFTEENTH ENTRY

I sat upon the bed and watched as Mama slept. I knew that soon I must waken her and tell her the truth about Tituba, but for now I was grateful for the peace that lay upon her beautiful face. Never had I seen such a calm about my mother. Mistress Black says that it is always that way with a woman who has borne a child, but I know nothing of that. I like to think that Mama had a few moments of joy before her terrors began.

When the baby began fussing, Mama awoke. She smiled at me as she held little Mercy to her breast.

"There now, you see Dorcas? Everything will be fine. I can feel it," said Mama contentedly.

"No Mama, it won't" I said shaking my head sadly.

"Whatever do you mean, daughter?" said Mama raising herself upon one arm and staring into my face. "What have you seen, Dorcas? Don't deny you can see that which is hidden to others. I know you see as my father did."

"Mama," I said slowly, trying to keep the traitorous tears that fell from my eyes hidden from her, "even you would know we must run away if you saw what I saw this morning."

"Whatever is wrong little one?" said Mama enfolding me and the baby into her arms. I could feel her heart beating madly against mine.

55

"Tituba has been taken for a witch, Mama. Oh please forgive me for not telling you sooner. I know I lied and God will make me burn in hell, but I didn't want to scare you and hurt the baby. Please don't be angry."

"Hush now Dorcas, Mama's not angry, I promise you. It makes me sad that Tituba is accused, but why do you say we must leave?"

"Because they are coming for you too, Mama!" I cried getting to my feet and looking about the room frantically. I felt like one of the small rabbits that Father would sometimes trap and bring home for supper. "We must leave now before they find you here and take you away. The Constable, Mr. Herrick, said he was going to arrest Goody Osburn and you today. It was only when the Reverend told him to wait until the morrow to come after you that I decided you had time to have the baby. Oh Mama, we must run away now before they find us. I saw how the Constable Herrick looked at Reverend Parris when he was told to arrest you tomorrow. He didn't like it at all. I feel sure he will come for you sooner. Hurry Mama! Get dressed and leave before it is to late!"

"What you want me to do is madness, Dorcas," said Mama settling back upon the bed. "The baby would die out in the cold and I might too. And then what would happen to you, a small girl wandering about with no home or family to protect her? Perhaps all this will come to nothing. I am innocent of any crime and there are just men in this town who know it."

"But it's not the men who cry out against you Mama," I said trying to wrap her things into a small bundle while I argued with her. "'Tis that evil Ann Putnam and those nasty girls, Abigail Williams and Mary Walcott. They are afraid that you and Tituba will tell of their bad games. Then they would be punished no matter whose daughters they are. I saw them standing at the door as Constable Herrick dragged Tituba off. The smile on Mary Walcott's face frightened me, Mama. I know she means evil to us all. Besides, you haven't seen the others things Mama, the things that come to me in my dreams."

"Oh my little love, I know what comes to you in your dreams, I know only too well. 'Tis the same evil that came upon my own father and drove him mad. 'Twas not until he drowned himself in the pond near his tavern that he found peace. Close your mind to the voices or they will drive you mad, and me along with you Dorcas."

"Then come with me Mama before it's too late. Come now," I begged grabbing hold of my mother's skirt.

"I believe you daughter, the voices within you ring as true as pure sweet water, just as my own father's did," said Mama, raising me to my feet and giving a great sigh. "If you say there is no justice here for us then we must leave. Fetch my shawl while I bind the baby for our journey."

"Yes Mama," I said flying into the next room on joyous feet.

SIXTEENTH ENTRY

It took us but a moment to gather our few things together. Mama even took Father's tavern money from the horde that he kept hidden behind a loose stone in the fireplace. I held my breath as she slipped the few precious coins into her pocket. If Father caught us we well might be beaten to death for our boldness, but it was to late to think about that now.

"Hurry Mama, hurry," I said as a fearsome panic overwhelmed me. Never had I felt such terror as I did at that moment. I lifted the latch and put my hands against the door. It was then that I was knocked over by the force of the heavy door being pushed in upon me.

"There you are my loving family," said Father as he stood blocking our way. "And what is this?" He said striding up to my mother and taking her by the shoulders.

"Why 'tis your new daughter, husband," said Mama attempting to back away as she watched two other men follow Father through the door.

"Then get you to your bed like a proper wife," said Father roughly pushing Mama back towards the bedroom. "'Tis no time to be moving about. Ye'll need all your rest to face the trials ahead of you, wife. These good yeomen have come to look after you until you be ready to travel, Sarah Good."

"Where am I to be traveling William?" said Mama trying to look shocked at his news.

"Why to Ingersolls' Tavern and mayhap to hell, you bitch!" said Father hitting Mama across the face. As she fell against the table, the money she had kept hidden in her pocket spilled onto the floor.

"And what is this, Sarah?" said Father standing over Mama with his legs wide apart and his hand raised.

"Now then William, 'twill go hard with us if we have nothing to deliver but a corpse to Reverend Parris tomorrow," said Constable Locker as he and Joseph Herrick blocked Father's way.

"Yes, I suppose you're right, " said Father as he backed away from Mama and gathered up his treasure. "Let the village take care of her now. I wash my hands of the bitch, and her whelps too. Neither are my trueborn daughters you know. Why this last one could even be the spawn of the devil," said Father, eyeing the newborn baby that had somehow survived Mama's fall.

"Tis yours and you know it," said Mama emboldened by the protection offered by Constables Herrick and Locker. "I've been a good and loyal wife to you, William Good. I swear before God and these folk that both Dorcas and little Mercy here are your trueborn daughters. May I rot in hell if I lie."

"That you shall, my lovely wife," said Father taking Mama by the hand and lifting her gently from the floor. Somehow his almost kind actions was more frightening than his curses. "You see Sarah, my darling, these two yeomen are here to take you and your foul tongue and wasteful ways off my hands forever. It is all up with you my wife. We know that you are a witch born and bred as was your father before you and the child by your side. Admit it now and the people of Salem may take pity upon your soul. That daughter of the devil, Tituba, has already given both you and Goody Osburn up. Go along quietly with these worthies and they may go easy upon you."

"Nothing shall go easy with such as she, not until she stops torturing poor little Betty Parris," said Joseph Herrick, with his eyes narrowing.

"I torture no one," said Mama backing against the wall as Herrick and Locker came towards her.

"Twill do no good to deny it," said George Locker as he grasped at Mama and tied a rope about her waist. "When the poor child could no longer speak for herself, those tormented along with her spoke up. How brave they were as they endured your evil bites and pinches."

"What others? I don't understand. I never hurt anyone!" cried Mama as Locker dragged her into the bedroom and tied Mama, still holding my little sister tightly, to the bed.

"Ann Putnam, Elizabeth Hubbard, and Abigail Williams have all cried out against you. Think not that the town will believe such as you, Sarah Good, when accused by the daughters of respectable folk. Lay ye still and think upon your fate while we take our rest. Remember, the more gentle your manner, the more chance those you love shall survive," said George Locker as he shut Mama into the little room.

"Now then, William, where is that rum you promised us," said Joseph Herrick as he put an arm around my father.

"Dorcas, fetch us my bottle," said Father giving me a vicious kick that sent me sprawling. "Be quick about it. It seems that we must wait upon your mother's rest and deliver her to the tavern on the morrow as the old Reverend demands. But that's no excuse to pass this night in mourning, eh friends," said Father giving a wink to Herrick and Locker. "First let us have a few cups and then I'll show you what tricks this little witch can show you."

"Yes Father," I said edging towards the door. To this day I know I had no choice but to run. There was nothing more I could do for Mama and the baby and I could see by the light in the eyes of the three men that what they had planned for me would cost me my soul if not my life. With strength that could only have come from the angels above, I grasped the heavy wooden door and opened it. I took a deep breath and started to run. It was as if someone or something ran with me, urging me on and warning me not to look back. In some far off dream I could hear my Father screaming, but I could not make out the words.

"Run Dorcas run," I kept panting to myself until I finally came to rest behind the same shack that had hidden me earlier that day. So what if it was but a stone's throw from the warmth and danger of Reverend Parris' home, it looked like heaven to me. I slipped inside the shack and by some miracle was soon curled up in a ball sleeping the sleep that only those truly innocent of the evils of the world can do. In my dreams I begged Mama and Mercy to forgive me and was rewarded with gentle smiles and sweet caresses that filled my quaking heart with a life saving peace.

SEVENTEENTH ENTRY

I was awakened the next morning by the sound of shouting. At first I thought it was Father come to get me, but then I realized it was the Parris family, fully dressed and assembling in their wagon for a trip to the tavern. It was less than a short walk away, but I could tell from the way Mistress Parris leaned upon the Reverend's arm, that she could not journey so much as a step without support.

As the horses and wagon went by the shack, I skittered to the farthest most corner and cowered. It was if I believed that Betty Parris and Abigail Williams could see me through the solid wood. It's no wonder I was afraid. Hadn't those girls been responsible for ripping me from my mother's arms? It was then than I felt the fury growing within me. How dare they! Why, I was as good as those spoiled girls who rode in that wagon. There they sat safe from danger while I was hiding from my Father. I was sick of misery, sick of cold and sick of abuse. I grabbed a heavy wooden stick that had been abandoned on the floor of the shack and began hitting the walls with an anger that must have come from the devil himself. As I battered the poor old shed I sobbed and screamed.

"I hate you, I hate you all!" I cried, feeling the fury surround me until the very air filled with it. It was then that I noticed the edges around a knothole begin to smolder and then burst into flames.

"Good," I cried, taking the burning smell as a sign from God that he liked my anger and wanted an invitation to my furious party. "Let them all be taken to hell and burned alive. They've taken Mercy and Mama away from me and should be punished. Thank you God!"

With those words I ran from the shack and watched as one by one the old rotted timbers caught fire. Perhaps the burning came from a pipe ash carelessly flicked by a passing stranger, but I prefer to think my anger alone started the blaze. I watched with a smile on my lips as the thatched roof began to crumble. Then I came to my senses. What if someone had seen what had happened? No one would understand that it had been a happy accident. I looked around in panic and realized that I was standing alone outside the Parris house watching their shed burn to the ground. I quickly gathered my skirts and fled down the path, stepping in the ruts that the Parris wagon had made only a few moments before. It was insanity I know, but even in my fear I could hear the singing of my heart. "Thank you God," it cried as I followed the wagon tracks towards Ingersolls' tavern. Now I knew felt that I was no longer helpless. From now on I had two new friends, anger and revenge.

EIGHTEENTH ENTRY

I realized, as I crossed Ingersolls green, that any hope I had of seeing Mama alone and telling her about my new feelings was gone. I watched as Mama, Tituba and Sarah Osburn were led out of Ingersolls' tavern. All three woman were weighed down by chains that shackled their hands and feet. I saw Mama stumble as she tried to hold little Mercy tightly to her breast. I could tell by Mama's face that the weight was almost more than she could bear. Where were they taking her? Was I too late? I gasped as a familiar hand slammed down upon my shoulder.

"There you are daughter," said my father smiling down at me. The few teeth he had left were showing as he attempted to give me a blackened grin. "See there my friends," he said nodding to Goodman Proctor and his wife Elizabeth, "I told you that she was about somewhere. Thank the Lord that the witch Sarah Good has done nothing to harm her. Come along daughter and look upon what happens when a woman ignores her betters and writes her name in the Devil's book," said my father as he held my hand tightly and began dragging me away from the other villagers.

"Speak not a word to anyone or it will go hard with you, bitch," said my father as he held my hand in a crushing grasp.

"Yes Father," I managed to say as we joined the crowd making its way towards the Salem Village meetinghouse. Never in my life had I seen so many people at one time. It almost took my breath away as I found myself pushed and prodded by the bustling crowd as they hurried towards the meetinghouse down the road.

"Tis a shame that we couldn't stay at the tavern, " I heard John Parker, son-in-law to old Giles Corey, mumble.

"Aye, that it is," replied his companion, Thomas Preston, giving John a nudge. "Say now, what hope do ye think we have of ridding ourselves of a few more meddlesome biddies?"

"Hah," snorted John with a peculiar light in his eyes. "I'd pay a pretty penny to see my wife's step-mother, Martha, up there in the docket. She's

65

a foul tempered old thing and threatens us daily with the loss of our rightful inheritance. Come to think of it, she could well be a witch."

"As could any in this town, John," said Thomas looking about him thoughtfully. "Why even such as my own mother-in-law, the good Rebecca Nurse, is not above suspicion. I know that most about here regard her as a saintly woman, but do you remember what happened with old Holten and the pigs? 'Twas not long after the beasts destroyed Rebecca's garden that Holten died sudden like. It was said at the time that old Rebecca's curses brought about his death. My words were in jest a moment ago, but I would grieve sadly if any brought misery upon our dear Rebecca. These are dangerous times we live in, my friend. It would pay to watch our step."

"They are confusing times, Thomas, what with the devil all about us," said John shrugging his shoulders and gathering his coat closely about him, "but I think such as Rebecca was just in a rare fit of temper. We all know she is as close to an angel on earth as any who ever lived in Salem. You certainly cannot compare her to such as the slave, the beggar and the old woman up ahead."

"Right you are friend," said Thomas slapping John on the back, "but will you just look at this crowd. There's more than one who knows something is amiss in Salem. I say 'tis a pity we must move down the road to the cold, damp meetinghouse. There'll be nothing to keep us warm but the stink of one another," he laughed as the two men jostled their way towards the largest building in the village.

"Watch it now!" cried Thomas Preston as he stumbled over me.

"Beg the Goodman's pardon, Dorcas," said Father as my eavesdropping ways caused me to bump into Thomas Preston.

"Oh, I'm very sorry sir," I stuttered as the men glared down at me.

"Well then study upon it little mistress and be more careful," said Thomas as he pushed me roughly out of his way and continued down the path. "What can you expect from the daughter of a witch," he said loudly as he turned his back on me.

"I'm not the daughter of a witch," I cried rudely after him. The anger that had welled up in me earlier was nothing compared to what I felt now. How dare he say such things about my mother! She was the most wonderful woman that ever lived! It took me many years to forget his remarks, despite the kindness' Thomas Preston was soon to do me.

"Keep your mouth shut, Dorcas," said my father as he struck me so hard across the face that I fell backward into a snowdrift.

"There now daughter, are you all right," I heard my father say as he glanced about at the villagers staring at us. "Tis clumsy you've become. Let me carry you, Dorcas, so that we are not late. 'Twould be unkind not to witness and comfort your mother in her distress." With those words my father scooped me into his arms and smiled down at me lovingly. "She's far too small to make her way alone," said my father nodding to the other villagers with a smile.

"'Tis a fine father ye are," said Mary Herrick, wife of the constable, taking in the sweet scene.

"I've often had to be both mother and father to the child," said my father looking at me benevolently and beaming at Mistress Mary.

"Why I suppose you have, " said Mistress Herrick with a sigh. "You are a fine man, William, and I hope your little daughter loves and obeys you as she should."

"She does most of the time Mistress," said my father sadly, "but there are times when the wickedness of her mother comes through and causes me much trouble."

"Well then, Dorcas Good," said Mistress Herrick looking at me sternly, "tis time to stop such foolishness and heed your father's words. Think well upon your mother's fate and thank the Lord that there may still be time to redeem your soul."

"Yes Mistress," I said from my father's grasp, aware of the pressure he was applying to my arms. I knew that one wrong move would result in my bones cracking beneath his thumbs.

"Come then daughter," said my father as he tipped his hat to Mistress Herrick, "tis time to see what this day shall bring."

"Bless you William," said Mistress Herrick as she smiled kindly at us both.

NINETEENTH ENTRY

It was then that my body began to shake. It was as if a fever had taken possession of my being. Try as I might I could not still the quaking that overtook me.

"Stop that, Dorcas," my father whispered in my ear as he held me tight. "Our words are over and we must be loving for all the village to see. 'Twill go badly for your mother if you are in distress. They will say that you too have been bewitched by her evil eye."

"But Father, you know Mama is not a witch," I said quietly, seeing the sense of his words.

"I know nothing of the kind," said my father.

As I looked into his eyes I saw something that brought terror to my heart. The eyes of William Good were oddly empty. It was as if he felt nothing for my mother's plight. They were the eyes of a man that would just as soon see my mother dead.

"But Father," I pleaded as I put my small hand upon his face and caressed it softly, "there must be something we can do to help Mama, I know that she's innocent of any wrong doing."

"Shut your mouth, daughter," said my father holding me tight. "You know not of what you speak. Look about you. See your neighbors and friends for what they really are, a pack of blood maddened dogs thirsting after their prey. Your mother and those other two have long been trouble in this village and 'tis time they were called into account."

"But Father," I said boldly, feeling the fear beneath his words, "why would anyone want to hurt Tituba, Goody Osburn and Mama? They are just harmless women. You've said often enough that woman have no rights except for those a man grants her, and poor Tituba is only a slave. Abigail Williams says she isn't even human, just some sort of clever animal."

"That's my girl, now you're beginning to speak like a child with some sense," said my father stroking my curls. "'Tis true that woman have no rights, but they can still be bothersome. Look at Goody Osburn closely. She seems innocent enough, but a blackened heart beats beneath her bodice. Why she's the worst of all creatures, an unnatural mother! 'Twas Osburn that cheated her own sons out of their birthright and gave it to that piece of trash she married after her first husband went to his grave. If those poor boys had not had the good fortune to be nephews of Captain Putnam they would have found themselves starving in the snow while their mother and her hired man helped themselves to the fortune. Now justice will be done and the sons of Sarah Osburn will be given what rightfully belongs to them."

"And as for that slave, Tituba, we all know that it is she who has brought the Devil down upon the whole village what with her strange ways and odd tasting potions. Why, some say she even murdered her own son to spite the Reverend. 'Tis said she would have rather seen the poor boy dead than working for a white man."

"But what of Mama?" I asked, amazed by what I was hearing.

"I know this may not rest easy with you child, but your mother is seen to be the worst of all," said William solemnly.

"I don't understand, Father."

"And well you shouldn't, innocent child that you are, Dorcas. But many's the time you yourself have been witness to the evil doings of Sarah Good. Her mutterings and curses are well known about this village. The list of those who could testify against her is long. 'Tis a great relief that she has finally shown herself for what she truly is. No longer must the village live in fear of your mother. Her torturing of those poor girls in both body and soul has sealed her fate."

"But Mama hurts no one!" I cried looking ahead as the meetinghouse came into view. "Those girls are the evil ones. I've heard them myself. They plot and plan against the villagers. Why, they even sit in the kitchen of Reverend Parris' house and tell each other's fortunes. I've heard them threaten to lay curses upon those who cross them. 'Tis they that are the witches Father, not my Mama."

"Never say that again, Dorcas, if you wish to live," said my Father savagely twisting my arm beneath his. The tears that came to my eyes as I nodded my head satisfied my father enough to release the pressure before my arm broke beneath his grasp. "The people of Salem believe every word those girls utter," said my father as he drew me away from the meeting-house to a small stand of bushes.

"Yes, Father," I said with downcast eyes. I realized that no matter what I said or did, it would only make things worse. I knew that Mama, Mercy and I were beyond any earthly help.

"Those are the most precious daughters of this town, you little fool," continued my father in a tone that almost bit into my flesh. "Elizabeth Parris is the Reverend's own daughter, and Abigail Williams is his niece. As for the other three! My God child, you might as well protest against the Governor himself. Ann Putnam's family is the most powerful in the village and her cousin Mary Walcott is also Ingersoll's niece. As for Elizabeth Hubbard, 'twas her own uncle, Dr. Griggs, who declared the Devil was afflicting those poor wenches. Let this be a lesson to you, Dorcas. Unless you are the daughter or the niece of a man with property, you have no power. No one cares what you say, so keep still. Remember that your words can only bring grief to yourself and your mother. It's time you knew that Salem will be glad to be rid of those three hags."

"And what of you, Father, will you be glad?" I said looking deeply into my father's eyes.

"Only after the constables have paid me what they promised to testify against them," said my father with a gleeful smile.

TWENTIETH ENTRY

By the time we entered the meetinghouse there was nary a seat left. Father and I were forced to stand in the back of the room. The door that kept opening and closing next to us made our spot cold beyond belief. I could see those about us shuddering, but I was too heartbroken to care about my own state. Where was the hope and love of mankind that Mama had taught me about? Certainly not here. The only things that filled the air, that first morning of March in 1692, were revenge and retribution. All at once the door swung open and two men appeared. I had never seen anyone dressed so finely. Were they here to save my Mama? They certainly looked like something that could come from heaven.

"Oh Father," I said tugging at William's arm, "who are those men?"

"Why 'tis the magistrates themselves," said my father in awe. "Yonder comes Judges John Hathorne and Jonathan Corwin, from Salem Town, to see that justice is done."

The crowd parted silently as the two men strode towards the front of the meetinghouse and took their places at the table set up on a platform. Surrounding the two men were the constables of Salem Village.

The man my father had said was Judge Hathorne cleared his throat and looked at the crowd with a stern frown that invoked a fearful silence.

"Bring in the beggar woman, Sarah Good," he said in a voice that sounded like God's.

All heads turned in the direction that Judge Hathorne looked and watched as Mama was led in. The chains that weighed her down made Mama appear smaller and more frail than she truly was. Little Mercy fussed and squirmed in her arms as Mama was led up onto the platform. It was to my horror that I saw spots of blood on Mama's skirt.

"Look Father," I said pulling at my father's sleeve. "Mama is still bleeding from having the baby. Can't they let her lie down and call Dr. Griggs to see to her? She needs help!"

"Hush now, Dorcas, 'tis none of your concern," said my father giving me a kick with the toe of his hard boot. "If all these worthies think your mother fit to be examined than fit she is. Take it for the witch's trick it is child. Sarah Good is just trying to make us feel sorry for her. Think upon yonder afflicted children instead and how they must be suffering."

"They don't look like they're suffering to me," I said glancing over at the buxom seventeen year old Mary Walcott. She was fairly bursting with good health and would have made two of my mother.

"Look at the old witch up there," I heard the man next to me say to his wife. "Why is it always the old ones who make their way to the Devils throne?"

"I don't know, Nathaniel," said his pretty, well cared for wife. "It's so shameful to do such a thing. Thank the Lord that none in our home is afflicted."

I looked at the couple and felt a moment of confusion. Mama wasn't old, the proof of that lay in her arms in the form of my little sister. To me she seemed the same age as the woman who had just spoken. Then I looked towards her and saw how those around me could feel that way. The men and woman who stood about me were dressed quite differently than my Mama and me. Most of the men had on tall black hats, warm woolen breeches and heavy dark cloaks. The white that shined at their collars and wrists bespoke of fresh linen beneath. Their woman were as well dressed as they, with woolen skirts and bodices encasing their bodies. Oh what I would have given to be able to see Mama with her hands buried deeply in a fur muff like the one warming the hands of the woman next to me. But not for Mama was such comfort. She stood before the crowd in her thin skirt and shawl, her hair hanging about her face and her body bound in chains. It seemed to occur to no one that she might be cold and in need of a few Christian comforts. The lines around her face and eyes had been caused by the hardships that few in this room had ever known. My Mama did look older than she should! She had lived a much harder life than most in this room. Then I looked at my father. For all his poverty he had managed to keep an almost boyish look about him. "That is because you let my mother carry your burden as well as your own," I whispered bitterly, looking up at him with narrowed eyes. "I hate you William Good," I hissed quietly, unable to stop myself.

"What was that, daughter?" said my father staring down at me strangely. He had not heard my words, but I knew that he could tell from the look on my face that they were not those of a loving daughter.

"Nothing Father, I was just sighing," I said turning my face away from him. Never again would I let him know what I thought or felt about anything. He had lost any right to my heart the night he first laid his hands upon my body.

"I would have quiet in this place," I heard Judge Hathorne say as he looked about the meetinghouse. It seemed that I was not the only one muttering. The crowd quickly hushed as the judge turned towards Mama and addressed her sternly.

"Sarah Good," said the judge, "what evil spirit have you been familiar with?"

"Why none at all sir," said Mama gently.

"What is that, Goody Good?" said a jeering voice from the crowd. "Speak up woman. We can't hear ye. Tell of how you and your evil spirits have cost my father two fine cows."

I stood on my toes and saw the speaker was Henry Herrick, the same Henry that had chased us away from his house. I remembered how Mama had cursed him and felt a shudder run through my body. "Oh Mama," I thought, "they all hate you."

"Aye, 'tis true. She did that and more too," I heard Mistress Abbey say. "We tried to act as Christians to the witch, but what did she do but thank us with spitefulness. Offered her shelter we did, and lost our livestock as thanks. Praise the Lord that you have finally brought her to judgment."

"That will be enough interruption," said Judge Hathorne. "Each that has a grievance against Goody Good shall be heard at trial, this I promise, but we must all conduct ourselves in a seemly and proper manner. Encourage not the Devil's ways in this place. "Now then Sarah Good, why do you hurt these children?"

"I hurt no one," said Mama lifting her chin and staring defiantly into the crowd. It almost seemed that she was daring them to say another word against her. How proud I was of Mama at that moment. Never have I known anyone more courageous that my mother, Sarah Good.

"I scorn what you say sir," she continued, "and further say to all in this room that they who accuse me falsely should look upon their own behavior before they judge mine. Why, there are many that turn their guilt into mine and see themselves through the mirror of my eyes. Ashamed they are to have turned a poor woman away with no food or warmth in the cold of a winter's night. More ashamed they should be to force a woman from childbed to stand before you. 'Tis filled with evil you all are." The

75

red spots that stood out on my mother's cheeks were fine to see and it was all I could do to keep from cheering as I listened to her brave words.

"Then," said Judge Hathorne, trying desperately to regain control of the crowd, "who does your evil work for you? Come now, Sarah Good, don't lie to us. We who know you well know the truth. It may be that you yourself do these poor children no harm, but you can't deny that something is causing them terrible distress. Who do you have do your dirty work for you, wench?"

"No one sir," said Mama glaring at the judge. "If I wished to hurt someone I would have the courage to do it myself and not employ the magistrates and constables to do my dirty work for me, which is more than I can say for those standing about in this room when there are chores to be done."

"Sarah Good," said Hathorne, ignoring Mama's words, "what creatures do you employ to hurt these children and do your evil bidding?"

"I employ no creatures," said Mama confused that the judge had not answered her words. I could tell by the look on Mama's face that she was weary beyond belief, despite her brave show. "I declare to this place, and to all the good people within it, that I am innocent of any wrongdoing. I am falsely accused and should be set free to tend to my little one," said Mama looking down at Mercy who was sleeping sweetly in her arms.

———-*Note from Hannibelle Black: It seems that any but Sarah's direct responses went unrecorded by the court clerk. But too much was said in meanness by Sarah's neighbors and friends later on to doubt that Sarah would not have fought back and tried to clear her good name. To me, the spitefulness of the testimonies against Sarah Good speak for themselves and lend truth to Dorcas' memories.*

— Dorcas:

"It was then that Judge Hathorne sat up squarely in his chair and turned upon Mama with the fury of an avenging angel.

"Why is it then, Sarah Good, that you scorn those who would help you," said the judge in a loud, intimidating voice.

"I don't understand," said Mama unconsciously shrinking back towards the wall. The judge's voice reminded me of the one father would use right before he would beat Mama with his belt.

"Let me say this so that you can understand what I mean," said the judge as he smiled at Mama. "There was a day, not so long ago, that your very own Reverend Parris offered you shelter and food, plus covering for the bodies of your child and yourself. Why I've heard it said that he took the shoes from the feet of his own niece and offered them to you. And what did you do but leave his home muttering curses against him."

"Tis not true, I swear it," said Mama looking at the group of girls huddled in the corner. "Ask Abigail Williams. She followed my daughter and me to the very gate of the Parris house and heard nothing but speech between Dorcas and myself. It was just that, and a few psalms I was speaking. I never muttered anything against the Reverend or any that live beneath his roof. All I did was thank him for his gifts of shoes for myself and my daughter and leave as quickly as I could so that I would be of no further trouble to those who had been so kind to us. Why, I've always thought that the Reverend looked upon my Dorcas kindly and have praised him for it."

"Then you declare that you have made no contract with the Devil?" said Judge Hathorne with a strange smile upon his lips,"

"I so swear, your worthy," said Mama. I could tell from the way her eyes sought out mine that she felt that now there would be an end to this torture and we should soon be making our way home.

"Then," said the judge, eyeing the 'afflicted' girls that Mama had just called to his attention, "I shall now ask the poor young souls, who have been so grievously ill, to look upon you Sarah Good. Let us see if your words are true."

It was then that a great commotion enveloped the room. The unearthly scream that came from Ann Putnam's mouth sounded like a wolf howling at the moon.

TWENTY FIRST ENTRY

To this day I find it hard to believe that the fits the five girls went into that day were not real. It was not until Ann Putnam stood before the village many years later and admitted her guilt that I was convinced. I was quite sure my mother had not caused the girls, sufferings, but their fits were surely born of the Devil. I know now that it was the devil that lay within them.

The crowd watched in horror as Ann Putnam and Mary Walcott rolled on the floor and foamed at the mouth. Soon they were joined by Abigail Williams and Elizabeth Hubbard. Only little Betty Parris stood away from the group as the girls screamed out their agony and begged my mother for mercy. Betty's face had lost all color as she watched her cousin and friends suffer. With no warning, Betty Parris quietly slid to the floor, senseless of all about her.

It was then that I looked at the faces about me. Those friends and neighbors I had known all of my short life were looking upon Mama as if she were something terrible. Even the two constables standing on either side of Mama backed away as the fits of the girls continued. The village tailor, Ezekiel Cheever, was busy scribbling something into a notebook as he watched poor Mama being accused by those vicious girls.

Suddenly it was more than I could stand. Mama needed me. She was so alone up there with only the baby to shield her from the hateful glances of the crowd. I tried to break free from my father's grasp, but it was no use. He was determined that I should stay where I was. All I got for my trouble was a bruised arm and a warning whispered into my ear.

"Try that again daughter and you won't be able to walk for a week," my father hissed as he displayed a concerned look for the benefit of the crowd.

I turned away from him and stared at my mother. The tears that ran down her cheeks as she watched the sufferings of those bad girls should have told Judge Hathorne that my mother was a woman of kindness and compassion, but even that was turned against her. Abigail Williams gave a scream and began rubbing her eyes furiously.

"They burn, they burn!" cried Abigail running in circles as she frantically sought relief. When Reverend Parris grabbed Abigail and tore her hands from her face the evidence was there for all to see. Abigail's eyes were a flaming mass of bloodshot pain.

"Sarah Good, do you see now what you have done?" said Judge Hathorne. "Tell us the truth. Why do you torment these poor children?"

"I do not torment them," said Mama raising her eyes to the rafters and then looking directly at the judge.

"Then who does, woman?" said Hathorne, trying not to let Mama's eyes meet his. "Do you employ someone else to do your work for you?"

"I employ no one," said Mama. "And I scorn you and these others for bringing me here."

"If there is no one else who harms these girls then why are they tormented?" continued Hathorne relentlessly. It was obvious what he meant by his words. Judge Hathorne believed that Mama was a witch!

I knew that unless Mama thought quickly she would be condemned then and there. "Oh Mama," I prayed silently, "think of something! Say anything that might save you."

Mama looked at me and I know, by her next words, that she must have read my heart.

"I am not the only one that was brought here today your worthy," said Mama hesitantly. "How do you know that I am to blame for the sufferings of these children?"

"Then who is?" said the judge with a slight smile touching his lips.

"I don't know," said Mama desperately, " but there were two other women brought in with me. Why am I seen as the guilty one?"

"Who torments these children, Goody Good?" said the judge looking at Mama in an almost kindly manner.

"It is Goody Osburn," cried Mama looking frantically into the crowd. How old Mama looked as she desperately shouted out the unfortunate Sarah Osburn's name.

"That may be so," said Judge Hathorne arranging the lace at his cuffs, "but you too, Goody Good, have much to answer for. Many in this very room hold you to be a witch."

"What proof have any of you that I should be called a witch?" said Mama realizing that there was no way to stop her trial. All she had done was help put the noose around Sarah Osburn's neck.

"Sarah Good," said the judge, "what is it you say when you go muttering away from people's houses?"

"Why, I pray, your honor," said Mama. "I say my commandments and a psalm.

"What psalm," said the judge. "Speak it now so that we may believe you."

"The psalm of death is what I speak your worthy," said Mama sadly. "I say it in memory of my beloved father who could not live this life God gave us. I pray for his soul today as I have prayed for it every day since his soul rose from the lake near our home.

The Lord is my shepherd, I shall not want.
He maketh me to lie down in green pastures:
He leadeth me beside the still waters, he restoreth my soul.
He leadeth me in the paths of righteousness for his names sake.
Yea though I walk through the valley of the shadow of death,
I will fear no evil, for thou art with me;
Thy rod and thy staff they comfort me.
Thou preparest a table before me in the presence of mine enemies:
Thou anointest my head with oil;
My cup runneth over.
Surely goodness and mercy shall follow me all the days of my life:
And I will dwell in the house of the Lord forever."

Never had I been prouder of my mother than I was at that moment! As I looked about the meetinghouse I could see that Mama's words had brought more than one villager to tears. Even Goodman Cheever had stopped his scribblings to listen to Mama's beautiful prayer. "Oh Mama," I thought, "maybe they will free you!"

But that was not to be. I could tell from the resolute set of Judge Hathorne's jaw that he had not liked Mama's prayer.

"What God do you serve Sarah Good?" he shouted at her in anger.

"Why the God that made heaven and earth!" shouted Mama equally angry. "And you know it as do all here abouts. 'Tis for no reason that I have been brought here. Those girls that pretend to swoon at my very glance are liars, your worthy. Why, it is only because I am a poor woman and helpless that I have been accused. Look to yourselves, and to Thomas

Putnam and Samuel Parris if you want to know why these girls suffer so. A bit of kindness may have kept them from their evil fantasies and wicked ways. 'Tis only to cover their own deeds that they accuse me now. Tell the truth for all to hear, Ann Putnam, before I tell it for you!"

"I will have order," cried Judge Hathorne as he beat his heavy gable upon the table.

"I will ask you once more Sarah Good, what God do you serve? Heaven help your soul if you cannot answer well."

"I serve the same God as any in this house your reverence," said Mama glaring at the villagers who accused her.

"Well then," said the Judge John Hathorne coughing as he cleared his throat. "Let us ask those who know you well whether your god is from heaven or hell. I call Goodman William Good to come forward to testify."

TWENTY SECOND ENTRY

I almost cried with relief as my father put my hand into Mistress Proctor's and bade me stay with her quietly until he was done. Now Mama would be saved and we could go home. Father may not like Mama, but he knew that she was no witch.

"There now, Dorcas," said Mistress Proctor stroking my hair, "don't be afraid. I'm sure that you will soon be out of danger."

"What danger Mistress?" I asked as I looked up at the pretty woman.

"Why the danger of possession by the witch, Sarah Good," said Elizabeth Proctor.

"'Tis my father who is to be feared, not my mother," I said, not able to still my words. "He's a cruel man and uses me harshly. 'Tis he who should be up there questioned and condemned before all. My mother is a good woman and has been nothing but kind to me."

"Hush now child," said Mistress Proctor letting go of my hand as if it burned her. I could tell from the look on her face that she wished no more to do with me and my foolish talk.

"Easy now little girl," said a warm voice next to me, "'twill go hard with you if those about hear you speaking badly of your father. Only a dutiful child goes unpunished in these harsh times."

"Right you are, sir," I said, looking up at the tall young man who had spoken. His warm brown eyes and golden hair made him look as if he were some sort of kindly archangel sent from heaven to comfort me. I surprised myself by not moving away as he placed a gentle hand on my shoulder.

"What you hear next, little one, may not be what you imagine. Steel yourself to silence, for to cry out would only hurt those you love."

"Yes sir," I said placing my trust in the unknown stranger. Somehow I knew, even then, that here was one who knew what I knew. I watched quietly as my father took his place upon the platform. It seemed strange to me to see him from such a distance. He didn't look like my father at all. Gone was the mean sneer from his lips and the flexed muscle of his arm. It was as if some sad and sober being had possessed his body.

"William Good," said Judge Hathorne, "look upon the prisoner and say what she is to you."

"She is the woman Sarah Good, whom I have called wife. It is to my regret that she has not been such to me for many a month gone by."

"And why is that, sir?" said the judge, warming to my father's plaintive tone.

"Because she is a mean spirited creature who abandons the vows she has made to me before her God in favor of a bitter tongue," replied my father with a sigh.

"Then she uses you harshly, Goodman Good?"

"Aye, that she does your honor," said my father staring directly into my mother's face.

"And what is your opinion of all that you have heard here today, Goodman," asked Judge Hathorne.

"That my wife Sarah is either a witch now or will be one very quickly, your honor," said my father with his traitorous lying tongue.

It was then that I felt the rage fill my body. I attempted to shout out against my father only to find my mouth covered by the hand of the stranger who had befriended me.

"Easy now maid," he said, stooping down next to me and cradling me in his arms. "They will say that your mother has driven you to fits if you cry out now. I know these people and have learned that for such as you or Jackie Quelch there is no justice to be found in this place. Silence now may earn you the freedom you need to help your mother later."

"Yes sir," I whispered back, realizing the wisdom of his words.

"Well then, William Good," I heard the judge say, "have you any proof of Sarah Good's witching ways?"

"Only," said my father with another false sigh, "that she has bad carriage unto me and," said my father as the lying tears welled up in his eyes, "that she has always been an enemy to all good. Clearly she must be a witch."

"Thank you Goodman Good," said Judge Hathorne solemnly as he motioned for my father to step down. "It has been hard upon you I know

84

to say such words against your helpmate and the Almighty himself thanks you for doing your Christian duty. Sarah Good," continued the judge, "you may now take your leave of us until the morrow when we will once again examine what is in your heart. Think well upon the fate that awaits you and your sister witches. Confession is the only way that you will be cleansed of your evil and brought back to the covenant of the Lord."

"I am innocent," cried my mother as the constables dragged her from the room. I will never forget the sound of her fading cries as Hathorne gave a solemn look towards Judge Corwin and once again banged his gavel for order.

"Come now maid," said my kind stranger, "let us leave this place before any does you harm." With those words, the man who called himself Jack Quelch whisked me into his arms and out the door before my father could make his way back to me.

TWENTY THIRD ENTRY

Outside the meetinghouse Jack Quelch set me on the ground and took my hand.

"Where are we going? I want to stay and see what happens!" I cried as I looked back towards the meetinghouse in time to see poor old Sarah Osburn being dragged forward meet the judge.

"A child of your years has had quite enough for one day," said Quelch with an odd set to his jaw. "Why I'll warrant your blackguard of a father hasn't even seen that your little belly has been filled. Am I right in that lass?"

"Yes sir," I said feeling it was useless to tell him that father had eaten all there was left in the house, leaving none for me. It sounds strange I know, but for some reason I felt that I was to blame for my father and his evil ways.

"Then it's off to Ingersolls for a bit of meat and drink, Dorcas Good."

"But what of my father?" I asked looking back.

"Twill be safe enough for a while. Such as he will stand eagerly to hear the other poor women questioned," said Master Quelch picking me up in his arms and making his way toward food and comfort.

The safety of his strong arms felt wonderful about me. Never before had I been carried in such a kindly manner. I think back on it now and realize that at the time Jack Quelch was a very young man, barely more than a child himself, but to me he seemed like a God. How big and brave he was as we journeyed towards Ingersolls.

It was not until I heard a door slam and the rumble of masculine voices that I realized I had fallen asleep. By the dark that filled the place I knew that I had slept the day away. I opened my eyes and looked around. Had I been dreaming? Was my mother's examination at the meetinghouse only another of my nightmares?

"Here now, lass," I heard a voice from nearby say," I thought you were going to sleep until the morrow."

I sat up and looked towards the friendly voice. Then I remembered. Master Quelch! The tavern! The trial! They were all as real as death itself. I gave a cry of disappointment and burst into tears.

"There now sweetheart," said Master Quelch as he protected me from staring eyes by standing in front of me and offering me a brightly colored bit of cloth, "tis right that you should weep. Go ahead little one."

"I can't cry," I said as I soaked his crimson handkerchief with my tears. "Father says only bad girls cry, and when you're bad you get what you deserve."

"Your father's a mean fool and a coward to boot," said Quelch as he sat beside me quietly. "Look at me, Dorcas Good, and remember my words. I had such as yours for a father and there was no good nor truth in him. Men like that tell lies to get what they want. 'Tis wrong to tell a little girl she is bad when she cries. You are a sweet child, both true and loyal to your mother. Many a day I've seen you by her side as she went house to house, begging for her bread, and thought what a fine daughter you are. It's ashamed I am that I did not reach out to you both sooner and offer you something to sustain you."

"But why should you?"

"Because you are a child and I am a man, Christian to the core despite what those around here might think. And what's more I knew what you were suffering lass. 'Tis not just little girls that find themselves ill used by those who should cherish them. There is a sickness in this town that goes far beyond those poor hysterical girls who accused your mother. They are possessed all right, but it has more to do with the madness of man than any Devil with a black book."

"Oh Master Quelch," I said suddenly afraid for my new friend, "don't speak so. That's how my Mama spoke and see where she is now. They punish people for telling the truth."

"Right you are my wise little friend," said Jack looking about him. It was true, there were many faces turned in our direction, eagerly trying to catch what was being said between the roguish young man and the daughter of the witch. "Now then, let's get to our victuals before Ingersoll runs out. I'll warrant that the day's work is over by the look of the villagers coming through the door."

"I am hungry," I said as I rubbed my empty stomach, "but in a way I'm not. It seems as if there is an ache that fills me and wants no food."

"That is your heart's yearning for your mother," said friend Jack as he motioned for bread, meat, and ale from a woman passing by our table. "If you are to stay strong enough to help your mother you must turn away from that ache and eat. Gather together everything you have within you that is strong so that you can live through what will come."

"Yes Master Quelch," I said as I picked up the piece of venison he placed before me.

"Tell me lass, have you any friends or kin that you can turn to?"

"No one sir," I said. "There has always been only Mama and me, and now baby Mercy of course. Oh and then there are my pets."

"Pets?"

"Yes Master Quelch. The three beautiful birds that live near our house. Mama and I feed them whenever Father is gone so that he won't beat us for wasting food. But Master Quelch, if you saw those birds you know that we were not wasting food. One is black, one yellow and one blue. They are the most beautiful things I have ever seen. I wish you could see how they eat right out of Mama's hand. And when she talks to them it's so wonderful! It's almost as if they understand what she's saying. How I wish I could hear Mama sing with her birds again. I must make sure they are fed so that they will be here when Mama comes home."

"How strange that they have not flown to warmer climes," said Quelch eyeing me oddly.

"Why should they, sir, when Mama feeds them. It's like my snake, Emily," I said removing my secret companion from my skirt pocket to show Master Jack. "Why should she run away from me when she can stay warm and safe in my pocket. See how happy she is. Mama found her one day and told me to keep her for my own. See the way she loves to suck my finger?"

"Put that away child," whispered Quelch, drawing his arm across my body and turning me away from curious onlookers.

"But why?" I asked, hurt by his motions.

"Because there are many about that will see such pets as friends of the Devil. Trust me in this Dorcas. Say and do nothing that those about you can use against you. They are out for blood, and many innocent villagers will perish before their hunger is satisfied. Free your snake and let the birds take flight."

"But they are all I have now," I said on the verge of a fresh outburst of tears.

"Sometimes we must leave everything we hold dear behind us is we are to survive, Dorcas. Never forget that."

"No sir," I said putting my trust in the warm brown eyes flickering with gold. I slipped Emily the snake back into my pocket, resolved to let her free at the first possible moment. To this day I can't tell you why, but I trusted Jack Quelch, and thank God for it.

"So, that's where you are, you little bitch!" growled a familiar voice from behind me. I knew from the expression on Jack's face that my father's mood was an evil one.

"It's young ye are to be sttin' in tavern with the likes of this no good, but if that's what ye want girl I can see to it that you turn your father a profit for your time." With those words my father grabbed me by the shoulders and set me on my feet.

"William Good," said Jack Quelch, "it's time you left off torturing this child and saw to yourself. There are many about this town that know you for what you are. Treat her well or you will pay, I promise you."

"And what business is it of yours, you whoreson," yelled my father standing nose to nose with the younger, taller man.

"If I choose to make it such then it is," said Jack putting his hand upon his sword and backing my father against the wall. "I'll be watching you, Good. See to it that the maid comes to no harm or you will pay for her every tear."

"Look here," said my father, his voice lowering to a whisper, "if you want her you can have her. She's a fine little bit and seems to like a poke. She's all yours if you can give poor old William fifty pounds sterling."

"Here now, what's this," said Nathaniel Ingersoll as he pulled Jack away from my father. Constables Herrick and Locker stood in front of my father and blocked Jack's way. It was a good thing too, for from the look on Jack's face he was ready for murder. That was the only time I ever felt grateful for the constables of Salem Village. The last thing I wanted now was to see Jack Quelch hanging from a tree at Gallows Hill. He was my only friend.

"I'll have no fighting in here. Sit down William and take your rest. And as for you, Master Quelch, leave these two alone. Enough has been done to Goodman Good this day."

"Remember what I said, " yelled my friend Jack as Constable Herrick dragged him towards the door.

90

TWENTY FOURTH ENTRY

"Sit down daughter," said my father as he smoothed his hair and eyed me strangely. "'Tis time you heard what the others have said of your mother. While you've been having a high time here, your poor old father has stood in the cold for hours listening to the fullness of you mother's evil deeds."

"My mother is not evil!" I said kicking him under the table.

"She's as evil as you are, bitch," he said reaching under the table and twisting my leg until I thought it would break. It was then that I remembered Jack's words. I refused to give my father the satisfaction of tears. Instead I smiled at him and said, "I'm sorry Father, what is it that you wanted to tell me?"

"Just that you mother has been condemned by the witches Tituba and Osburn." said my father with a satisfied grunt.

"I don't believe it.! You're a liar!"

"Softly daughter," said my father as he patted my head and made quite a show of smiling at me for the benefit of others to see. "Aye," he sighed, "'tis true, Daughter. Your mother has been found guilty enough to be held over for more examination. She rests now in Salem jail, and it is my guess that she will soon be taken to Boston to await her time of judgment."

"I don't understand, Father," I said softly, "has she already been found guilty? I heard no one say she was."

"Sarah Good, the witch, will be questioned tomorrow, but her guilt is plain for all eyes to see. If you had stayed with your poor grieving father, instead of running about with the likes of Jackie Quelch, you would have heard what the old woman and the Indian said."

"What did they say?" I asked as the room begin to spin about me.

"Well daughter, if you must know, it seems that your mother has long been in league with the Devil. Oh, Goody Osburn tried to act as if she were innocent, but when she heard that your mother had said that she and Osburn were in league, Goody Osburn's face went white. Then the poor afflicted girls shrieked as they were pinched and slapped by unseen hands. Who else harmed them but your own sweet mother? She was the only one left unchained at the time of the poor girl's misery. Sarah Good had been left free in hand to ride the horse to the jail where she was to be kept until the morrow. It was plain for all to see that Osburn and the Indian were held fast by their chains. Your mother was the only one who could have hit those sweet innocent girls."

"But Father, that's impossible, Mama wasn't even there.!"

"'Tis the sign of a witch that she can harm those who are not near her," said my father sadly. "And then," he continued," there is the matter of Tituba's testimony."

"What of it, Father? Oh please tell me everything."

"Well," said my father warming to his task, "even I would not have imagined such blackness in your mother's heart if I had not heard it with my own ears. 'Tis a blessing that either of us are still alive, child. Tituba took the stand and soon admitted that she was a witch and that your mother and Goody Osburn were witches as well. It seems that at night they ride upon sticks high up in the air to do their mischief. It is your mother who has been torturing poor little Betty Parris and Ann Putnam. It seems that she also plotted to kill Ann with a knife. She wanted to cut off the innocent child's head! Lord forgive me that I was so often away from the house and at prayer. If I had stayed closer to your mother those girls would not be suffering now."

"At prayer, Father? I thought you were just out getting drunk."

"Careful, little Dorcas," said my father looking at me again with his false smile and sad face, "even now it may be too late to save you. An evil tongue on a woman is a sure sign of witchery, and yours is as sharp as a serpent."

"Now then," I said quietly, afraid that his words might be true, "what else did Tituba say?"

"That she and your mother came together last night and sent your mother's three birds to torture the afflicted girls. Don't deny that you have seen your mother's birds come right up to her and eat out of her hand. Tituba said that she watched as the black bird sucked your mother's hand between the forefinger and long finger of her right hand."

"But that's impossible!" I said, furious at the foolishness of my father's words. "Mama was giving birth last night. You know Tituba is lying!"

"What of the little cat that follows your mother everywhere, daughter," said my father with that smile that I was beginning to hate. "Surely that cat does her bidding."

"You know it just follows her because Mama is kind to it," I said beginning to be weary of the whole conversation. It was becoming quite clear to me that the Salem villagers were going to believe what they wanted to.

"Daughter, you might as well resign yourself to the fact that your mother is a witch. She has been seen torturing the village girls, cavorting with
animals and signing the Devil's own book. Tituba herself saw the name 'Sarah Good' blazing form the pages of the dark man's bible. Be prepared for the worst, Dorcas, for it shall come soon. There are many more waiting to testify upon the morrow and all of them have no good to say of your mother. Come now, it's a cold journey home and I'm tired."

"But what of Mama?" I said realizing with horror that I would have to spend the long night alone with the brutal William Good.

"Why daughter, she's as good dead," he said as grasped my hand tightly and pulled me towards home."

TWENTY FIFTH ENTRY

I know it may sound strange, but I was becoming used to my father and his animal ways. The terror I felt as he hurried me towards home was soon replaced by the echo of Master Quelch's words. It was as if there was a small angel whispering in my ear, "survive Dorcas, survive". Even as I stood before my father, naked and alone, I knew that he could no longer harm the real me. The strength I found in my far away dream island, and the reality of Jack Quelch's words carried me far away from my fathers putrid breath and sweating body.

It was almost with pity that I watched my father's face as he lay next to me in Mama's bed. His snores and grunts seemed so base, so simple. I knew now that I could be free of my father as long as I saw to it that he had his fill of food, drink and me. Mistress Hannibelle has said that managing men is not so easy, but I have always found it so. To me, most men are nothing more than predators looking for a feeding. All men, that is, but Jack Quelch.

I was strangely peaceful as I lay in that bed next to my father and listened to the cries of the brittle March wind. I felt almost guilty for the content that filled me as I watched the flickering of the hearth fire through the open door. The worst that could happen had already happened. Mama and baby Mercy were locked away in some cold small cell and I was alone with my father. All my life I had lived in fear of such a moment and now that it had come to pass I found that I could not only live through it, but find strength in the thought that I could survive. I know now that I can thank my mother for such strength. From the day I was born she had been preparing me for such a moment by teaching me how to care for myself and cope with my father's ways.

"Thank you Mama," I whispered to the passing wind as I turned on my side and fell asleep. It was then that I heard the voice.

"Dorcas, Dorcas Good!"

"Who is it?" I said, as my dream self sat up in bed.

"Tis but a small man come to warm himself by your fire," said the tiny figure standing almost in the flames.

The small man could not have been more than three feet tall, for I could look him straight in the eye as I moved closer to get a better look at him. He was dressed all in black and had the ruddy complexion of someone who spent most of his time outside. The white of his hair almost hurt my eyes with it's brilliance. It reminded me of snow on a sunny January day. Next to the man stood a woman with wings who wore a black silk hood lined with white. Something told me that I should stay far away from these two, but I felt myself being drawn closer and closer as the man hummed a strangely bewitching tune. "I must ask him what it is," I thought.

"Excuse me sir, what is it you are humming?" I asked the man who ignored me and turned his back.

"Sir," I repeated," I must know the tune," I said loudly as I touched his sleeve.

The man gave a deep laugh as he turned to face me. It was then that I saw that in place of eyes the man with the snowy hair had deep empty sockets. Out of each socket crawled a snake that looked like my own pet Emily.

"Stay, my dear, and Nick will sing you an even prettier tune," laughed the man as he made a grab for my arm.

"No," I cried as I managed to jump away from him and run to the far end of the room.

"Yes dear, come here and let poor Mary get a feel of your firm lips," said the lady with the white and black hood. I could see that her eyes were a beautiful brilliant blue, but the mouth that she offered me was dripping with white pus.

"No," I cried," as I backed into the wall, "I won't. And anyway, I don't believe in you. You are just a dream."

"That may be so, little one," said the black man, "but ask Betty Parris how real a dream can be. You cannot run forever, Dorcas Good. You belong to us."

"Yes, little girl," said the woman stretching her arms toward me. "There will be a day when you invite old Nick and his sweet Mary to abide with you always."

"Never," I cried as I watched the two turn to each other and begin to smolder. The next thing I knew they were stepping into the flames and riding them up the chimney. I knew when I heard Master Nick's tune blend in with the melody of the wind that they were gone.

I stood there shivering a moment or two and became aware of another voice. It sounded to me like the voice of the doctor's niece, Elizabeth Hubbard. Her form came into view and I saw that she was pointing to another form standing on our table. To my amazement I saw that it was my mother, bare legged and naked to the waist. I watched in horror as a heavy staff flew through the air and struck my mother on the arm, causing it to bleed from elbow to wrist. The specter of my mother gave a sob and disappeared.

"Remember Dorcas," I heard a voice whispering in my ear, "you are not alone." At first the voice sounded like my mother's and then the lower tones of a man's voice joined in. I realized, to my delight, that both Mama and Master Quelch were with me, holding up my spirit and filling my soul with hope. It was true! I was not alone. The fear that had filled my heart disappeared and I felt myself wandering back towards the bed, shaken but calm. I knelt beside the bed and closed my eyes.

"Dear God," I said with silently moving lips, "help us."

TWENTY SIXTH ENTRY

Any peace I felt was drained from me as I watched Mama being led into the meetinghouse the next day. I thought it strange that she was holding the baby in her left arm until I noticed that there was a bloody rag wrapped around her right one. Mama's poor arm was bloody from elbow to wrist

"See, there's the proof," I hear Elizabeth Hubbard cry as she fell to the floor and began pulling out her hair.

"Tis the witch I saw lying on the ground before me last night," cried the cooper, William Allen, as he stood protectively in front of the writhing Elizabeth.

"I saw her too," cried a nodding John Hughes. "Twas Sarah Good that appeared before me in lewdness this night past. Of that I am sure."

"You're a fool, Johnny," I heard my mother say in a scolding tone. "Tis only your rum addled brain that makes you speak so. Hush now before you bring me to harm."

"The accused will be silent," yelled Judge Hathorne. "Wasting God's own time is an act of the Devil and I'll have none of it. Master Allen, you and Master Hughes will soon be brought to testify and have your say against Sarah Good. Until then please take your seats and wait patiently."

"And what of me, your worship?" asked Samuel Braybrook, the weaver.

"You will all have your say in good turn," said the judge, "but first I wish to call William Good."

"William Good is so called," said Constable Herrick as he struck his staff on the ground three times.

"Now don't go wandering off as you did yesterday, Dorcas," said my father as he patted my head and handed me over to the unsympathetic Dr. Griggs.

"Guard her well, sir. She is a gadabout and a runaway with need of a firm hand," said my father sternly.

"So I can see," said the old doctor as he closed his hand around my arm like a vise. "Let us pray that she holds none of her mother's poison within her."

"Yes, let us pray," said my father as he turned and made his way to the front of the room.

How I hated his swaggering, arrogant form. The peace of last night had totally deserted me and in its place was a disgust for everything that assailed my eyes and ears. How could these people be such fools? Couldn't they see that Ann Putnam and those other mean girls were lying?

"Now then sir," I heard Judge Hathorne say as he motioned my father to face frontward. "What is it you have to say for yourself and the woman you call wife?"

"Only that I have been tricked the same as any in this room as to her deeds, your honor," said my coward of a father.

"In what way is that, Goodman Good?" said the judge, nodding his head as if he felt true sympathy for my father's plight as a betrayed husband.

"Just that I know her for what she is now," said Father, "a witch who wanders about with the black man and rides upon a stick. The truth of it came to me when I saw the Devil's own mark upon her where her skin had been fresh and clean only a fortnight ago."

"A mark, sir?" said the judge fairly drooling in anticipation."

"Aye your honor, a mark. Examine the witch and see it for yourself. There is a strange lump on her right shoulder. Surely Goodwife Ingersoll must have seen it when she searched Sarah."

"Why, so I did your honor," came the voice of Goodwife Ingersoll from out of the crowd. "I thought it just a lump left by a fall or a beating, but now that I think of it, 'twas surely a wart or tett left by the devil himself."

"There, you see your honor," said my father, "Sarah Good does carry the witches mark upon her body."

"'Tis not true, Judge!" I heard my mother cry. "'Tis the mark of my man's whip upon my body and nothing else. You should be ashamed, William Good, to use such a thing against me!"

"The accused will be silent or find herself gagged," said Hathorne looking from husband to wife in dismay. "You may step away from here William Good. Once again the people of Salem Village thank you for your honesty."

I watched as my father slowly stepped down from the raised platform and made his way towards Thomas Putnam. It was disgusting how Putnam put his arms about my father and offered him consolation. Who was there to comfort my mother? Baby Mercy and I were but helpless children.

I watched my mother closely and prayed silently for her to look at me. I thought that if I could just catch her eye and smile at her she might gather some strength. Wonder of wonders, she did look my way and smile. It was as if the sun had shone down upon me and warmed my very soul.

"Hear me Mama," I said in my mind. "You are not alone. No matter what happens, Mercy and I love you and believe you."

A strange tunnel of light seemed to appear and block out everything but my mother's gaze. It was as if we were linked together by our hearts and our minds. Nothing else existed outside of our special world. I could hear the testimony of John Hughes and William Allen, but I could not feel it. Their droning voices, describing of how Mama had come to them and then disappeared, made no impression upon me. It was not until Samuel Braybrook took the stand that the light faded between Mama and me and the room took on its former dismal tone.

"And how did Sarah Good attempt to take her own life?" I heard the judge say.

"By jumping not once, but three times from the horse we had set her upon to take her back to jail," said the worthy Samuel. "Either she was trying to bring upon her own death or escape into the night with her guilt."

"Oh Mama," I thought, "not that! If you die I shall surely die too!"

"Twas the madness of the moment, daughter," I heard Mama's voice echo within me as I looked toward her and saw that she was mouthing the words with her lips.

"See, the witch is talking to her master!" screamed Abigail Williams as she tore at her clothes and held up scratched arms for the whole gathering to see.

"She pinches, she pinches!" yelled Ann Putnam rolling about on the earthen floor.

"Take the woman from here, Constable," said the judge in a steady voice. "We have learned all we need to know for this day."

"I hurt no one," I heard my mother cry as I watched her being dragged from the room for a second time.

TWENTY SEVENTH ENTRY

The next few days were more of the same. Daylight was spent listening my mother's closest friends and neighbors betray her, and nighttime was spent in the rough, hot hands of my father. Between dark and light I felt that I was battered in both body and soul. It was with amazement that I caught a glimpse of myself in a patch of ice and saw that I still looked like the same four year old Dorcas I had been a month ago. I felt older than grandmotherly Rebecca Nurse. The only thing that roused me from my stupor was when I heard that Mama was to be taken even farther away from me. Judge Hathorne had ruled that Mama was bad enough to stand trial for witchcraft and must be taken to the real jail in Boston. He might as well have said the moon! Boston was another world. I felt in my heart that if they took Mama there, I would never see her again.

"I must do something to stop it," I mumbled, as I walked with my father from the meetinghouse.

"What is that, Daughter?"

"Nothing Father," I said, not aware that I had spoken aloud.

"Be careful with your mutterings, Dorcas Good," said my father as he pushed me towards home and his filthy bed. "There are many that think that as the child of your mother you are already half a witch."

I listened in silence as he went on and on about my mother and her foul ways, but my mind was far away. I was desperately casting about for some way to save my mother. Then a wonderful idea came to me. If Ann Putnam could make my mother guilty, why couldn't she make her innocent? All I had to do was find her and get her to say she had made a mistake and my mother was not a witch. I would slip out this very night after my father had fallen asleep and beg her to save Mama. Her family was the most powerful in the village. Surely she could do anything she wanted to. Father had said often enough that Reverend Parris did whatever Master Thomas Putnam told him to. Why not turn that to my advantage and to free Mama! And I knew how I would make Ann do it! Unless she said the words that returned Mama to me, I would tell everything I knew about the her fortune telling parties and the casting of spells done by Ann and the other girls.

"I can save Mama," I thought as I began to skip and laugh, "I know I can."

The moon lit my way as I struggled through the heavy wet snow. Father had been especially lively this night and had used me hardly. My legs shook with the pain. As I looked up, I thought I saw a shadow flicker across the moon. I stopped and rubbed my eyes and looked again. What was it? It must have been a bird, but if it was, it was the biggest bird I had ever seen. It was more the size of a man than anything that had feathers. I shrugged my shoulders and moved on, terribly aware of the cold stillness of the night.

The Purnam house lay almost a full mile beyond that of Reverend Parris and his family. It had taken me far longer than I had thought to get there and I could tell by the angle of the moon that there was perhaps only an hour or two before the sun would begin to rise. I knew well the window that belonged to Ann Putnam. It lay at the back of the house behind the kitchen. How lucky was spoiled Ann to have a room to herself. Few in the village ever dreamed of such a luxury. Only rich girls could enjoy the bliss of a bed to themselves and a room alone.

As I passed the stable I noticed that there was a stall that sheltered more than one horse. I recognized the small brown mare that Mary Walcott rode standing beside the tall black stallion of Thomas Putnam's. "So," I thought, "I will get two for the price of one." Mary must be visiting her cousin Ann for the night. The whole village knew that Ann and Mary often visited each other and kept company for as long as a week. It was strange, but small as I was, I no longer felt afraid of twelve year old Ann and seventeen year old Mary. True, they were almost as big as grownups, but their fits had shown me that they were full of childish fear. Only two girls desperate to protect themselves would have resorted to such mean ways to protect themselves from punishment. I would have never done such a thing no matter how bad my punishment would have been. Mary and Ann were nothing but liars and cheats for all their fine clothes and fancy ways.

As I approached Ann's window I saw a single candle burning. It cast a warm glow out onto the snow piled high against the Putnam house. I eagerly climbed upon the snow and peered in, fully expecting to see Ann and Mary fast asleep. But that is not what I saw.

Ann Putnam and Mary Walcott were completely naked and wrapped in each others arms. The look on their faces was just like the one I had seen on my father's on many a night, right before he would tear me apart with his hard flesh. I gasped silently as I watched first Ann, and then Mary slide down each other to the place that Father made me touch while he watched. In turn, each girl kissed and fondled the other until they both arched in some sort of pleasure. How could they like what they were doing to each other? When Father did such things to me I only felt pain. But what Mary and Ann were doing had nothing to do with pain. It was obvious to me that they liked playing their game. The happiness on their faces as they sank deep into each others embrace made me feel that some-day I would like to find out what this game was all about.

"Dorcas Good!" I heard a voice in my head shout, "come ye to your senses and get about the night's work. 'Twill soon be to late to do any-thing but grieve for you mother and your sister unless you make haste."

"Dear Lord," I gasped as I lost my footing and crashed down the snow bank.

"What was that?" I heard a voice from within say as the sash of the window went up and Ann Putnam looked down.

"Tis only Dorcas Good come to get justice for her innocent mother," I said boldly, secretly relieved that now I could not avoid confronting Ann.

"Your mother is as guilty as sin," said Mary, joining Ann at the window.

"Far less guilty than either of you. I've seen your wicked games and spell casting, Mary Walcott," I said in as loud as whisper as I could. "And what's more what I saw just now was surely lewdness. Say the words that will free my mother or I will tell everyone in the village what I know of you and
your friends. If my mother goes to Boston jail I swear that you will soon join her."

"Fine words from the child of a witch," laughed Ann as she put an arm around Mary. "Tell your tales, Dorcas Good, and I promise you that you will live to regret it. You certainly look like a witch to me. Why else would you be wandering around in the moonlight spying on innocent folk. Get out of here before I wake my father and have you arrested."

"You wouldn't dare!" I cried as I backed away from the window. I could tell from the half insane look on Ann's face that she meant every word. "Oh, what have I done," I thought as I turned away from Ann and fled toward the rising sun.

I must have run over two miles before I looked back over my shoulder. I knew that Ann Putnam was more than capable of sending something evil to track me down. The pounding of my heart was thundering in my ears as I sat down behind a thicket of holly to take my rest. It was then that I spied the heavy brown horses of Constables Locker and Herrick. Between them rode three women on mangy nags. The Indian, Tituba, was supporting a sick looking Sarah Osburn and looking from side to side. The third woman was my Mama! She was having a hard time holding the reins and the baby at the same time. Every time she tried to wrap the old rags more tightly about my sister the reins would slacken and her horse jump forward.

"None of your tricks, witch," I heard Constable Locker say as he struck my mother on the leg.

"I'm just trying to warm my babe," I heard my mother cry defiantly as she held the baby closer.

"Then do a better job of it or I'll see to it that Boston jail has one less prisoner. It would be a mercy for those poor girls if you died before we got there."

"Try as you might, Goodman Herrick, I will live through this and see you suffer for your ill treatment," said my mother.

"Silence, witch," he cried as he struck her again and knocked her to the ground.

"That's no way to treat a prisoner," said Constable Locker as he got off his horse and helped Mama back on hers.

"Remember what the judge said. We get paid by the delivery. No delivery, no gold," said Locker with a smile.

"Right you are," said Herrick as he grasped the reins of my mother's horse and pulled her forward. "Keep you mouth shut, witch, and perhaps I'll let you live." With that he made off down the road dragging Mama behind him.

I watched in stunned silence as Mama disappeared. I must have looked at the point where she disappeared for almost an hour because when I tried to move my whole body was stiff and cold. It was then that a deep despair flooded my soul and I knew that there was no reason to go on. I lay down in the cold, comforting snow. I knew now that if there was a God he had deserted me, and if there wasn't I had nothing to fear. The bliss of blackness seemed sweet indeed. "Good bye Mama," I whispered through cracked lips as I closed my eyes.

PART THREE

BETRAYAL

TWENTY EIGHTH ENTRY

It was not until many days later that I awoke to find myself wrapped in blankets and lying by a roaring fire. At first I thought that I had been punished for my evil deed and landed in hell until I heard the familiar rumble of my father's voice.

"There now, you see Quelch," I heard Father say, "I told you she would live. Any child of Sarah Good's has too much meanness in her to go quietly. It's in your debt I am to you for finding her."

I looked up from the blankets to see my father and Jack Quelch playing some sort of game. A bottle of rum stood between them on the table. I could tell by the firelight shining through it that the bottle was almost empty.

"I'll have none of your smooth words to trick me from my game, William," said Master Quelch as he glanced at me quickly and then looked away. "If I win this toss the lass is mine as you promised."

"And if you lose, you owe me more than you have, Quelch," laughed my father. It was then that someone began pounding on the door.

"Damn," said my father as one of the game pieces fell to the floor. "Bide a bit, Quelch, and we'll finish this yet."

My father opened the door and I saw his face go white as he ushered in Constable George Herrick.

"I'm here to make an arrest," he said solemnly, looking from my father to Jack Quelch.

"But I'm guilty of nothing," said my father, backing away from the door and towards his rifle.

"'Tis not you we wish, but Dorcas here," said the Constable with a red face.

"That's ridiculous," said Jack, leaping to his feet and scattering the game pieces on the floor.

111

"'Tis true, Master Quelch," said the Constable as he was joined at the door by William Allen and Samuel Braybrook. All three men carried sidearms and swords.

"Masters Edward and Jonathan Putnam have both signed the warrant. Dorcas Good is under suspicion of witchcraft and is to be taken for questioning."

"Master Jack," I cried as I leapt to my feet and ran towards him. "Don't let them take me."

"She's my daughter and I must see to it that justice is done," said my father tearing me from Jack's protecting arms and thrusting me towards the Constable.

"Take her now and do with her what ye will. I'll not have this Devil's spawn under my roof a minute longer."

"Well said, Brother Good," said Samuel Braybrook as he picked me up in his arms and carried my squirming body away.

"This is not the last you hear of me, William Good," I heard Jack Quelch shout as he stared into the barrel of the musket my father had shoved against Jack's chest.

The next stop the Constable made was at the home of Rebecca Nurse. How my spirits lifted as I saw that George Herrick meant to turn down the familiar pathway that led to the large brown house. I had always delighted in any visit to the Nurse homestead. The house stood at the end of a long pathway lined with apple trees. It had been built on a small rise overlooking fertile cleared fields that represented the bulk of the Nurse family's power. I knew, from listening to Mama, that Rebecca Nurse and her family had not always been so well off. They had gained their lands and beautiful house, with sparkling diamond cut windows, through hard work and honest living. Mama would often sigh and say that if Rebecca Nurse had married grandfather, we would be respected daughters of the town and have a special place to sit in church on Sundays. Mama liked and admired old Rebecca Nurse and would often stop at the house to see how she was feeling. I smiled as I thought of the day that Goody Nurse had been well enough to sit outside the front door and teach me to knit. It had been a glorious day, all aglow with the spicy heat of the changeable September sun.

"Remember, Dorcas," I could still hear Goody Nurse saying, "always make small loops for warmth. 'Tis the only way you can hope to keep out the chill once the wind begins to blow."

"Yes ma'am," I had said hoping that she could hear me. Goody Nurse had been almost deaf last fall, but there were still times when she could hear if you spoke loud enough and looked her in the eye. I remember she had gazed down at me and touched my shoulder gently as I struggled with the small bit of blue yarn she had given me.

"No, Dorcas," she had said as she untangled the small balled up mess that had wound itself around my fingers, "'Tis not that way at all. Leave off with this task and look up at the sky. I can see that you are still too small for such work."

"Mama says I'm a big girl, and smart too," I said, stung by her words.

"That you are, sweeting," said Rebecca as she put her arm about me and tipped my eyes towards the sky, "but there is a time for everything. Knitting will come soon enough to your clever fingers. Tell me, young Dorcas Good, what do you see in yon sky?"

"Why, clouds and sun and sky, Goody Nurse. What else is there to see?"

"Oh many things, child, if you know how to look. Take that strangely shaped cloud above us. Both you and I know that it is just a cloud to most folks, but I find that if I look at it long enough it becomes a mist that encircles my mind and carries me away to far off places.

"I know just what you mean!" I said, excited beyond belief. "It's not clouds that carry me away, but that moment before I dream, or when I stare into the dying embers of the fire. I know my dream places are really real."

"Just like your grandfather Solart," sighed Goody Nurse as she gave my shoulder a hug.

"My grandfather?"

"Yes child, I knew him well. There was a time when I thought of setting my cap for Johnny Solart. I still think of him and wonder if things might have been different if I had," said Rebecca with a smile on her face that made her look like a young girl.

"Oh," I said nodding my head in understanding, "you mean that he might have been happy and not drownded himself."

"Yes Dorcas, that is exactly what I mean. How clever you are to know that."

"Mama said that my grandfather was always sad. He would stare into the fire and go away just as I do. She says that when he would come back, he would go for walks so that no one could see him cry. Do you know why he was sad, Goody Nurse?"

"I think I do Dorcas, and perhaps you do too. Think upon it child. The things you say you see in your dreamland, or in the fire, are not always happy are they?"

"No, they're not," I said thinking of the time I had seen Father beating Mama with his belt, long before the welts appeared on her back.

"Well then, you see how it is. Your grandfather's gift was strong and true. He could see folk's misfortunes before they happened, just as you and I can. Sometimes the burden of that can be too great for a man. A man always feels that he should be able to fix whatever is wrong."

"Why did he drown himself, Goody Nurse?"

"Because his visions became to strong for him to bear, little one. I remember the times that we spent walking along the lake, speaking of the Indian raids to come and the failures of crops not yet planted. At first he would try to warn the villagers, but no one believed him. I tried to tell him that people only want to hear good news, but he kept on and on until finally he fell silent. That is when he turned from me to marry your grandmother and open the tavern. I remember well when Johnny fell to using rum as a way to silence the voices within him, but I could tell it never really worked. Death was the only path to peace for such as John Solart."

"I think I know what you mean," I had said quietly. "I've seen things that make me want to run away lately. I've tried to tell Mama, but she just makes me hush, or tells me that my mind lies to me. But what I see and hear and feel is the truth. I know, right now, that there is a nasty dark thing right here in Salem Village, but no one would believe me if I told them about it. I've seen it in barns and bushes, and once I saw it sneaking up behind Ann Putnam in the meetinghouse. It looked like some sort of black slimy snake, only I knew it wasn't real."

"I believe you, Dorcas Good. I too have seen the darkness you speak of," said Goody Nurse turning to me and covering my tiny hands with her large wrinkled ones.

"Will it hurt us, Mistress Rebecca?"

"Yes, I believe it will. But I also see that we will go through it together. Whatever happens, I will be with you unto death, Dorcas Good."

It was then that I looked into Rebecca Nurse's face and realized that we had spoken together with our minds, not our voices. I now knew that Rebecca Nurse could hear anything I said to her with her mind alone. And I could answer her with mine. She would never be deaf to my words.

"Somehow," said Rebecca tenderly, "you will survive the storm that is to come young Dorcas. This I know."

Rebecca Nurse's words echoed in my mind as I watched Constable Herrick hammer at the beautiful wooden door of the Nurse homestead. Why were we here? Surely no one in the Nurse home had done anything wrong!

I gasped in horror as I saw the Constable dragging Rebecca towards me. Goodwife Nurse shook with the cold despite several warm shawls wrapped about her. The cold of late March was too much for an old woman taken from her sickbed.

"Good day to you, Dorcas," she said as Constable Herrick put chains around her thin wrists.

"Good day to you, Mistress Nurse," I said trying to match her cheerful smile. There was something about Rebecca Nurse that suddenly inspired me with courage.

"Come now, Constable," she said turning towards George Herrick, "make haste before you find the Putnams have replaced you with a quicker man."

"I can't think of what you mean, Mistress Nurse," said Herrick as his face turned bright red.

"Of course you can't, George," smiled Rebecca as she turned her face towards the road. "Place your trust in God, not your neighbors, Dorcas," she said as we headed towards Ingersolls' tavern.

TWENTY NINTH ENTRY

How cold it was in the small room that Rebecca Nurse and I shared that night. Beyond the darkness we could hear the laughter of the village men as they drank to each other's health and talked about what was going to happen tomorrow.

"Did ye hear," I heard a low voice growl, "I heard that they've gone and taken an old grandmother and a baby!"

"I wish they'd taken my fat sow of a wife while they were about it," I heard another voice shout.

"Hey then, why not take them all," chimed in a third. "Just leave a few likely wenches for service and away with the rest I say!"

"Right you are, fellows," said a voice I recognized as Nathaniel Ingersoll's.

"What do they mean, Goody Nurse?" I asked as I shook with fear in the cold, dark room.

"Pay no attention to them, Dorcas," said Rebecca holding me tight. "They are just a group of drunken fools who deserve the swelled heads and sick stomachs they will wake with. Close your eyes, my child, and listen to the songs inside of you."

"What songs?" I asked as I felt calmed by her touch.

"The songs we both hear, my dearest," said Rebecca as she began to hum softly. "Can't you hear them? Why, they have become my sweetest companions since I can no longer hear the real sounds of God's creatures. Thank the Almighty for your gift, Dorcas, it can be a blessing if you use it rightly."

"But how do I do that, Goody Nurse?" I asked as I snuggled closer to her and passed my thoughts wordlessly to her mind.

"By waiting until you know how to control your power, Dorcas. Remember little one, that all our gifts are from God, and that used

117

rightly, they can bring you great joy. That was your grandfather's mistake. I knew from the day that he began using it on games of chance, to win a pence here and a farthing there, that his gift would turn against him. And it did too! Why would anyone choose to believe that John Solart, who they drank and gambled with, had the gift of prophecy and second sight. Ordinary men cannot be believed when they speak extraordinary words. That is why I have kept myself apart all these years and only spoken when the Almighty's voice was so loud that it echoed like an angel in my head. And it is because I broke my own vow that I am sitting here with you now."

"What happened, Goody Nurse?"

"Why, I spoke against those in this village who want nothing but their own way, no matter what it might cost others. I never did trust Samuel Parris and his strange ways. No Christian man I have ever known should own slaves the way he does. Tituba and Indian John are humans with souls just the same as you or I. How could I let such a man as Parris tell me what God's word should be? There were many in this village who held it against me when I urged my family to have none of his preachings."

"Oh, now I remember," I said. "Father said that it was your fault that all your family was now going to the Topsfield church. He said that it was bad of you to take your money out of the village and give it to another town. But I thought you were very brave to stand up against the mean people in the village."

"What else could I do when they began shouting 'sorceress" and taking such as your mother, fresh from childbed, for a witch. A man who would own slaves sees nothing wrong in hanging a few useless women."

"No! No! They can't hang Mama. Please say they can't, Rebecca," I cried wordlessly, my head pounding with the force of the thoughts flying from my mind to Rebecca Nurse's.

"I hope they won't, darling," said Rebecca trembling slightly, "but now is the time to know the truth and be prepared for it. Look into your soul, Dorcas Good, and tell me what you see."

"I see nothing," I said, turning away from her and putting my thumb in my mouth. Let the foolish old woman try to scare me if it gave her pleasure. I would have none of it. What did she think I was? Some baby that could be frightened by tales of witches and boogie men. I was Dorcas Good, daughter of Sarah Good, who had stood more pain and trials in her short life than most folks went through in a lifetime. Father had taught me well how much pain I could stand and keep on living.

Whatever Rebecca Nurse had to say had nothing to do with Mama or me. We were going to escape and run away from this evil place. Someday soon Mama, Mercy and me would find that beautiful land with the sand and the sun.

"That place only exists in your mind," came a small voice that tickled me with it's truthful edge. The voice was not that of Rebecca Nurse. It was a younger voice, even younger than mine. It was as if a baby's coos had shaped the sounds that made the words.

"Who is that?" I said out loud.

"Tis Mercy Good, your true and loving sister," came the voice swelling in my head, louder and more clearly than before.

"But that's not possible," I whispered back, terrified that one so young could be calling to me here in this dark and lonely place.

"No more possible is my gift than yours, dear sister. We both share what we share and must stand what we must. Listen to Goody Nurse and heed her words. 'Tis the only chance we may have. Poor Mama is even now beyond feeling with misery and pain. I fear for her sister. Come to us quickly and protect us before it is too late."

"But what can I do? I am only a little girl?"

"Ask Goody Nurse, Dorcas, and follow her lead." With those words, my sister's voice faded into the darkness, but it left behind a faint glow of hope that grew as I turned my face towards Rebecca Nurse.

"She is right, Dorcas," said Rebecca smiling calmly. "Listen to me and survive. If you live, I promise you that someday what happens in Salem Village will become a gateway for the righting of greater wrongs. You must be silent and remain as a child for all to see. Only in that way will they leave you alone, Dorcas. Think upon it. If you say nothing, there will be no answer to those that accuse you. The judges will think you only a poor bemused baby who has fallen under an evil spell. You may be jailed and chained like an unruly pet, but I doubt that any will say the words that will put a noose around a baby's neck. Be a silent and sweet child. Cling to those about you for protection if you wish to live."

"But I'm not a baby and I do know what is going on!" I cried. "I know that Mama is innocent, Goody Nurse. Maybe I can say something that will save her!"

"All we, the accused, say from this day forward will be used against us, child. This I have seen in my waking dreams. From this day on the guilty are innocent and the innocent are guilty in Salem Village. Your only hope is to remain still and hide behind the protection of your child's body. Please promise me that you will do this Dorcas. It is the only hope you have. And remember child, you must live if your sister is to live. Who is there but you to care for her?"

"There is Mama, and Father too," I said in breathless in a panic.

"Your Mama is helpless and your father is evil, Dorcas. Wake to these truths and live, daughter of my soul."

"I don't want to live anymore if all that you say is true."

"But you will live, Dorcas Good," said Rebecca putting her arms about me tenderly as she pressed her cheek to mine. "I too know what it is like to be the daughter of an accused witch. My own mother was dragged from our home and tortured just as yours is now. It was only a miracle that she was returned to us, but she was never the same. There will be a day when the anger will swell within you, just as it did in me, and when it does it will be Dorcas Good who avenges the innocent of Salem Village.

THIRTIETH ENTRY

"Revenge, revenge," screamed my mind as the two woman raised my skirt and began pinching my thighs.

"Easy now," said the first woman as she looked up from her work. The face was that of Goodwife Sibley, wife of Samuel. It was rumored that Goody Sibley had actually practiced witchcraft. It was said she had formed a 'witches cake' from grain and little Betty Parris' water to find out who had been tormenting the Reverend's daughter. Why was Mama in jail and Mary Sibley here in this dark room hurting me so?

"Unless you stop twisting, Dorcas Good," came a voice I knew as Deliverance Putnam Walcott, stepmother of Mary Walcott and aunt to Ann Putnam, "I shall be forced to call in my husband and Uncle Ingersoll to hold you down."

"No," I cried as I tried to hold still beneath their prodding hands. What were they doing to me? Nothing that Father had ever done felt as bad as this. I gasped as the two women held my legs far apart and inserted something long and cold inside of me. I could hear myself screaming silently as a bladelike instrument ripped away at my insides.

"Stop that now you cruel bitches," I heard Rebecca Nurse command through my painful fog. "Can't you see she is but a child and too tender for such things. Take me to the table and do as the Judge Hathorne commands, but spare that innocent child."

"Twill be your turn soon enough, Rebecca Nurse," I heard Deliverance Walcott say as she gave the blade within me a savage twist. "We must know if the child feels pain. A cry or two from her now could be proof of her innocence later. Don't you want to see her free, Goody Nurse? 'Tis evil you do the child if you stop us now. Only a true witch would stay my hand."

Deliverance Putnam then turned back to her evil work. Try as I might I could not keep the tears from falling from my eyes. How I hated to give those two woman the satisfaction of seeing me cry. Goody Nurse came to my side and began weeping as the blade went deeper into my being. "Cry out Dorcas, cry out," she whispered into my mind.

"I won't," I wordlessly screamed back at her, stubbornly believing that if I humbled myself before these women all was lost.

"You must if you are to live. Think of your sister and live!" commanded Rebecca Nurse as she crushed my small fingers in her hand.

To this day I thank God for the cruelty of Deliverance Walcott and Mary Sibley. If the next few moments had not occurred I might have stubbornly refused to cry out and lost my life as a result. I have found that pride is the greatest of all sins and all virtues. I realize today that if my pride had kept me from my screams I would have perished in the summer of 1692.

"Why, what's this?" I heard Goody Walcott say as she withdrew a bloody knife from my tiny womb.

"Tis a growth of some sort, perhaps it is the 'witches mark'," said Mary Sibley looking at the bloody mass closely. "Can you tell us what this is, little witch?" said Goody Sibley holding a part of my own body before me.

"I don't know, I don't know!" I screamed, realizing that whatever it was, the small piece of flesh had come from within me and was part of the womanhood I would now never have. I stared at the small bloody piece of myself and screamed and screamed. Such screams as I cried that night in the cold and damp of Ingersolls' spare room should have torn my voice from me for all time, but the horror that lay behind the voice gave it a supernatural strength.

"You fools, you idiots!" I heard Rebecca Nurse say as she slapped Mary Sibley. "Don't you see what you've done. You've cut away the door to this child's womb. Now there is no entrance for seed or exit for babe. You have destroyed any hope she might have for marriage or motherhood. 'Tis you that are the true fiends from hell in this village, not this poor mutilated child."

"You're nothing but a wicked liar, Rebecca Nurse," said Mary Sibley hiding the bit of flesh in her hand as she motioned for the old tan hound that had been laying across the door. I watched in disgust as she slipped the bloody mass of flesh to the hound and he swallowed it whole.

"Tis not my fault," continued Mary, "that the child had no maiden's curtain to protect her from such things. Who would expect one so young to be such a wanton. She is certainly not the virgin one her age should be.

Think upon it as a blessing that we know what we know about her now so that she may be punished for such wicked behavior. Who would have thought that one so young was a fornicator."

"Yes," said Deliverance Walcott as she released my throbbing legs, "only a wicked girl would have struggled so against us. Sit up now Dorcas and make way for Goody Nurse, 'tis her turn to be found innocent."

"Yes Mistress," I heard myself say through a light blue mist. "Whatever you wish, Mistress." I remember trying to lift myself from the table only to fall back upon it as a mist enveloped me in its soft calming light. Unlike my other dreams, this one was both waking and sleeping. I could still hear the strident voices of Mary Sibley and Deliverance Putnam arguing with the calm voice of Rebecca Nurse, but I could no longer make out their words. It was as if what they said no longer mattered.

"Well done, Dorcas Good," I heard an unfamiliar voice say as I stared into the pale blue mist. From a distance I could make out three figures coming towards me. All three were female. The tallest was a woman about my mother's age with a clear and intelligent look upon her face that made me want to ask her questions about all those things I didn't understand. Her long, thin limbs were delicate but strong. She moved with the grace and serenity of a dancer. The second woman was small and round. She seemed quite young until she moved close enough to me to reveal her face. The lines around her eyes and lips spoke of age, but the smile that lit her face was the youngest I had ever seen. The third being was a little girl who looked like me. The only difference between this child and myself was the halo of golden hair that floated about her and almost swept the ground beneath her feet. Never had I seen such a cloud of pure light before. It made me think of a sunrise on a bright June morning.

"Well done sister," I heard the child say as she grasped the hands of her two companions.

THIRTY FIRST ENTRY

"Sister?" I heard myself say to the child as she drew me towards her.

"Yes dearest," replied the child in a voice exactly like mine," you are Dorcas and I am Mercy, children of William and Sarah Good."

"Children of the Goddess, as your mother was before you," laughed the smaller of the two woman as she stroked my sister's hair. "How quickly you forget your lessons, Goddaughter. Heed not small Mercy's carelessness, Dorcas. She is young yet and knows not our ways."

"How can I learn if what is to be cannot be changed?" asked my sister turning first to one woman and then to the other in confusion. "You said I would always be young."

"Ah," said the tall woman with a nod of her head, "but someday your wisdom may outmatch your age if you listen closely and bide with us. Learning comes from doing. Ask Sister Dorcas here if you don't believe me, little Mercy. She is young in years, but knows more than most who belong to the Goddess. Great pain brings great understanding. Why, if it were not for what has been done unto her this day she may have never known us."

"Come then, Sister, and teach me," said Mercy Good taking my hands and lifting me far above the table.

I gasped as I felt my soul rise from my body and hover above it. How small I looked from this height. I could see that Goody Nurse was still speaking to Mary Sibley and Deliverance Walcott, but I could not make out her words. I watched as the two women left, followed by the hound who now held a part of my womb in his stomach.

"Don't grieve, little Dorcas," said the small, kindly woman as she pointed towards Rebecca Nurse. "There is more than one path to marriage and motherhood. Those poor fools think they have done a righteous deed, but woe unto those that try to interfere with the Maiden, Mother or Crone. Believe that you will have more of the gifts of womanhood than those two woman ever dreamed of."

"But how?" I said scarcely understanding her words, but knowing that the sweet woman spoke the truth.

"By the grace of the Goddess, my dear," said the taller woman putting her arm around me and leading me away from the small woman who had begun to play a game of hide and seek with my sister.

"It is as Goodwife Nurse has told you," continued the woman as she drew me down onto the misty grass beside her. "There are those who die in the service of the Goddess and those who must live. Yours is the harder task. For those who enter the eternal mists of the otherworld there is peace and goodness and a doorway to a new and better life. For those who must remain behind there is work to do that will bring you earthly pain beyond belief and an eternal reward of great majesty. It has been given to you, Dorcas Good, to bring your sisters out of the darkness into the light. Many will be the days and nights of pain and horror, but in the end you will prevail. The dark times that we now live through will someday give way to an age of light and understanding where all such as we will be honored, not tortured and killed."

"Oh, does that mean I can save Mama and Mercy?" I said, suddenly filled with joy.

"In a way it does, Dorcas, but not in the way you think. Whatever happens, you must accept your lot. I promise you that your mother and sister will know happiness, no matter what happens to them in the life they now live."

"But will I be with them?" I asked, not liking the way the wise woman was answering my questions.

"All I can tell you is that they will always be with you, Dorcas. You must pray to the Goddess to reveal the rest."

"I'm beginning to hate the Goddess, whoever she is, if all she can do is hurt me and take Mama and Mercy away."

"But she loves you, Dorcas Good. Know that you and she are entwined both on this earth and in the next."

"What do you mean?"

"I mean that you are she and she is you. The bond of mother and daughter is one that can never be broken."

With those words the mist around the wise woman began to swirl and she disappeared with a soft sigh. The last thing I heard as I fell back into my deep sleep was the laughter of my sister as she played in the mist.

THIRTY SECOND ENTRY

The morning of March 24th, 1692 was a glorious one. It was as if winter had finally released poor little New England for a moment and handed it over to the gentle winds of spring. I blinked my eyes furiously as Constable Herrick placed me on his horse for the short ride to the meetinghouse. It was there that Rebecca Nurse and I were to be questioned. I found the ride almost unbearably painful. Every time the horse moved I wanted to cry out in agony. If it had not been for the words of the tall woman in my waking dream, I would have been awash in tears by the time Constable Herrick reigned his horse in front of the Salem meetinghouse. I waited quietly while the Constables Herrick and Locker helped old Rebecca Nurse from her mount. How small and feeble she looked in the bright morning sun. The glaring light unkindly showed every wrinkle and pock mark that the old woman had acquired in the service of her loved ones. Mama often said that only the rich had the blessing of looking younger than their years. Folks like the people of Salem were doomed to grow old before their time. Such was the legacy of the cruel New England coast. Mama liked to call it, "a God forsaken rock that beat to death all that fell against it".

"Hurry now, wench," growled Constable Herrick as he grasped me about the waist and lowered me to the ground in rough fashion. It was only then that I became aware of a bit of blood shining wetly on my skirt. It marked the place where the two women had cut me with their knife. My first thought was to cry out, but then I remembered the words of my dream friends. To speak was to die, and to seem to be aware of what was going on about me was to seem less then an innocent child. I looked about and realized that none but myself had noticed my spotted skirt, so I quietly folded my skirt over itself and took the hand the Constable offered me. Heeding again the voices of my protectors, I placed the thumb of my unused hand in my mouth and widened my eyes in childish fashion.

Rebecca Nurse caught my eye and gave me a smile that heartened me greatly. If she could face our accusers with such serenity then so could I.

I tried to smile back but found it difficult with my thumb in my mouth, so I gave her a bit of a wink instead.

"No stumbling, witch," I heard George Locker say as he dragged Goody Nurse towards the open door of the meetinghouse. "You are to wait here while the judges have their say about the girl," he said as he entered the building and motioned for us to follow. Constable Locker made his way towards two chairs set slightly behind the crowd as Constable Herrick tried to move forward through the crowd.

"Make way for the accused, make way for the accused," he shouted as he grabbed my hand tightly and pushed aside the good citizens of Salem.

"Pick her up you fool, do you want the child crushed before she's judged?" I heard a familiar voice shout over the din of whispers that filled the room. I turned my face towards the dear voice of Jack Quelch, but I could see nothing but dark wool breeches and skirts. It was not until Constable Herrick lifted me into his arms and held me aloft for the crowd to gawk at, that I saw Master Jack. By then it was too late to speak a word to him. I was being carried away towards the front of the room where the judges awaited me. I know now that it was a lucky thing that Jack and I were separated so quickly. Even then Jack Quelch had a reputation for thievery and twisting the truth. No innocent child would have ever hailed him as a friend. And innocent I must seem if I were to live through this day.

It was then that I saw two other friends in the crowd. One was the tall wise woman, dressed in heavy white muslin hardly warm enough for the cold March day. The other was her small round companion with the kindly smile and twinkling eyes. She was swathed in some sort of dark blue cloth with a bit of red wool wrapped around her neck. They both looked younger than they had appeared in my dream, but I was sure the two women who stood to the far right of the judge's stand were the same friends who had come to me last night. Any doubt I had was immediately taken away when I heard a calm voice whisper, "courage Sister, your moments in this place will be few if you do as we say."

I turned my head to stare at the smaller of the two woman just as the Constable stepped onto the platform. He tried to put me down, but I let out a childish cry and snaked my arms tightly around his neck.

"Stay there Constable," said Judge Corwin as he adjusted his spectacles and stared at me. "Twill be easier on us all if this bit of unpleasantness is over with quickly. 'Tis only Christian to give one so young comfort at such a time."

"Yes sir," I heard Herrick mumble as he shifted my weight so that it rested upon him in an easier fashion.

"Dorcas Good," said Judge Hathorne as he peered at me sternly, "do you know why you are here?"

"She's here because she's a witch," I heard someone in the crowd shout as the rest of the villagers answered with laughter and whistles.

"Don't answer," came the voice in my head, as I opened my mouth to say a word in my defense.

I quickly placed my thumb back in my mouth and turned my face towards Constable Herrick's coat. I buried myself there and pretended to sob like a baby.

"Turn its face toward the Judge," came another voice from the mocking crowd. I recognized the voice as belonging to my own father. William Good had come to watch my agony. Where had he been last night when those fiendish woman had cut me so cruelly? Why hadn't he defended his small daughter against such a thing? All I had ever been to my father was a thing, an it to be used or beaten for his pleasure. Was I really only an it?

"Why torture yourself with questions you already know the answer to?" came the voice of the tall wise woman from deep within my own mind. "Know that you are precious beyond words to us and that William Good is no friend to you. Your father is afraid for his life and seeks to see both you and your mother destroyed before the people accuse him of having the evil eye. Speak not to him. Seek your own salvation."

That was enough to keep me from looking up from the Constable's coat and in my father's direction. If it had been only me I might have chanced it, but there was Mama and the baby to think of. Well I knew the mind and soul of William Good, and well I knew that he would like to see his wife and daughters dead.

Again I was turned towards the judges, and again I was asked the question.

"Dorcas Good, do you know why you are here?" All I could do was stare at Judge Corwin.

"She answers not, Judge Hathorne," I heard Judge Corwin say in a respectful tone to the larger man.

"Tis no matter," said Judge Hathorne, "she is the daughter of a witch and must be questioned closely. Who knows what wiles are hidden beneath her beguiling form. Dorcas Good," said Judge Hathorne turning his black eyes upon me, "why to you afflict these children?"

It was then that my childish confusion became real. The thumb I had placed in my mouth to appear senseless suddenly became a thing of comfort as a great commotion filled the crowded meetinghouse. First Ann Putnam, and then Mary Walcott and Mercy Lewis fell on the floor as the room echoed with their shrieks.

"She bites, she bites," I heard Ann scream as she rolled forward and stopped just short of the platform where I was being held.

"Stop it, you daughter of a witch!" yelled Mary Walcott as she grasped her throat with her hands and began making choking sounds. When Mercy Lewis attempted to pull Mary's hands away from her own throat, I saw her thrown across the room and stumble against the wall.

"The heat, the pain," she whimpered as she sank to the floor grasping her nether regions with a look of wide eyed terror.

What was the matter with them? Were they truly possessed? I looked towards my two dream friends and saw a slight smile cross the face of the kindly lady. The tall woman next to her gave a stern look and the unfinished smile froze on the smaller woman's face. So, they did have the power to torment as well as comfort! "Thank God for it", I thought as I watched the three girls writhing on the ground. Well I knew that they had faked their agonies and used them to put my mother in some faraway cell. Let them suffer the real agonies of hell for their evil deeds!

"She sticks us with pins," cried Ann, holding up a small silver pin. "Dorcas Good comes even now to torment us. Make her stop, oh won't someone chain her limbs and set us free?"

"Stop this nonsense, you wicked trollops, and confess that it is none but yourselves that bring about your agony. Confess before it is too late, " came the voice of Jack Quelch as he pushed the villagers who stood in front of him aside and made his way to the front of the room.

"Can't you see these girls are making fools of you all?" continued Jack, coming nose to nose with Judge Hathorne and placing his hand on his sword. "This girl is but a babe and no more guilty of anything than the Christ Child. I don't know why these girls wish this baby ill, but I know, as a man of this village, that I must defend her."

"Sit down Quelch before you are accused as well," said Judge Hathorne with a shaky voice. "Look to William Good for your example. See how he stands silent, rightly ashamed for bringing an imp from hell into this world to do evil to the righteous girls of Salem Village."

"So it's down to that, is it your worthy?" said Jack with a strange smile as he turned towards the crowd. "It's ashamed you should all be to be here this day. This child has committed no crime save that of being born to a poor mother and a drunken lecher of a father. Shame on you all, I say, and to you too most worthy judges. Let her go before the sins you have committed this day weigh you down and damn your souls."

"Leave this room, Quelch, before I have you arrested," said Judge Corwin as he motioned towards three yeomen standing to his left.

"Arresting me will not free your hearts of your evil deeds," cried Jack as two yeoman grasped his arms firmly and started to lead him towards the door.

"Mark my words," I heard him cry as the crowd swallowed him up, "there will be a day when you beg the forgiveness of Dorcas Good."

It was then that my own father stepped forward, hat in his hand, and made his way with mock humility to the judging platform.

"May I say a word your worship," said William Good with a pious whimper in his voice.

"Of course, Goodman Good," said Judge Hathorne with obvious relief. "Tis indeed time for cooler heads to prevail."

"It is heartily sorry I am that such as my wife and daughter have brought affliction to the Village. If I had but known of their deeds I would have cried them out for all to hear. But what is done is done and I thank these young ladies for having the courage to bring the witches down. Look you to poor Ann Putnam, stuck through with my daughters pins. I have seen Dorcas hold them in her hands many times and roll them about on her lap. If only I had known that she tormented others with them I would have torn them from her and cut off her hands to stop her wicked ways. It grieves me greatly to say this, but say it I must. Take this child of my bosom, this Dorcas Good, and do with her what you will. The curse of witchcraft must be burned out of Salem so that God will once again shine his light on its true believers. Take my daughter, my wife and my newborn if you must to free these poor innocent victims from the devil's hand."

"Well spoken, Goodman Good," said Judge Corwin with a satisfied smile as he looked upon me in an almost kindly fashion. "Tis a blessing that we have such true souls as you to defend God in this lonely place."

"Dorcas Good," said Judge Hathorne with a nod towards Corwin, "it is the decision of this court that you be guilty of a witch's ways and a signer of the Devil's book. From this day forward until you are brought to trial for a final time, you shall be imprisoned. You shall be chained hand and foot so that you can no longer afflict these poor girls. Your years may be young, but your deeds are those of your master, the Devil. What say you, Witch Good, to this ruling?"

"Silence!" I heard a voice scream in my mind so loudly that I shook with it's force. The two women in the crowd were staring at me with a ferocity that could not be mistaken.

"Away with you then," said Judge Hathorne, looking into my blank face with a dissatisfied frown.

It was only when I realized that my examination trial was over that my mock tears turned real, soaking Constable Herrick's coat as he carried me towards the back of the room. My tears turned to screams of anguish as I entered the witch's dungeon of Salem.

THIRTY THIRD ENTRY

"Hold still, witch," said the fatter of my two jailers as he chained my small wrists to the damp moldy wall behind me. I knew the man as Nicholas Noyes, sometime preacher and full time bully in the village. He had often tormented and teased Mama and me when we were begging.

"There, that will hold you until their Honors come to visit."

"Visit?" I said, my curiosity stopping my tears.

"Why yes, my sweeting," said Noyes rubbing his dirty hand on my leg. "You are to be honored by the Judges Hathorne, Corwin and Higginson, all three. Conduct yourself well and tell them all you know, that is my advice to you. That is unless you want to be made to talk."

"Made to talk?" I said trying to pay no attention to the hand that was pinching my small chest.

"Yes dearie, talk," he said blowing into my face a breath as foul as a dead fish.

"What should I talk about?" I asked trying not to pull away as his hand tried to move my skirt to one side.

"The witches teat, you little fool. Surely you must have one somewhere. We all know you are a witch born and bred. The sooner you show us the proof, the easier it will be for you."

"Oh, I see," I said not seeing at all.

"Then of course, there are the birds."

"What birds?" I said giving him a coy smile and praying that his hands would stop short of the pool of blood that was now drying about my thighs.

"Your mother's birds, of course. The witch Tituba spoke of them, but the Judges wish to hear more. 'Tis quite a pretty thing you are, Dorcas Good, and old Nicholas can help you if you are nice to him. They say that

133

you have already known a man and find it pleasing. Pleasure me well and I'll see to it that you have an easy time here. Your mother did, and she escaped all but the prison walls. Believe that old Nicholas will see to it that you even get a bit to eat now and then if you make him happy."

"Where is Noyes?" I heard a voice shout just as I was about to empty what was left in my stomach onto the smelly jailer's shoes.

"Coming your Honor," he called as he took his hands from me and adjusted the front of his pants.

"Remember to save some for me sweetheart," he said as he turned around and shuffled out the prison door.

What did these powerful men want of me? I was just a small girl who must have seemed an ignorant child to them. What could I possibly tell them that they did not already know? I recognized the voices of Judge Hathorne and Judge Corwin mumbling to the jailer outside the prison door. The other voice that came to my ears was a mystery to me. How small I felt at that moment, one four and a half year old girl faced with being questioned by three large men. It was then that the truth of my situation began to overwhelm me. Here I was chained to a wall, helpless and alone. Why, these men could do anything they wanted to me and none would be the wiser. Had not Nicholas Noyes already given me a taste of things to come? What more would three judges, powerful and rich, do to me in this lonely, sad place? And what of my poor Mama? What had they done to her? If Mama was helpless against such as these men then there was no hope for little Dorcas Good.

I closed my eyes tightly as the prison door swung open. I could hear the footsteps of the men as they moved towards me.

"Open your eyes, Dorcas Good," said the voice of Nicholas Noyes as he placed his greasy hand on my face and poked at my eyes. The pain of his ragged fingernails forced me to open my eyes and face my tormentors.

"There now child," said Judge Hathorne as he stroked my hair gently, "we are not here to harm you. All you need to do is tell us want we want to hear and we will go away."

"I want my Mama," I whispered quietly, looking at the Judge who I guessed to be named Higginson.

"Later, child," said the man in a kindly tone as he stooped down next to me and looked me straight in the eyes. "Tell us where your witch's teat is and I promise that you shall see your mother. Can you do that?"

"I don't know what you mean?" I said, suddenly filled with wild hope. What if I could make up something that would please them and bring no harm to anyone? Was it true that if I told them what they wanted to hear they would return me to my mother?

"Of course you know what they mean, sweeting," said fat Nicholas as he began to unlace the front of my small bodice. "Show us what you have you little slut!"

"That is quite enough, Noyes," said Judge Corwin as he removed Nicholas' fat hand from my tiny breast. "There is no need to be rough. I am sure that Dorcas is more than willing to help us. What do you say, Dorcas Good. Would you like to show us where your familiar sucks upon your body, or would you like us to leave you to Master Noyes here? I assure you that you will find it far more pleasurable to help us."

"Is that all you want," I said with a childish whisper as I searched my mind desperately for some way to satisfy the men who loomed over me.

"Yes child, that is all we want," said Judge Hathorne as he looked first at Corwin and then at Higginson. "Show us the devil's mark and you shall be left in peace."

I looked at the men who stood so close to my small body and shifted my weight, first this way and then that, to buy some time. "Come to me voices," I cried silently, praying for some direction in this matter. How, oh how, could I give these men what they wanted and still seem an innocent child. It was then that the cruelest truth of all was revealed to me.

"Use me Dorcas," I heard the voice of my mother say as I lay on the ground before the judges. "I shall not live through these times, but you must for your mother's sake. Give me the comfort of knowing that you will live! Tell them about my gift to you, the little friend in your pocket. Tell them about the birds too, if need be. 'Twill do me no more harm than has already been done and 'twill save your life, beloved daughter."

"But how can I betray you Mama?" I answered back silently, horrified at the very thought of speaking against my beloved mother.

"'Tis not betrayal but obedience you do, my daughter. I order you to speak against me and save your life. Speak quickly, darling child, before these men bring you to torture and burn the very heart from your mother's soul."

"Yes Mama," I whispered, heart sick but resolute. So be it. I would do as she wished. I would now speak the words that would brand me as a traitor to my mother in the eyes of the world. Surely no other child has ever been more put to the test that I was at that moment.

"I think what you seek is here, kind sirs," I said as I held out my small hand for examination. On the lowest joint of the forefinger was a small red welt no bigger than a flea bite.

"And how did you come about this?" asked Judge Corwin, twisting my hand towards the light with a puzzled look on his face.

"Tis the suckling place for my little snake," I answered softly, trying not to cry out as the Judge almost snapped my small wrist.

"And was it the Devil that gave you your pet?" asked Judge Hathorne peering at me with a look that made me feel naked.

"No," I answered, suddenly sure of what my mother had asked me to do, "it was my mother. She said the tiny thing would keep me company in those times when she had to be away from me. I never thought that it might be a bad thing. I'm sorry I did a bad thing. Please take my pet if it pleases you. He's right here in my pocket."

"Remove the Devil's serpent!" commanded Judge Higginson as he and the other two judges looked at Nicholas Noyes.

"I'll not be touching the Devil's disciple," protested Noyes as he backed away in horror. "There's no telling what it might do to me."

"There's no harm in it, you fool, if your are a Godly man," said Judge Hathorne as he pushed the jailer aside in disgust and reached into my pocket. Sure enough, my little snake was there and willingly wrapped itself about the Judge's finger as he drew it from my pocket.

"There now," said Hathorne as he threw the snake on the ground and crushed it beneath his boot. "Tis but dust now, as are all the Devil's creatures. Our work here is done and it is far past my time for supper. Thank the Lord that you saw you way clear to be an obedient child, Dorcas Good."

"But what of the birds? You said she must know about the birds, "said Noyes. I could see in his mind a picture of me naked and bleeding before him.

"Why I had forgotten about them completely," said Hathorne with a bemused look upon his face. "I am beginning to weary of all this and hope that soon I will be quit of this place. I suppose you are right, Noyes. We must do our duty, tired or not. Young Dorcas, can you tell us willingly about the birds that flock to you mother's call, or will it be the strap and tongs for you to make you speak?"

"I know of Mama's birds," I said in what I hoped was a sweet voice. "They are her dearest friends and sing to her even when the snow falls upon the ground and the others of their kind have flown south."

"What else do you know?" said Corwin, obviously relieved that soon they would be out of the cold, damp dungeon.

"Why, just that one is black and one is yellow and Mama speaks to them in whispers." I knew there was a third bird, bright as a red leaf in autumn. He had always been my favorite. I was afraid that my little bird might be captured and destroyed if I told about him.

"And that is all?" said Nicholas Noyes as he eyed me suspiciously.

"Yes sir," I replied quietly, giving a small yawn and fluttering my eyelids.

"That is enough," said Judge Hathorne moving towards the door as he pulled a heavy gold watch from his brocaded vest. "Come sirs, it is time to leave this place. Dorcas Good is a child tainted with the blood of witchcraft and ignorant of her crimes. Let us spend our time on those who torment the innocent with malice and cunning. Say your prayers, Dorcas Good, and perhaps God will forgive you your wayward spirit."

"Yes sir," I said in a respectful voice as the prison door shut behind the three judges and my cruel jailer. I knew now that Mama had been right to ask of me what she did. For the moment, I was safe.

THIRTY FOURTH ENTRY

The next time I saw Master Noyes, he was dragging Rebecca Nurse behind him. I watched silently as he chained her to the wall beside me and left with a grunt. Nicholas Noyes was a bully, but he was not stupid. As long as Rebecca Nurse was chained beside me I was safe from his fondling paws.

Dear Goody Nurse, how ill she looked. I knew that they had taken her from a sickbed to meet her accusers, but it was not until this moment that I realized how old and frail she was. The Rebecca Nurse I had always known was a strong and decisive woman, still beautiful despite her great age. The woman who sat chained next to me was but a pale imitation of the strong matriarch of the industrious Nurse family.

"Goody Nurse," I said gently with my thoughts, "are you well?"

"Well enough, Dorcas, considering the strain of the day," came her answer though our 'mindspeak'. Rebecca opened her eyes and looked about the moldy cell with water dripping from the walls. "Pray that we leave this place soon, little Dorcas. To stay here more than a fortnight could be the death of us both."

"We will soon leave this place" I said silently, glad that I could give the old woman some comfort.

"How can you know such a thing, child?"

"Mama has spoken to me and I can feel us moving closer together. I know that soon both you and I shall leave this place and join her in another cell. It will be a bit more crowded, but its comforts will be greater than this underground swamp."

"I believe your words, Dorcas. Pray God that they come true. The mad light in Mary Walcott's eyes seems to make me wish for the blessed peacefulness of death. If ever the Devil walked in a soul, it does in hers."

"I know what you mean," I said with a shudder. "She scares me most of all. She's not like the others. Ann is pressured and harassed by her mother, and Abigail feels that she will be seen as more than a penniless orphan if she make herself important in the eyes of the villagers, but Ann and Abigail seem to get no great pleasure out of what they do. Mary Walcott is different. Have you seen the smile that she gives when one of us cries out in pain. It's as if she finds joy in it."

"It has always been so with Mistress Mary," said Rebecca, staring out into the darkness of the cell. "Even as a small child she would take pleasure in the pain of others. I remember one day I came upon her laughing so hard that I thought her sides would burst. When I asked her why, she said nothing and ran away with the merriment still upon her lips. It was only later that I found out that her poor brother's puppy had been found with a broken neck by the side of the road. The beast had been covered up with leaves and left but a few paces from where I came upon our happy Mary. Pleasure and pain are the same for young Mistress Walcott, as well as many others in this Village."

"And how was she at your trial, Goody Nurse?" I asked, thankful that at least old Rebecca had roused herself from thoughts of dying in this damp cell.

"The same, Dorcas. 'Twas she that brought to mind the matter of my neighbor, Benjamin Holten, and his garden-destroying pig. Mary reminded all who would listen that I scolded Holten for letting his beast roam on my property. She made it seem that it was my fault that Holten took a fit and died. If I had known that my words would put a noose around my neck I would have bit off my tongue and swallowed it whole."

"But I've never heard you be mean or scolding to anyone," I said looking at Rebecca and trying to imagine her scolding her neighbor Holten to death.

"I have kept my tongue to myself for many a year now, but it seems that it only takes one slip to condemn the daughter of a witch. Remember that, Dorcas."

"Was your mother really a witch?"

"I don't know child, but I don't think so," said Rebecca thoughtfully. "She was never brought to trial, but the taint of being accused followed her all her days. It has also followed myself and my two sisters. I remember as a child the other children of the village following sisters Sarah, Mary and me about. They would taunt us and call us witch and sorcerer. It is no easy thing to be the daughter of a woman accused, my dear."

"Well I know," I said pulling at my chains in the hope of getting some relief. To my delight, one of them slipped off my wrist. It was with increulous joy that I pulled at the other one and found that it too was soon hanging from the wall with no Dorcas attached.

"Don't do that child!" said Rebecca as she looked at me with alarm.

"Why not," I said defiantly shaking my hands with fury in an attempt to bring back some feeling.

"Because those who wish you ill will take it as a sure sign that you are a witch. Who else but a witch could free herself from these heavy chains?"

"But any fool can see that they are much to big for me," I said sulkily, determined to stay free from the mean things that had hurt me so cruelly.

"The folk of Salem see only what they want to see right now, Dorcas. Put your hands back against the wall before you wind up like the children who have gone before you."

"What children?" I asked, still determined to have my own way.

"Why the children of Wurzberg, Germany. You are not the first innocent to find herself in such a cell, Dorcas Good. Do as I say child, or you may pay for your willfulness with your life."

"What happened to those children in Germany, Goody Nurse?"

"Well," said the old woman taking a deep breath, "according to the tale my old grandmother told us, there was a great witchhunt in Germany over sixty years ago. Many were accused and died, including the Bishop of Bamberg's own chancellor and burgermeister. But the worst of it was the children of Wurzberg. Many were accused and imprisoned as you are now, and forty-one were executed. A few may have been hanged, but most were burned. They suffered for hours in the flames as they slowly suffocated to death."

"I don't believe you!" I screamed as I stared at her in horror. Why was kind Goody Nurse making up these nasty stories at such a time? I was frightened enough without her torturing my poor mind.

"I'm telling you these things so that you can save yourself, little girl," she said softly. "Slip your hands back against the wall child before it is too late."

"What is going to happen to you and Mama, Goody Nurse?" I asked as I reluctantly put my arms back against the slimy wall and squeezed my flesh into the cruel chains.

"The worst that can happen to us is that we will be hanged. Your mother and I are both innocent of any crime, but that seems not to matter. Hanging is an easy way to die. On the other side awaits comfort and peace. Both your mother and I have lived our lives, Dorcas, and in a way may be glad to be quit of this earth. Death must come to us all sooner or later. I feel it is better to have a truthful death than a deceitful life. I'll not betray my Lord and say I signed the Devil's book no matter what those lying judges promise me in return."

"Neither will Mama," I thought, knowing now that the forces that gathered around Salem Village were truly the dark ones that I had seen flow through the bodies of my mother and sister a few months before. Nothing but a human sacrifice would ever satisfy such a black and hungry beast.

THIRTY FIFTH ENTRY

I was left alone the next day when they came to take away Rebecca Nurse. She was to be examined again because there were many in the village who were saying she must be innocent.

"Pray God that I never see her in this place again," I thought as I watched Rebecca hobble from the gloom of the moldy prison cell into the sunshine that glowed beyond. I lay down on the floor and sank into a dreamless sleep that took me to a land of dark softness. Rarely since have I been so blessed with comforting nothingness. It was as if I had passed to the gentle land of sleepless death. The kick of a boot roused me many hours later. To my horror I saw the toothless grin Nicholas Noyes leering down
at me.

"Come to me now, Dorcas Good. It is time you were punished for being a bad girl," I heard him say as he unchained my hands from the wall and lay me across his lap, face down. The leather strap he slapped across my naked buttocks was but the beginning of his tortures. I cried to my dream friends to take me far away from the pain that seared through me as his beatings with the strap went higher than I could count, but I was only answered with silence. It was not until I felt his fat member enter my beaten and bleeding buttocks that I screamed out loud for my friends to save me.

"Yes, that's it little wench," I heard him pant wetly, "scream for Satan himself. No one will hear you in this place. It makes old Nicholas warm to hear you. Scream bitch, scream!" he cried as his ragged nails scratched and tore at my small breasts.

When he was done he fell upon my body, crushing it into the muddy floor of the cell. I was smothering beneath his weight. It was only when his snores began that I tried to move myself from under his slimy form. It was useless. I was trapped beneath his huge body and the weight of Nicholas Noyes was crushing me to death.

143

"Scream, Dorcas my love," I heard my mother call just as a cloud of darkness began to fill my head. I lifted my face from the mud and managed to give a cry mightier than any I had ever given before. I heard the lock on the prison door turn and someone enter the cell.

"Will you look at old Nick," I heard the voice of a woman say as she gave him a vicious nudge with her foot. "Get off the babe, you fat fool, before someone catches you. I'll not starve because of your little games." With those words the stout lady hauled the grunting Nicholas Noyes out the door and left me bleeding in the dark.

PART FOUR

ONLY THOSE WHO
LIE
SHALL LIVE

THIRTY SIXTH ENTRY

A few days later I was taken, along with Rebecca Nurse, to join Mama in the dungeons of Boston Town. Not even the joy of seeing my mother could mend me. I now lived in a land where silence ruled. It filled my body, mind, and soul with a silence so great that I knew it must be madness. The torture I had endured at the hands of Nicholas Noyes had released a waiting savage within me that would someday send me back into his arms followed by all the demons of hell. I would live, just as Mama and my dream friends wished. But no longer did I live for the sake of finding a life beyond the horror of Salem Village. I had a purpose, a quest. It was to bring down all those who had hurt me so cruelly. It was hard to hide these thoughts from Mama and Goody Nurse, but I found in the days that followed my torture

I had acquired powers far greater than theirs for hiding my feelings. It was as if my unspeakable pain had lifted me into some strange land where I could wander at will, free from any earthly feelings save that of cold, calculating revenge.

I was now shackled to the walls with smaller chains. Tituba said that they had been specially forged for me by order of Cotton Mather himself. She said Reverend Mather was a powerful man. Fancy such a man taking such an interest in me and my imprisonment! Tituba said that he must be very afraid of me to have given such an order for my small chains. Silently I added the name of Mather to my list of enemies as two large yeoman shackled my hands to the wall and loaded the rest of my body down with chains.

Now it seemed that those days when I had run at Mama's side in the sunshine of Salem Village had only been a dream. The chattering, chubby little girl who had gathered flame red leaves, joyously running to show her mother her priceless treasures, had been replaced by a bony, blank eyed wraith. I could tell from the look on Mama's face that round little Dorcas was gone and in her place was a small starving monster that pretended to be Dorcas.

I was afraid to speak. I knew that if I let go of the blessed silence that stood between me and what was happening around me I would retreat into madness forever. My friendly, misty silence seemed to drain the pain out of my mind and body and leave me numb to where I was and what was happening about me. It was only when I rocked to and fro, or beat my head against the stones of the wall behind me, that I could rouse myself enough to hear Mama's words or try to eat the maggot ridden food that she pushed towards me.

"You must eat, Dorcas," I could hear her say through my mist. "This food has cost me dearly my beloved child. Eat and live. Do you hear me Dorcas? Oh, say something, anything my darling!"

Often I was tempted to answer Mama, but I knew that if my words cost me my soul she would be even more saddened. It was Goody Nurse who finally came to the rescue and tried to tell Mama what had happened to me and why I needed to be far away from the prison, even if it was only in my mind. I heard them muttering and I could tell, by the look of horror on Mama's face, that she finally understood. Now it was her turn to rock back and forth in that dark, cold place, knowing that she was as helpless as I.

Poor Mama. I wished that I could bring her with me into my land of dreams and healing quiet mist, but there was the baby to think of. Everyday the baby grew weaker and weaker, making sounds that were but an echo of the cries that should have come from a hearty newborn. When she did cry, the sounds were more like that of a sick kitten than the baby my Mama had given birth to. I knew that soon I would be saying farewell to my treasured little sister.

We were the poor of Salem Village and had no one to send us extra food and fine blankets. Goody Nurse shared what she could, but she had little despite the great sums her family paid to make sure she had only the best. Both baby Mercy and Goody Osburn would die soon unless something changed. Looking at them I knew that Salem Village had invited the Devil in and he sat by us daily, drawing the life out of us in the cruelest possible way.

Every once in a while Mama would be unchained and taken to another room where I could hear grunting and moaning accompanied by the now all too familiar sound of beating. It was never long after that Mama and I would receive our food, crawling with maggots, but enough to keep us alive for another day. Mama would hand me the baby when she was taken away. My dear little Mercy who had changed from a fat squalling treasure to a white creature that could only stare at me with almost lifeless eyes. I think it was her eyes that finally began to rouse me from my silent mist. One day I found myself crooning to her, praying that the sound would bring the spark of life back into her. Then I began to rock her, and finally, I found myself screaming at her.

"Cry, Mercy, Cry!" I screamed, terrified by the sound of my own voice. I held the baby tight and began to cry myself, soaking us both through with my tears. "At least you won't grow big enough for them to hurt you the way they hurt me!" I was still screaming when the prison doors scraped open and the yeomen brought my mother back from her daily torture.

"Hush now, my love," said my mother as she broke from the guard's grasp and cradled me in her arms. "What is done is done and now we must think of your future. They may overlook you, my angel," she whispered in my ear. "Mama may have them bemused enough for that. See here," she said as the guards waited for her to finish with me, (a miracle in itself), "Mama has a friend for you that will take care of you when she's not here. Whatever happens, our friend Osiris will protect you. Go now, my precious pet," she said as she slipped a small snake into my hand and turned towards the guards.

"Thank you for your kindness," she said as they chained her to the stone wall.

The snake that Mama had given me was the twin of the one that had died beneath Judge Hathorne's boot. I hid it quickly and smiled at Mama.

"It's too late for your sister and me, my child," said my mother, Sarah Good, with a bitter laugh, "but swear to me that somehow you will live and avenge us.

"I swear Mama," I said as I closed my eyes and began rocking to and fro.

THIRTY SEVENTH ENTRY

My sister, Mercy Good, died the night before Mama was taken for her final trial. It was somewhere close to dawn when I was awakened by Mama's sobbing. At first I thought that she was sad because she would have to leave me alone again, but then I noticed the dark blue blanket that usually swaddled my sister was lying on the ground. Mama was holding my baby sister's wasted body tightly, rocking back and forth much the way I often did. My sister was no longer a healthy baby pink. Her little face was as white as a statue, and the curved lips that had so often smiled up at me with her sweet baby's smile were as blue as the blanket that lay at Mama's feet.

"She's gone," said Mama as her anguished eyes met mine. "My little angel is gone.

"She's only gone over to the Otherworld," I said to Mama in a desperate attempt to comfort her.

"And what other world is that Dorcas Good!" screamed my mother as she began to tremble like one palsied.

"The one I see in my dreams, Mama," I said, suddenly comforted myself by the visions I had seen. "You must believe me. Mercy is now with two kind ladies who will care for her until we come for her. One is tall and wise and the other is small and kind. You must believe me Mama. I have seen them, truly I have."

"You are a fool, Dorcas," said Mama raising her voice and shouting into the gloom. "This is all there is, can't you see that! And because of these evil people your sister will never get a chance to know the world as you or I have. Never will she smell the flowers of spring or dip her toes into the salt of the ocean on a hot August day. The people of Salem Village have robbed little Mercy of her life now and forever. I curse them all for it. And as for you, my daughter, they've stolen your innocence and your childhood. Never will you be as you were before. I curse them for that too, and mourn the grandchildren I will never have. DO YOU HEAR ME," my Mama screamed, "A CURSE UPON YOU ALL UNTO THE THIRD GENERATION, JUST AS YOU HAVE CURSED ME.!

"Hush now, Goody Good," said Rebecca Nurse softly as she stretched her hand towards Mama. "We both know there is a God and that now his angels have taken your small daughter to be with them."

"I know nothing of the kind," said Mama as she placed my sister on the blanket before her. "Look at this little thing, murdered by Salem Village. I'll not take back my words nor feel badly about them. I meant what I said and am glad I said it. I'm sorry that I scolded you, Dorcas. If you wish to believe that Mercy has gone to a happier place than so be it, but don't ask me to believe it. I welcome the blessed nothingness of death. What else is there for me now."

"There is your other child, Sarah," said Rebecca.

"And what can I do for her, chained and helpless as I am?"

"Just what you have been doing, Sarah. Each day you make a sacrifice so that this daughter of yours may eat and live. Surely such goodness will be rewarded. Promise me that you will not curse God, even if right now you feel you can't believe in him. Perhaps he believes in you."

"What nonsense," said Mama picking up the baby again and covering her tenderly with the blanket. "Give me quiet so that I may say good-bye to my babe. Daylight will come soon enough, and I know that her poor body will be thrown somewhere far from any ground we would call hallowed."

"Not if I can help it," said Rebecca. "My son-in-law, Thomas, promised to go with me to trial this day. Let not any know that the babe is dead and I will see to it that she is buried on our farm. I'll even have the words said over her. Let me do this for you, Sarah."

"Why would you be so kind to me, Rebecca?" said Mama.

"Because our Lord said to love our neighbors as ourselves, Sarah. I have known you all your life and seen what you have walked through. You are a brave woman and deserve more out of this life. The least I can do is offer you this. The enemies that surround us are the same. They are the instruments of my destiny as well as yours. Your fate and mine are the same. We have become sisters."

"Thank you, Rebecca," said Mama as she held my dead sister to her breast and smiled at me." And thank you daughter. I didn't mean to hurt you. 'Twas the madness of the moment."

"I know, Mama." I said raising my head and looking towards the sounds that came from outside the door.

THIRTY EIGHTH ENTRY

"Hide it before she comes back!" I said to Rebecca as the woman quickly hid the precious tobacco beneath her skirt.

"Now Dorcas," said Goody Nurse, "you know your Mama won't be back for awhile."

"You never know," I said smiling, "sometimes the guards are interrupted."

"Aye, little one, 'tis true."

"Just think, Goody Nurse, tomorrow is Mama's birthday. I never thought we'd be able to get her such a fine gift. I can't thank you enough for it. How wonderful it will be to see Mama smoking her pipe again."

"I can't believe it myself," said Rebecca. "'Tis a wonder my daughter wasn't searched when they brought her in, but it does seem that as our time grows closer the guards have been kinder."

"Oh please, don't talk so," I said as the familiar panic rose in my breast. "Something may yet happen to save you both."

"Dorcas, you must face facts. Six days from now your mother and I are to be hanged."

"Not if you confess to witchcraft," I said as turned my face from Goody Nurse.

"To do so would be to sacrifice our immortal souls, you know that child."

"I only know that you and Mama are choosing to die when you could live. I don't understand how Mama could be cursing God one second and then determined to die with a pure soul, so that she can be with him, the next."

"Your Mama has always believed, Dorcas. The words she spoke when your sister died were from her great grief, not her lack of faith. Both your Mama and I are determined to die rather than live a lie."

"So, what you are saying is that only people who lie are allowed to live."

"That is what I'm saying, Dorcas."

"Then let me die with you. Please, Goody Nurse. I don't want to be left alone in this place. Please make it so I can die too!"

"That is beyond my power, child," said Rebecca sadly. "Your path is different from ours."

"Why?"

"I don't know, but trust in God's plan and pray for our souls when we are gone. That is the only answer I can give you."

"At least we can give Mama her birthday party first," I said, happy for the small comfort."

"Yes," said Rebecca. "It's hard for me to believe that the little Sarah I knew when she was as small as you will be thirty-nine tomorrow. I have grown too old."

"Oh not you Goody Nurse," I said with a wave, "I will always think of you as spry and youngish.

"Thank you, Dorcas," said Rebecca with a laugh as we turned our faces towards the door and watched as Mama was brought in and reshackled to the wall.

"There now, Sarah, 'twas a goodly turn you did us this day," said the tall skinny yeoman we had come to know as Matthew.

"Just remember your promise," said Mama with a wink.

"That I will," said Matthew as he looked me up and down. "Ye have kept yours to the letter, Sarah Good, and there's no one about here who doesn't feel that you deserve better than ye are getting. We'll see to it that the child is fed. You have my promise upon the holy book."

"Thank you, Matthew," said Mama, looking almost happy.

"What did he mean, Mama, when he promised that I would be fed?" I asked realizing suddenly that soon Mama would no longer be there to protect me.

"It is nothing for you to worry about darling," said Mama quietly. "'Tis just that I made Matthew promise that you would receive your food after I'm gone."

"But I don't understand," I said. "Why am I to get my food for free when everyone else has to buy theirs?"

154

"Because Mama has been kind to the guards and made them promise to be kind to you. Oh Dorcas, don't plague Mama anymore with your questions. I've said all I'm going to about it. Just be thankful that there are still a few souls about who keep their promises."

"Yes Mama," I said, realizing for the first time how much Mama and Goody Nurse had stood between me and the cruelties of prison life. As bad as the last few months had been, I had been covered with blankets and given food to eat. I was luckier, by far, than many of the folk housed deep within the dungeons. At night I could hear them crying for food and water.

"Mama," I said, too frightened to stop my words, "am I going to live here forever?"

"Forever is a long time, Dorcas," said Mama avoiding my stare.

"But am I, Mama?"

"I don't think so, Dorcas," said Mama sadly. "Not even the people of Salem Village would leave a little girl in prison forever. Sooner or later this madness will end and then you will be set free."

"But what will I do then, Mama?"

"Live Dorcas, live."

The next day was July 14th, 1692. It was Mama's thirty-ninth birthday. The warmth of the outside world had seeped through even to our cold dark place and Mama awoke with fewer aches than she had experienced in months.

"Can you hear them, daughter?" she said as she opened her eyes.

"Hear what Mama?" I asked.

"Why the birds singing their birthday song to me, Dorcas."

"Why yes, I do hear them," I said, happy that Mama looked so happy. It may sound strange, but in the past few weeks Mama's face had taken on an almost unearthly beauty. It seemed that once the trial was done and Mama sentenced, she had stopped worrying about everything. Even her concerns about me seemed to have melted away. I suppose her great calm had something to do with all the time she spent praying. Mama prayed day and night, sometimes to God and sometimes to other spirits that she said had no name. It was all the same to me. I knew now that nothing could stop the terrible thing that was going to happen to Mama and Rebecca. More powerful people than me had tried to stop the hangings and failed.

The Nurse family and their friends had filed petition after petition in Rebecca's favor and gotten nowhere. Poor Rebecca had even been found innocent at one point. How happy she must have been! And how sad she must have been when the judge ruled she must be found guilty, no matter what anyone else said. No one cared whether Mama and Rebecca were innocent or guilty, they only wanted to get rid of them. And now Rebecca lived with the fear that her sisters, Sarah and Mary, might be accused and hanged as well.

"Mama," I said looking towards Rebecca as I try to shake away my sad thoughts, "Goody Nurse and I have a present for you."

"A present my love? However could you manage such a thing in this place."

"Twas no easy feat Sarah, I can tell you that," said Rebecca, "but your little one nagged and scolded until I finally gave in. Thank my daughter, Rebecca, for this boon."

"Well, what is it, let me see!" said Mama like an excited child.

With great slowness, Rebecca Nurse drew the precious bit of tobacco from her skirt pocket, followed by some flint.

"See now Mama, you can smoke your pipe while we wish you happy birthday," I said as I squirmed in my chains. It was so hard not to jump up and down in them, but to do so would have brought me painful bruises.

"Ah," said Mama as she drew her old corncob pipe from her own skirt and placed it between her lips. "Throw my gifts to me Rebecca. 'Tis a fine birthday I am having. Indeed it is."

I watched with delight as Mama filled her pipe and brought the small flame she had mustered close to it. We all held our breath as the first bit of tobacco caught fire and began to glow and then smolder within the corncob bowl. Then Mama put the pipe back between her lips and drew the blessed stuff into her lungs. She held it there a moment and then breathed out, making small circles with the blue smoke.

"Oh Mama, look! You're making halos."

"That I am Dorcas, that I am," said Mama with a delightful chuckle. "Remember how Mama showed you. When you grow up to do it, think of me."

"Oh, I will Mama, I will," I said suddenly sobered by what she said. It was Mama's last birthday. Soon the woman who had been my whole world would be nothing but a lifeless bit of bone and dry flesh. Try as I might I couldn't keep the terrifying panic from overtaking me.

"Mama, make it all stop!" I cried moving about in my chains, not caring if I was bruised. "I can't bear it if they kill you. Oh Mama, they can't kill you, they can't! There must be some way you can stop them. If you really loved me you would find a way." Then I burst into tears and began beating my head against the wall.

"Dorcas, my love," said Mama in a voice that was near to tears. "There is nothing I can do. You know that. Please don't cry my daughter, it only makes it harder. I don't want to leave you. Can you believe that?"

"Yes Mama," I said in a small voice, realizing with dismay that I had ruined Mama's party. "I'm sorry Mama, I didn't mean to be such a baby. It's just when I think I will never see you again, I can't stand it."

"But you will see me again Dorcas, you said so yourself."

"But that was only in my dreams, Mama. I don't believe them anymore. You were right. They are just bad things that drive a person mad like grandfather John. I know that now. The only real things in this world are the mean people who hate us. Everyone hates us."

"That's not true Dorcas, not everyone hates us," said Rebecca. "Think on it child, there are many who are good. Why even as I stood in the meetinghouse after I was tried, excommunicated and damned in the eyes of man, I knew God was looking after me. Let Nicholas Noyes and his like think that I will go to my hanging without the comfort of heaven, I know otherwise. You see, we Puritans have our rules, but none is as strong as the word of God....."

"Or the Goddess," said Mama.

"Or the Goddess," said Rebecca nodding. " Even the Puritans believe that if I have a vision, brought by heaven itself, my soul will be saved. And my dearest I have had one. I know that your Mother and I are to die, but you will carry on for us and someday, when your work is done, you will join us in a better world. And as for the earthly cruelty of man, think on the reprieve that Sir William Phipps tried to grant me. He thought me innocent when everyone's hand was turned against me."

"But those bad girls made such a fuss that he took it back," I said determined to believe in the evil of the world.

157

"Only because Master Noyes lied to Phipps and told him that the girl's were being tortured. If fat Nicholas had remained silent I would be sleeping in my own bed this night."

"So you see, there is only evil around us and when you are gone I will be alone," I said sinking into self pity.

"No daughter," said Mama, "there is one who is our friend and risked his own life trying to save me. Remember what I say darling and when you finally set your feet outside these walls, search this man out and stay by
his side.."

"Who is it Mama? Who tried to save you?" I asked excited by
the thought.

"Twas that young scamp, Jack Quelch. When Mary Walcott cried out against me and told all who would listen that I had stabbed her in the breast with a knife, the crowd would have hanged your Mama, then and there, if it had not been for Master Quelch."

"What happened Mama?"

"Well," said Mama, enjoying the story, "young Jack came right up to Mistress Mary and asked her to show him the knife. When Mary drew a bit of blade from her bodice the crowd gave a roar of anger and pressed towards me. That was when Master Quelch showed the court the handle of a knife from which the blade had been broken away. He told the court that the day before he had broken his knife and thrown away the useless blade. Then he grabbed the blade from false Mary's hand and fit the two parts together. Jack Quelch showed Judge Hathorne that Mary Walcott was a liar."

"Oh how brave of him, Mama. I knew Master Quelch was our friend the first time I saw him. Then what happened, Mama? Are they investigating the bad girls and their lies. Will you be set free?"

"No daughter. I told you before that we are no match for the judges. Their authority comes from King William and Queen Mary alone. No one, not even a Governor Phipps or an honest Jack Quelch is a match for them. All that happened was that Judge Hathorne told Mary to stop lying and go on with the evidence that she knew to be truthful."

"How could you stand it, Mama?"

"By thinking of you, my darling, and knowing that you would be safe once you get free of this place. Between Mama's making sure you shall eat and Master Quelch's friendship, there will be a day when you walk in the

158

sunshine again. As long as you live, Dorcas, I shall never die. And, if the dead can come back to earth, I shall always be with you. I will be in the sunshine that falls on you face and the breeze that whispers by your cheek on a spring day. My spirit will be with you in darkness and in light, and when your end comes I shall help guide you to that happy place where I live with your sister. Take comfort in that, my love, and give up your fear. It only weakens us both and makes what we must face harder. Can you do that for me? That would be the best birthday present I could ever have."

"Yes Mama, I can," I said, trying to sound happy for her sake.

"I love you, Dorcas," said Mama.

"I love you too, Mama."

THIRTY NINTH ENTRY

The night before Mama's hanging my dreams returned. I dreamed of Mama in a long blue robe. She was dancing in a silvery dappled sunlight. To her right stood Rebecca Nurse. They looked happy and carefree as they danced among the violets that covered the ground under their feet. A long way off a bell was tolling. It chimed in rhythm to the dance as the women made their way through the lavender flowers. My 'dream' Dorcas was running after the women but I couldn't catch them. The violets that welcomed the others were slippery and wet under my feet and I kept falling and sliding back down the rocky hill that Mama and Rebecca had climbed with ease. I could see Bridget Bishop, dressed in her bright red bodice, at the top of the hill laughing at Mama and Rebecca and urging them to hurry. It was only when I stood up that I saw that they were climbing Gallows Hill. I watched, helpless, as Mama placed Rebecca's head in a noose and then her own. Mama waved at me gaily and then took Rebecca's hand. The bells tolled wildly as Mama and Rebecca jumped, hand in hand, from the gallows. The wind at the top of the gusty hill turned their bodies in a wild imitation of the dance they had done through the violets and then knocked me down. I rolled and rolled until I finally came to rest on the dock at Salem wharf. The sound of the bells turned into the shrill piping of a boson's whistle and I knew no more.

"Wake now little one," I heard a kind voice say to me as I strained to hear one more tone from the whistle. "'Tis time to bid your mother good-bye."

I opened my eyes and stared into the roguish, but pleasant face of Matthew the yeoman. Mama had said that we were very lucky that Matthew had been chosen to bring us from the jail in Boston to the dungeons of Salem Town. If not for that, all Mama's plans and sacrifice for me would have come to naught. But lucky we were, and now he stood before me urging me wake.

"I'm awake, sir," I said, blinking towards the open door of the prison. I saw that dawn was still some time away.

"Well then, sweetheart," said Matthew shaking me again and drawing several keys from his deep pockets, "old Matthew wants to do you a favor, but first you must promise me that you can keep a secret."

"Of course I can," I said, insulted that he thought so little of me. I had been keeping secrets all my life. "I'm four and a half you know."

"Right you are lass, I had quite forgotten you were so very old," he said as he slid a steel key into the lock that secured my chains to the wall. With a thump, my hands were released and fell into my lap. Then Matthew went about fitting his keys into the heavy irons that weighed me down and forced me to sit on the cold, slimy floor.

"There you are now, Dorcas Good, light as a feather ye feel don't ye."

"Why yes, I do!" I said waving my arms in the air and twirling about like an unsteady windmill.

"Careful now girl," said Matthew as I whirled into him, pushing us both against the damp stone wall.

"Am I free sir?"

"No little one," said the yeoman, "but I thought the Almighty and your Mama might think more kindly of me if I let your Mama hold you close until they come for her. And what's more, Sarah," said Matthew looking at Mama with tears in his eyes, "I promise that I will try and look after the mite and see that she is free of her chains from time to time. Ye are a fine woman, Sarah Good, and it is to my regret that they take you away this day. If things had been different I would have been proud to call you wife."

"Why Matthew, I had no idea," said Mama with a smile that made her look quite beautiful.

"Neither did I until our journey from Boston Town," said Matthew as he took his hat from his head and held it with both hands. "When I saw you in the sunlight, so full of life and singing to the child, I knew that I had wronged you greatly. I'm a simple man and have always followed the way of the King's soldiers. There's been many a woman pass through my hands and I thought nothing of it, 'twas the only way I knew. When first we met all I saw was a witch accused, not the saint who caressed and lost her babe, nor the desperate mother who was willing to sell her soul for her daughter's bread. I knew no better Sarah, but I know now that being an ignorant fool is no excuse. I used you basely when I should have cared for and loved the woman you are. It's a great idiot I am that I let the time pass without trying to help you. It's planning your escape I should have been doing, not diddling my time away thinking about my own pleasures. And now it's too late. I beg you to find it in you heart to forgive me."

"I do, Matthew," I heard Mama say as the burly yeoman kneeled before Mama and took her hand. "With all my heart I do. It's little either of us have known of this world's comforts. Think not on what night have been, but on what we have had. What started out as lust has turned into love. Cherish the treasure we both share. Most never find it, even in the shadow of the gallows."

"There, you see," said Matthew taking Mama's hand in his, "I said you were a saint and I am right."

"Not a saint, Matthew, a woman who has been hard-used and knows that there is too little of love in this world."

"Mayhap it's not too late, my love," said Matthew jumping to his feet and looking towards the open prison door. "We could make our way to the docks and jump aboard ship. There is a fine vessel there, right this very moment, that has could take us far away from here."

"But Matthew," said Mama as the frantic man struggled to undo Mama's chains. "We would be caught before we cleared the prison grove. We are surrounded by guards and those who are waiting for the hanging. Think on it man! All you would do is get yourself hanged if we tried such a thing. And think of the child. If we took her with us she would be caught and hanged too. And if we left her behind, Nicholas Noyes would surely see that she was tortured to death. Can't you see there is no hope for us, save in the next life."

"Then let me die with you, Sarah."

"And leave my Dorcas alone? No, Matthew, if you truly love me as you say you do, you must bear this day as I must and care for my daughter. Be brave for my sake and know that I will be waiting for you on the other side."

"Then marry me now, Sarah, so that I may be sure of seeing you again."

"That's not possible, Matthew. I am already married, as well you know," said Mama taking the man's rough face between her hands.

"Not in the Catholic way," said Matthew as he brushed Mama's hands away and helped her to her feet. "Tis only the puritan ceremony that has joined you to another. That counts not, if what my mother said is true.

163

She was a papist and always regretted that she married a cold puritan with no love in him. Many the time she begged him to be married in the old way, but my father would have none of it. He said that the puritan words were good enough. I remember my mother reciting the true vows while she knitted and watched us children play by the fire. She said that if she did it every day the Lord might forgive her. We could do that now, couldn't we Sarah?"

"Do what Matthew? Recite the papist vows to one another?"

"Yes, my love.

"Then do it, Matthew. I'd far rather be joined to you than that scoundrel, William Good."

I watched as Mama and Matthew knelt down in the mud of Salem dungeon and grasped each other's hands. They put their heads together and touched cheeks as Matthew whispered the words that made them one.

FORTIETH ENTRY

Mama and Matthew slept in each other's arms until daylight. I stood guard over them until I saw the gentle dawn casting it's light into the prison through the open door. I knew that if Matthew were found with Mama and me unchained he would be punished harshly. Thank heaven that poor old Goody Nurse was ailing and had slept through the whole business.

"Mama, wake up," I said as I tugged at her sleeve.

"I'm awake, daughter," said Mama as she put her arms out and gathered me to her breast. The sleeping Matthew roused a bit and turned on his side, giving me room to press my body tightly against Mama's.

"Shouldn't we wake him?"

"Not yet darling," said Mama caressing my hair. "There is still time and I want this moment alone with you."

"Mama, I don't want you to go," I said trying desperately to keep from crying.

"I know you don't, my love," said Mama holding me tightly, "but I'm afraid there is no help for it. Promise me that when I am gone you won't lose hope, no matter what happens."

"I promise Mama," I said with a gulp, as a traitorous tear rolled slowly down my cheek.

"There's a brave girl," said Mama as she turned my face towards hers. "And promise me, Dorcas Good, that you will never forget your Mama."

"Oh never, Mama, never!" I cried as I wrapped my small arms around her neck. "Why did this happen to us, Mama! It's not fair. I hate them all and I wish they were dead."

"Don't wish that, child," said Mama, "to wish ill to others is to fill your heart with bitterness and hate. Sooner or later you became bitter and hateful and might as well be dead yourself. Forgive them all, Dorcas, and live free of their folly. That is the greatest gift you can give your Mama."

"But they deserve to suffer, Mama, you said so yourself many times."

"And they will, Dorcas, but leave the punishment to the Almighty. As soon as you get out of here live by their rules until you are big enough to get away. When that day comes leave Salem Village and make your own way in this big world. I know it will be scary, but there is nothing for your here. Look at Goody Nurse. Her mother was accused of witchcraft many years ago and it followed Rebecca and her sisters all their lives. She sits here now ending her life as a witch condemned. Don't let that happen to you, my daughter. When it is time, run from this place. Save yourself from our fate. Do this for me and I feel that my life and my death will have not been wasted. And when you are far from here and the curse laid upon this town, find joy and laughter."

"But how can I Mama, with you and baby Mercy gone? I'm so afraid that I might forget you. When you were locked so far away from me there were days when I couldn't remember your face no matter how hard I tried. Oh Mama, sometimes that scares me most of all."

"How can you ever forget your Mama, sweet child? You have but to look at your own face and listen to your own voice to know you are her daughter. You are the image of me, Dorcas Good."

"I am, Mama?" I asked, never having thought about such a thing before.

"Yes , my love, there is nothing of evil William in you, thank the Lord."

"I'm so glad Mama, but it's not enough. What will I do without you?"

"Do, child? Why live, of course. Gather the violets that I love and sing to the birds with our voice. Laugh and love and bring joy to the spirit of your mother who will be watching over you all the time."

"You will, Mama?"

"Yes Dorcas. No matter what you do or where you go I will be there beside you. Do you think Mama would ever leave you? Believe that I am with you always and have courage. Can you do this for me? Can you be a brave girl and believe that I will always be with you?"

"Yes Mama," I said with a lighter heart, knowing that Mama had never lied to me. How I would miss her sweet smile and the laughter that we had shared, but if her words were true then I had nothing to fear.

"That's my girl," said Mama hugging me tight and giving me a great kiss. I kissed her back and settled back into her arms while we watched as the sweet dawn turned into burning daylight.

FORTY FIRST ENTRY

"Tis time Matthew," said Mama as she shook the sleeping yeoman gently.

"Time? Time for what?" asked Matthew as he sat up blinking.

"Time for you to say good-bye and lock us up, my love," said Mama stroking the Matthew's shaggy head tenderly.

"I'd forgotten," said Matthew.

"Matthew, you must hurry," said Mama, as the poor man looked about him in confusion.

"Yes, I must," said Matthew slowly, as we took our places against the wall and waited for our chains. "It's just that I can't bear the thought of seeing you chained after knowing you free, Sarah."

"No matter, my love," said Mama looking up at Matthew with glowing eyes. "You have freed my heart and given me hope. Soon I will be free of all earthly care and know nothing but paradise."

"And so shall I, when we meet again, Sarah Good," said Matthew as he bent down and fastened her chains as tenderly as a lover.

"Don't forget Dorcas' chains," said Mama as Matthew moved towards the door.

"But surely no one will check the mite," said Matthew. "I promised she will go free and free she will be as long as there is breath in my body."

"But Matthew," said Mama, "Tis Nicholas Noyes coming for me. I know he will check her chains twice over. You know what delight he takes in such things. Chain her quickly before you are both beaten."

"Right you are, Sarah," said Matthew coming full to his senses and taking the key to my chains from his pocket. "It's a wonder you can think of such things at a time like this."

"My head is clear and my heart at peace, Matthew, as long as I know you and Dorcas live and remember me."

"You will fill my every thought from this day forward, Sarah. And such thoughts they will be for this empty old head. I thank you for bringing me such joy."

"Hurry now," said Mama, blushing a pretty pink. "Off with you before we all start crying.

"Right you are, my darling," said Matthew as he snapped my chains shut and made for the open prison door. "I love you Sarah Good."

"And I you, Matthew Taylor," said Mama as she gave Matthew a brilliant smile.

I watched Mama's face as Matthew shut the heavy door and turned the key from the outside. As soon as Mama heard Matthew's heavy footsteps moving away she buried her face in her skirt and sobbed.

If only I could have run to her and put my arms around her! Of all the cruelties we had suffered, this was the worst. I knew that I would never be able to find it in my heart to forgive Salem Village for this last evil act, To deny my Mama comfort on the morning she was to die was something that must be avenged.

"No Dorcas," said Mama as she raised her head and looked at me with her clear eyes. "There will be no vengeance for this moment. Remember that any deed you do to another in malice will be visited upon you three-fold."

I am sure that my mouth hung open as I listened to her words. Mama could read my thoughts as clearly as Goody Nurse! Why had she never told me?

"Because it would have done us no good, said Mama. "You see what being different gets you in Salem. Never let any know that we have this gift. Be a good girl and act the sweet simpleton until you see the last of Salem. You promise me that, Dorcas Good, and I promise that even after I cross over into the otherworld we will be as one, traveling our journey together."

"Oh, I promise, I promise," I cried, full of joy. Now I knew that my Mama could never be taken from me as long as we could feel each others words.

"Hush now daughter," said Mama as we heard the loud voice of Nicholas Noyes coming towards us.

FORTY SECOND ENTRY

"Wake up old woman," said Nicholas Noyes as he kicked dear Goody Nurse. I watched as the poor woman grabbed her side and rolled over, entangling herself further in the heavy irons that weighed her down. When she tried to sit up, she found it impossible.

"Please, won't you help me?"

"And why should I help such as you who tortures and harms those innocent, unfortunate children," said Noyes, laughing at the helpless Rebecca.

"Those 'children' are neither innocent or unfortunate," said Mama. "You help Goody Nurse right now, you fiend."

"And what business is it of yours what I do or I don't do, whore?"

"'Tis the business of any Christian woman to demand decency for an elder. Do your Christian duty, Reverend Noyes, or I swear that the villagers will hear of your actions from the top of Gallows Hill."

"Shut your mouth, witch!" yelled Noyes, crossing over to my mother and slapping her hard across the face. A trickle of blood ran down her chin and fell into the lap that had so recently been filled with tears.

"It's all right Sarah, truly it is," said Rebecca who had somehow managed to pull herself into a sitting position. "See Master Noyes? Here I am, alert and ready. Leave off from bothering Goody Good and do what you have to do."

"Well spoken, Goody Nurse. 'Twas always a sensible one you were before the devil got his hooks into you. I must say that it's with some regret that I'll see you hanged this day," said Noyes with false compassion.

"The same regret that forced you to drag me from trial to meeting-house and demand that I be shamed and excommunicated before my friends and family?" said Rebecca with more life in her than I had seen in days.

169

"Oh come now, Goody Nurse, you know I was only doing my duty as a teacher and God's minister. Besides," said Noyes as he sucked in his stomach and drew himself to full height, "you and all like you must be made an example of. You are the Devil's handmaiden and a witch tried and convicted. If you had shown any sorrow or remorse there might have been some mercy we could have shown you, but you insisted on being stubborn. A stubborn woman is one of the Devil's best tools, as we all know. It is you who chose to go to the hangman unrepentant and full of guilt, not I, Rebecca Nurse. Don't try your wiles on me or try to hand me the burden of your crimes. You and Goody Good are to hang today and I can tell you that Salem is glad of it."

"What it is you are glad of, Brother Nicholas?" said Matthew as he entered the cell.

"Why of being permitted to do God's work this day and all the days of my life, Brother Matthew," said Nicholas as he slapped Matthew Taylor on the back.

"Yes, well," said Matthew as he looked at Mama's bloody chin and swelling cheek, "perhaps part of God's work would be for you to lead us in prayer."

I could tell by Matthew's clenched fists and moving jawbone that it was taking all his strength to keep from killing Nicholas Noyes. Only his promise to Mama could have stayed his hand at that moment.

"I'll not do such a thing," said Nicholas as he stepped away from Matthew in shock, "and I'm surprised that you would suggest such a thing. We all know that to pray before a witch, unrepentant and guilty, is to mock the Lord. Think how these demons would glory in twisting our words."

"'Tis not so," said Rebecca with a hopeful light in her eyes. "Lead us in the Lord's own prayer, Nicholas Noyes. It would bring me great comfort to go to my death with God's words upon my lips."

"Yes, do that Nicholas," said Mama, realizing what prayer would mean to the old woman, "and I will take back my words of disrespect and follow you meekly."

"I'll not, I say! I'll not!" said Nicholas backing towards the cell door. "'Tis a trick to beguile me and make me lose my way. The next thing I know you will be urging me to sign the Devil's book. Unchain the bitches, Matthew, and let us get on with the Lord's work."

"Yes sir," said Matthew as he moved towards Rebecca Nurse. Gently he unchained the old woman and helped her towards her feet. Then he turned towards Mama and did the same. It was not until that moment that I finally realized that Mama was to die.

"Mama," I screamed, "don't leave me!" Don't go! Please don't go!" I fought against my chains and miraculously succeeded in pulling one from the wall.

"Shut your mouth," said Nicholas Noyes as he stood over me and banged my head against the wall.

"There now, let that be a lesson to you, Devil's imp," was the last thing I heard as blood filled my eyes.

FORTY THIRD ENTRY

Mistress Black and Goody Phillips have told me that Matthew went mad when he saw me slump against the wall and fall lifeless to the floor. In a fit he grabbed fat Nicholas and began banging his head against the stones. Matthew stopped only when the other yeomen heard the noise and rushed in to save Nicholas. Matthew was taken out and flogged until the blood ran down his back. Then he was put into the stocks for days. He was finally released when the honorable Nicholas Noyes declared that Matthew must have been bewitched by me!

But I knew nothing of all this as I lay senseless on the dungeon floor while Mama and Rebecca Nurse were led away to their death. All that I tell of now was told to me by Hannibelle Black and Mercy Phillips, my dearest friends and companions. I thank and bless them for making Mama's last moments live for me.

Outside the prison, Mama and Rebecca Nurse were joined by three other women. They were Susannah Martin, Elizabeth Howe and Sarah Wildes. Five women were to be hanged on July 19th, 1692. It was such a day that makes your heart sing and your feet want to dance. Even from my prison cell I had felt the warmth and smelled the sea breeze. Susannah and Sarah were much like Rebecca Nurse. They were good women whose only crime was that of helplessness against their accusers. Elizabeth Howe was a bit more like Mama in that she said what she meant and dared anyone to challenge her. I had always liked Goody Howe and it made me sad to think of the black hood being drawn over her beautiful violet eyes.

Mama, Rebecca and the rest were loaded into an old rickety cart and began their journey towards Gallows Hill. The cart swayed this way and that under their weight. Dear Rebecca sat in the bottom of the cart with her head buried in her lap, but Mama stood upright, weighed down though she was with her chains, and stared at the crowd. Hannibelle says that it was as if she were trying to remember the faces of all she saw. Mama's eyes burned black with her passion.

At first the cart rumbled past many houses filled with the people of Salem Town. The townsfolk had invited their friends and relatives to see the witches hanged, so each house was filled with people jeering and shouting oaths at my Mama and the other women. Hannibelle said that one man fell out of his second floor window as he tossed a rotten apple at my Mama. He blamed his broken leg on her evil eye. Many of the townsfolk threw things at Mama and Rebecca as they passed by. I have never been able to walk through the town without thinking of that. Never could I look at my neighbors without thinking, "did you hit my mother with a spoiled egg, Goody Wilson? Was it you, Goodman Allen, who cursed my Mama on the way to her death and made her last moments even worse?" Those thoughts alone would have been enough to drive me mad had not Goody Phillips warned me against such things.

"Think of all that later when the pain lessens," she would say, tricking me into believing that somehow, someday, the pain would be less. It never has been, but I thank her just the same for her kindness.

Mama and the other condemned women traveled down Prison Lane and turned onto Essex street, the fine wide road where Judge Corwin's house stood. The Judge's house was made of stained brown and had real glass windows that were held together by pieces of lead. Often Mama and I had walked by that beautiful house and admired the sparkling glass shaped like diamonds. It was behind those windows that Mama was taken to be examined one last time for her witches mark. It was also there that she saw the last of my father as he said, once again for all to hear, that she was a witch and so was I. Mama said that she stood in Judge Corwin's fine parlor while the finest ladies of Salem Town lifted her skirts and poked and prodded her with their fingers and with sticks. They made Mama turn round and round while they did their cruel work, not believing that her body was free of blemish. I can just imagine Judge Corwin, Judge Hathorne, and my father looking on as Mama was exposed so shamelessly. Hannibelle says that it takes more than expensive pewter and carved wooden chests brought from England to make a gentleman. Corwin may have had those sitting in his parlor, but his fine belongings will never excuse his base behavior. How I wish I had been there, full in my womanhood as I am now. I would have murdered all those who hurt my Mama and taken her far away. I could say more, but Mercy Phillips says to think such thoughts will only drive me to madness so I must abandon them. It is so hard to tell of Mama's last day without feeling the anger I do now, but I just heard her spirit in my ear urging me back from vengeance to truth. "Tell on, my daughter," she says," do not cloud my memory with what might have been. Such things drain away the power of the tale that must be told."

"Yes Mama," I answered in my heart, "it is time to go on."

Soon, Mama and the rest turned onto Boston Street and started the last of their journey. Mercy said they were made to get out of the cart and walk beside it as the way grew too steep for the old horse to pull them. They had been weighed down with chains far heavier than the ones that had held them fast to their prison walls and found it almost impossible to move, much less walk. But somehow they were made to go forward, urged on by the whip of Nicholas Noyes.

As the five women struggled on they were taunted and tripped by the townsfolk. Hannibelle said that Mama fell several times, but no one offered to help her up. It was only when a strange young man, with a hat pulled low upon his brow, came close to Mama and Rebecca Nurse and offered his arm to them, that the townsfolk stepped back a few feet and let them pass. By the description of the man I have guessed that he was Master Jack, but I cannot be sure. I do know that Mama and Rebecca passed through the orchards that led to Gallows Hill in relative safety once the young man took his stand with them. The same cannot be said for Susannah, Elizabeth and the other Sarah. They were cruelly pelted with rocks and offal as they made their way up the rocky slope of Gallows Hill. At the top of the hill Rebecca Nurse fell to her knees and tried to lead the other women in prayer but she was knocked to the ground and shouted down by the bloodthirsty crowd.

"Let them burn in hell!

"No prayers for the witches, they have signed the Devil's book in blood! Let them pay for it now!"

"Worse than a thousand whippings is what you'll get after you die!"

"Get on with it before we do it for you!"

Mercy said these were but some of the shouts that came from the crowd. There must have been worse, but my friends have always remained silent when I begged them to tell me more.

The crowd became quiet as Susannah Martin was led to the bottom of the ladder that leaned against the great oak tree. Susannah had been accused of taking spirit form and laying with the men of the town at night. When I think of the beautiful Susannah, with her thick auburn hair and large green eyes, it is not hard to believe that many men in the town would have had lustful thoughts about the lovely widow. It was their unfulfilled lust that Susannah was paying for now. I have learned that to turn down a man's lust is a dangerous act that can cost a woman her life.

"Susannah Martin, you have been judged guilty of the crime of witchcraft. Confess now and receive God's forgiveness," cried Nicholas Noyes above the crowd as he approached Susannah.

"I am innocent as well you know" said Susannah, ignoring Nicholas and facing the crowd. "To die with a lie on my lips would be to burn in hell for eternity."

"Then you refuse to confess?" said Nicholas with a gleeful smile.

"That I do, you fat fool."

A great burst of laughter came from the crowd as Nicholas shoved the black hood over Susannah's face and carried her struggling form up the ladder. There were muffled cries from under Susannah's mask, but the crowd could not hear her words. A hush fell over the crowd as Nicholas Noyes grabbed the noose and lowered it over Susannah's head. When Susannah felt the rope tighten around her neck she began to scream. The crowd was delighted by the sound and began to cheer. Their cheers turned into a roar as Nicholas pushed Susannah off the ladder. She hung down, suspended from the rope with her arms swinging from side to side, as she slowly strangled. Hannibelle said Susannah was one of the lucky ones. It only took her a few minutes to die.

Now Elizabeth Howe must die. She was an honest woman with more than her share of intelligence. Hannibelle says that Elizabeth had faced her accusers at trial and said, "God knows I am innocent of anything of this nature," as Ann Putnam showed the judges a pin that had been stuck into her arm. Why Elizabeth was accused was always a great mystery to me until I heard that her family owned lands that were coveted by the Putnams. In the crowd was Elizabeth's ninety four year old father-in-law and her blind husband. Often I had seen kind Elizabeth leading the poor blind man about the town, seeing to his every need and caring for him in a kindly manner. It has always made me sad to see the old man and his blind son stumble about the town since, alone and inconsolable.

Elizabeth went meekly to her death and spoke only of forgiving her enemies and seeing her loved ones in heaven. Nicholas allowed her to climb the ladder by herself and then gently placed the hood over her face and the noose around her neck. The crowd watched in awed silence as Elizabeth was pushed away from the great oak and swung in the bright July sunlight. She gave a few gasps and then she died as sweetly as she had lived.

Mercy Phillips says that after Elizabeth breathed her last, Nicholas quickly grabbed Sarah Wildes and hurried her up the ladder. The quiet death of Elizabeth Howe had set the crowd to muttering about the saintliness of her earthly manner. How could one who died so gently be a witch? What if the judges had been wrong?

Nicholas Noyes shoved the hood over Sarah Wildes face while the afflicted girls, sensing the mood of the crowd, began to weep and scream. They cried that even now Sarah Wildes was tormenting them. The crowd took up the girls' cry and began chanting "die witch die," as Nicholas pushed Sarah's body away from the tree. In his haste, Nicholas had not adjusted the knot of the noose tightly around Sarah Wildes' neck and it slipped, causing the poor woman to struggle in the air for almost a quarter of an hour before she died. The crowd watched in delight as Sarah Wildes twisted and turned to the cries of the afflicted girls. Hannibelle says Ann Putnam and Mary Walcott put on a wondrous show while Sarah Wildes died her lengthy death.

"See how a witch should die!" shouted Judge Hathorne above the noise of the crowd. "Only a soul bound for hell suffers such a death. Bring on the witch, Rebecca Nurse."

Dear Rebecca! How it hurts to relive her death. But it is what I must do if I am ever to be free of the horror. I am glad that at least she died surrounded by her family and friends and must have taken comfort in that. How good it must have been for her to see so many children and grandchildren standing on Gallows Hill mourning her passing. She spoke her last loving words to her family and then forgave her accusers. Rebecca prayed to her God to receive her that day in paradise just as he had his own beloved son who had also died as an innocent. Then Rebecca turned towards Judge Hathorne and pleaded with him one more time to be allowed to be buried in the ground of her own sweet farm, but even this she was denied.

"You shall be covered by the hard rocks of this unhallowed ground as are all the others," said Hathorne as he avoided looking into Rebecca's eyes.

"She shall not," murmured yeoman Preston, (who was standing next to my own friend Mercy Phillips). Preston was the husband of Goody Nurse's namesake daughter, Rebecca. It was then that he stepped forward and pushed Nicholas Noyes aside. It was Thomas Preston who gently carried his mother-in-law up the ladder and tearfully shaded the old woman's eyes with the hood.

"Jump up as ye feel yourself pushed, Mother," said Thomas for all the crowd to hear, "that way your neck will snap and you will die easy."

"Thank you, son Thomas," said Rebecca as she leapt from the ladder with the step of a young girl.

What Thomas had said was true and Rebecca died instantly, bestowing a gift upon my mother. She smiled as she watched the limp body of Rebecca Nurse being cut down from the great oak tree. Now she too knew the secret of dying quickly and stealing some of the joy from the face of Nicholas Noyes.

"Pile her body with the rest," said Noyes to the gravediggers as he turned towards my mother and grabbed her arm.

"Not so hasty, Nicholas my lad," said Mama loudly. "I'm no Goody Wildes to follow you meekly up the ladder without my final say."

"The only words we want to hear from you are those of confession, witch!" screamed Noyes into Mama's face.

"Confess witch, confess," came a cry from the crowd that Hannibelle said belonged to John Indian, Tituba's husband.

"Confess witch, confess," chanted the crowd after him until the chant became a shout and the shout became a roar.

"Then I shall confess," screamed my mother as she turned towards the crowd. She moved so suddenly that she almost fell off the ladder Nicholas Noyes was forcing her to climb.

"Silence," said Nicholas to the townsfolk as he smiled at my mother, never letting go of her arm. "Now then, Sarah Good, you have seen what happens to those who have gone before you. Confess now and save your life."

"Aye," said the great justice, Cotton Mather, who had come personally to see to it that the law was satisfied that beautiful July morning, "confess loudly for all the world to hear, Sarah Good, and I swear that you shall live."

"So," said Mama, "all I have to do is tell you I'm a witch and I will be freed?"

"Not freed, woman," said Mather, "put away where you can do no more harm. You shall remain imprisoned and chained all your life, unless of course you repent and do penance."

"And what would my penance be, sir," said Mama in hopeful tones."

"I have need of servants and you would make a fine one, Sarah Good. Confess now and I will indenture you to me," said Mather, looking lustfully at Mama's fine form and still lovely face.

"And what of my child, my Dorcas? What becomes of her?" asked Mama.

"Why, she must face justice like all the rest. But she would no longer be any concern of yours. You would be my servant, free of all that you had before, including husband, home and child."

"What chance would the child of a confessed witch have in your courts, fine sir," said Mama as her face turned red with fury. "You see what has become of Rebecca Nurse! It is said that her two sisters may soon follow her if you have your way. To confess to witchcraft would be to sign the death warrant of my only child, innocent as we all know she is. No sir, I will not confess to something I'm not. What good are a few more years of living in this earthly hell when I may enter a better place this day with the truth upon my lips. I'll not damn the soul of myself or my child for any earthy promise. I know how much those are worth. I curse you, Cotton Mather, and all like you who prey upon the weak and helpless for their own earthly reward. It is you who should be standing upon this ladder, not I!"

"Shut up witch," said Nicholas Noyes striking my Mama in the face and bosom. You are a witch and you know it."

"You are a liar!" screamed Mama. "I am no more a witch than you are a wizard, and if you take away my life, God will give you blood to drink!"

"You'll not live to put a second curse upon me," said Noyes as he hit Mama again and dragged her the rest of the way up the ladder. Hannibelle says that Mama put up a terrible fight and bit Noyes' hand when he tried to put the hood over her face, so Mama had the noose placed around her neck while her eyes still glared at the crowd. Those I know who watched that day said they could hear Mama's faint whisper above the sudden hush. She was repeating her favorite twenty third psalm, "Yea though I walk through the valley of death I shall fear no evil," were her last words as Nicholas kicked Mama from the ladder. She tried to jump up, but Nicholas caught her body and she fell heavily with the knot of the noose falling behind her neck as it had Sarah Wildes. Mama's death was a terrible one that was talked about in Salem for years after the hangings. No one had ever seen a person hanged without a hood and the shock of it added a special flavor to the day for those that enjoy such things the way Salem does.

179

Mama fell down with her feet but a few inches from the ground and began to choke. Her face began to swell, not only from the blows given her by Nicholas Noyes, but from the effects of the rope around her neck. Then her ears and lips turned red and took on a grotesque character, becoming three times their normal size. The gentle, loving eyes that had been my only comfort now turned red from the pressure and then were forced forward, seeming to fall from their sockets. Mama's hands kept clenching and unclenching in a strange fashion until finally she grasped them together in a prayerful position. It was only when the red frothy blood ran from her nostrils and her mouth that Mama began to die. The last thing that stopped moving was her tongue that now protruded, fully extended, from her mouth.

"Now you see who shall die drinking blood, witch!" shouted a triumphant Nicholas Noyes as he gave Mama's body one last yank and snapped her neck

The Robert Prince House, home to Sarah Osborn at the time of her arrest. It still stands on Maple Street, Danvers, Massachusetts.

The Rebecca Nurse Homestead, Pine Street, Danvers, Massachusetts.

Higginson Book Company, Washington Street, Salem, Massachusetts. George Corwin, High Sheriff and arresting officer of Sarah Good and many others, was buried in the cellar of this building. It is said that his ghost can be seen wandering through the halls to this day.

DEACON NATHANIEL INGERSOLL.
1634 — 1719.
GAVE THIS LAND TO THE INHABITANTS OF
SALEM VILLAGE AS
A TRAINING PLACE FOREVER
TO THE MEMORY OF HIM AND OF THE BRAVE
MEN WHO HAVE GONE HENCE TO PRO-
TECT THEIR HOMES AND TO SERVE
THEIR COUNTRY. THIS STONE
IS ERECTED BY THE TOWN.
1894.

The sight of Ingersoll's Tavern, Centre Street, Danvers, Massachusetts. This land was given to Salem Village by Nathaniel Ingersoll to be used as a training field.

The site of the Blue Anchor Tavern. It stands on the corner of English Street and Derby Street, Salem, Massachusetts.

The Jonathan Corwin House. This is the house of Judge John Corwin, magistrate of the Salem Witch Trails. It stands today at its original location on Essex Street, Salem, Massachusetts.

The Salem Witch Memorial, Charter Street, Salem, Massachusetts. The five stones shown represent Sarah Good, Rebecca Nurse, Susannah Martin, Elizabeth Howe and Sarah Wildes, all hanged on July 19th, 1692.

Detail of Judge John Hathorne's gravestone.

The gravesite of Judge John Hathorne, presiding justice of the Salem Witchcraft Trails, Old Burial Point, Salem, Massachusetts.

Died in jail previous to July 19, 1692

INFANT DAUGHTER to Sarah Good
of Salem Village

Hanged July 19, 1692

SARAH GOOD of Salem Village

ELIZABETH HOW of Topsfield

SUSANNAH MARTIN of Amesbury

REBECCA NURSE of Salem Village

SARAH WILDS of Topsfield

Detail of the Danvers Witch Memorial.

The Danvers Witch Memorial, located at Hobart Street, Danvers, Massachusetts. It was the site of many events of the Salem Witch Trials.

Gallows Hill, Salem, Massachusetts.

PART FIVE

THE ECSTASY
OF
ALONENESS

FORTY FORTH ENTRY

"Open that door before I knock your teeth out!" were the first words I heard as I came to. I had no idea how long I lay unconscious on the muddy prison floor, but I could tell by the blackness of my cell that it was night.

"I'll not let you in without a pass," said the voice of a yeoman I knew as John.

"Come now man, all I wish to do is bring my niece some comfort on this dark night. Is that so much to ask. Think of it. The child lies in there alone and friendless with nary a soul to talk to. Let me enter so that we may pray for her poor mother's soul. Do this for me and this is yours."

"Double it and I'll take the risk," I heard John say."

"Done," said the stranger.

It was then that I recognized the voice. It was my friend, Jack Quelch! What was he doing here? Where was my Mama? Then I remembered. Mama had been taken away to be hanged.

The prison door swung open and Jack Quelch entered, bringing the smell of fresh salt air into the dank room.

"Dorcas, my darling niece," he said winking at me, "how I have missed you."

"I've missed you too, Uncle Jack," I said loudly for the benefit of the yeoman.

"Would it be possible for me to have a moment alone with my niece so that we might pray, good sir?" said Jack turning towards the yeoman.

"I suppose so," said John as Master Jack tossed another coin at him, "but make it quick. I've no wish to wind up in the stocks for this."

"Right you are, lad. We'll be but a moment, I promise, " said Jack with his beautiful smile. "Come Niece, we must get on our knees if the puritan God is to hear us."

189

"Yes Uncle," I said, trying to follow his example as Jack knelt next to me. Despite my heavy chains I managed to stumble to a position that resembled his. I held it bravely until we heard the yeoman leave. Then I looked at Jack and began to cry.

"I want my Mama, Master Jack! I want her so badly. Please tell me they didn't kill her!"

"How I wish I could tell you that, little one, but I'm afraid she's gone," said Jack dragging me into his lap, chains and all, and hugging me tight.

"And what's this," he said as he stroked my curls.

"What?"

"Why this, child," said Jack as he drew his hand from my head. It was red with my blood.

"'Twas there that Master Noyes hit my head against the wall. I guess I wasn't a good girl when they took Mama away. Oh, I hope it didn't make things worse for her."

"Of course it didn't, child," said Jack as he took out a clean linen hand-kerchief from his pocket and began cleaning my wound. "This looks worse than it is, thank Judas," said Jack as he felt my head for any other bumps. "Tell me Dorcas, when you look out can you see clearly?"

"Yes."

"Does your head hurt badly?"

"Only when you touch it like that," I giggled as Jack rubbed away the blood.

"Then I guess you'll live, you minx," said Jack giving me a bounce as he sighed. "How I wish I could take you from this place, Dorcas Good, but I'm afraid I've only come to say good-bye and tell you I'll do everything I can to free you while I'm gone."

"But you can't go! I've already lost Mama and I don't know where Matthew is. You are the only one I have left"

"I must go, little one," said Jack, "but I promise that when I come back you will be free.

"But why are you leaving?" I asked, frantic at the thought of being abandoned by last friend.

"Because I have broken the law, and if I'm caught I won't be able to help you."

"What did you do, Jack?"

"I saw to it that Goody Nurse and your Mama were buried in hallowed ground. Your mother now lies sleeping peacefully with your sister in her arms."

"Thank you Jack," I said formally, struck to the core by his words. Mama really was dead, but Jack had seen to it that God knew she should be in heaven that she would be waiting for me when I got there.

"How can I ever thank you?" I asked, trying to act like a big girl as I fought the tears that threatened behind my eyes.

"Why, by returning the favor someday, my little friend," said Jack with a hearty laugh.

"Oh, I hope not," I said horrified that Jack might someday be hurt the same way Mama was.

"There now, sweetheart, I'm just making a joke, and a poor one it is at that. Don't you want to hear where your Mama rests so that you can visit her once I free you of this place?"

"Yes Jack," I said, suddenly happy at the thought that there was some spot on this earth that I could visit Mama. How wonderful it would be to cover Mama and Mercy's grave with yellow flowers and sing to them when high summer warmed the earth.

"Well," said Master Jack as he hugged me tight, "as you know all who are witches must be buried in unhallowed ground, but Thomas Preston, Rebecca's grandsons, and your humble servant, Jack Quelch, were having none of that foolishness."

"Of course not," I said as I nodded my head.

"So, we waited until nightfall and started out to bring your Mama and Goody Nurse back to the Nurse homestead."

"Weren't you scared you'd be caught?"

"Yes lass, but it was worth the risk. I could have never have looked you in the eye again if I had left your Mama out there alone. Now then," said Jack, continuing his tale, "Thomas and I knew that if we went by land we were sure to be caught, so we decided to go by boat. We took the lead in that old green boat Rebecca has always fancied, while Samuel, Isaiah and Andrew followed in a smaller boat. We carried poles and nets with us in case we were stopped and questioned."

"How clever of you Jack, "you could say you were fishing,"

"Right you are lass, but we still would have had a hard time explaining why we had chosen the middle of the night to cast about for supper."

"But you could have fooled them, I know you could!" I said, beaming at Jack with hero worship.

"Well, yes," said Jack gruffly as he looked down at my bright face. "Anyway, we muffled our oars with old rags and set out from the Nurse farm. First we traveled down the Endicott River to the Wooleston and then held our breath as we turned onto the North. That was the most dangerous part because there were the homes of the townsfolk along the banks.

Finally we came to the section of the North River that comes closest to Gallows Hill. We pulled the boats ashore and covered them with branches. Then we grabbed the nets and began climbing Gallows Hill."

"Was it very steep Jack? Did Mama have a hard climb before she died?"

"No dear," said Jack, "your Mama was shown an easier way. All was quiet and easy for her this morning."

"Truly, Jack?"

"Truly, my little love," said Jack as he lied through his teeth for my sake. "On with it now, eh girl?"

"Yes Jack"

"Now then," he said," when we got to the top of the hill it was easy to spot where the poor women lay. The gravediggers had done a poor job of it. There, in plain sight, was a hand reaching out from the rocks, looking alive as ever you please. I swear that if it had not been full moonlight I might have turned back. The place has an evil feel."

"Mama's not evil!" I said protectively.

"Did I say that, Dorcas? No, I didn't. It is the place that is evil, not the poor souls who have died there. It's as if that hill holds all the venom that the people of Salem hide behind their black wool and white bonnets. The place is evil and that's a fact. It seems to reach out for your soul with hungry arms. I knew that the sooner your Mama and Goody Nurse were quit of that place the sooner we would rest easier."

"Thomas and I stretched out the nets while the boys uncovered the women. We were in luck there because your Mama and Goody Nurse lay atop the rest."

"How did Mama look?"

"Like she was at peace at last, Dorcas. I could tell that her soul was happy that we had come for her. Soon she would be buried properly and Thomas had the book with the words that would ease her soul."

"I'm so glad, Jack. She wasn't always happy here, you know. Father was often very mean."

I know, lass," said Jack, wiping his eyes and going on with the story. "Thomas and I picked up your Mama and Goody Nurse and laid them in the nets while the boys put the rocks back over the other women. I wish there had been room for them all, but to load down our small boats further would have been to sink us. After the rocks were replaced, and more piled high to make up for your Mama and Rebecca, we made our way back down the hill and uncovered the boats. Then we loaded ourselves in and started back down the river. This time we knew that if we were caught there would be no way to lie our way out of what we had done."

"What would have happened to you, Jack?"

"Lord only knows, what with the mood in the town this day. Maybe a beating and the stocks, but I have a feeling it might have been worse."

"So do I," I said as the shivers ran down my back.

"On we went, guided only by the moonlight and the kind spirits of your Mama and Rebecca. It's strange, but I could almost feel them urging us on and protecting our way. For all the danger, I had the oddest feeling that we would make it."

"And you did!"

"Yes we did, child. Our boats sailed back down those rivers like they had wings attached to them and we landed, sweet as you please, on the shore right next to Goody Nurse's garden."

"And that's where you buried them?"

"No Dorcas, we went a bit further. We chose that spot, high on the hill overlooking the orchard, where Goody Nurse helped you and your Mama pick apples last summer. On either side of the graves we put three small polished stones and then covered the stones with grass."

"That's so no one but you could find them again."

"That's right, my clever girl, but now you know where Mama and baby Mercy lie and you can visit them whenever you want."

"And did Master Preston say the words, Jack?"

"That he did lass, each one loud and clear. We stood in a circle and removed our hats and said them twice, once for Goody Nurse and then again for your Mama. Then we sent the boys in to tell Rebecca's daughter that all was done. That is when Thomas and I went down to sink the boats."

"Why did you do that, Jack?"

"It only seemed fitting. They seemed more than just boats now. To ride in them after what we had done would have been a sacrilege. When the last bit of wood was sunk, Thomas and I sat at the edge of the water and smoked a pipe together in memory of Rebecca and your Mama."

"Oh how I wish I had Mama's pipe now," I said, suddenly feeling the rush of all the sadness I had held back.

"Well then, Dorcas Good, your wish is granted," said Jack as he pulled Mama's old corncob pipe from his pocket. "Here you are lass."

"Thank you Jack, oh thank you!" I cried as I grabbed the pipe and put it between my lips. It tasted of old tobacco and stale air, but it was the sweetest taste I had ever known. Just having it close by my made me think of Mama at her happiest.

"Now, sweetheart," Jack as he gave me a fierce hug, "tis time for me to leave. I've stayed overlong already. Be brave, my fine girl, and know that old Jackie will come for you. I promise that on your mother's grave."

"I am brave," I said, feeling the hope of his words and suddenly knowing that somehow, someday, I would be free of this place and make a life for myself.

"That's for certain lass, ye are the bravest little woman I have ever known. 'Till we meet again, eh Dorcas Good?"

"Till we meet again, Master Quelch,"

FORTY FIFTH ENTRY

Thank God Jack Quelch left when he did. It was not five minutes later that Nicholas Noyes entered my cell, red with drink and full of fury.

"There you are you Devil's spawn," he yelled as he stumbled towards me.

"I am not the Devil's spawn," I yelled back, full of courage and trying to be as brave as Jack Quelch thought I was.

"Then what do you call this!" screamed back Nicholas Noyes as he lifted my skirt, revealing the bruises and scars that he had inflicted on me over the past months. "These are the Devil's marks for sure. Tell me young Dorcas, just when is it that you let the Devil sup upon your body? I've had you watched and none has seen so much as a twitch out of you. Does he bewitch us and cause us to sleep while you have your foul orgies, or are you so powerful that you leave your body and fly about the town taking your pleasure where you may?"

"You're mad, Master Noyes, if that's what you think," I said quietly, not liking the gleam in his eyes.

"Mad is it I am? I'm as sane as any man in this town. The only madness here abouts is the one you and your kind are afflicting us with. Only by hanging you all will we ever be free."

"You shall never be free of what you have done, sir," I said, suddenly not caring about what Nicholas might do to me. It had been too hard and too long a day to be cautious any longer. What could Nicholas do to me that hadn't been done already? Rape me? Beat me? Torture me? There was nothing left he could take from me but my life and what good was that, sitting in this dark cell alone and friendless. I knew, despite Jack Quelch's brave words, that it would be a long time before I breathed free air again, perhaps longer than I could stand. If this is how Nicholas Noyes wanted to play the game than let him play it. I was tired of being afraid. No longer would I show him my face of fear. If he was going to kill me then let him be done with it. The sooner I died the sooner I would see Mama and Mercy.

"Go ahead, you little bitch," said Nicholas as he put his hand upon my shoulder and began to squeeze, "I dare you to curse me as your wicked mother did. An evil death it brought her and may it bring you the same."

"Oh no, Master Noyes," I said forgetting myself, "I happen to know that Mama's death was a sweet one and that she died peacefully, so don't try to torture me with your lies."

"Sweet and peaceful was it, you bitch? I'll tell you how peaceful it was. Your Mama took a full half of the hour to die. Conscious she was too, conscious to the very last minute. She flapped her arms up and down like an old crow when the blood ran out of her. It was really quite funny, and fitting too. Never again will anyone curse old Nicholas for doing his Christian duty. Your mother promised that I would be sorry for hanging her and swore that I would die with blood in my mouth. Die indeed! Here I stand before you, witch's daughter, hale as ever if you please, while what's left of Sarah Good lies beneath a pile of rocks waiting for the dogs. So you see, little bitch, you would do well to be a good girl and mind me," laughed Nicholas as he fumbled with his belt.

Now it was my turn for mirth as I watched the disgustingly fat man lower his pants. What a fool he was if he thought his tales could hurt me. One way or the other Mama was dead and beyond pain, and Jack Quelch and Thomas Preston had made sure that Mama, Rebecca, and Mercy were honorably put to rest. My tongue itched with the urge to taunt fat Nicholas with the truth but I knew to do so would only hurt Jack Quelch.

"Now then, Devil's bride", said Nicholas with his pants around his ankles, "what is it that brings such a smile to you? Is it that you like what you see?"

"Dear heaven," I thought as I looked at Nicholas' fat stomach and almost invisible manhood, "keep me from laughing." But it was no good. The strain of the day, combined with Nicholas' sweating flesh was just too much for me. The feeling bubbled up inside me and I started to giggle. Then I started to laugh. Then I started to hiccup and laugh at the same time.

"Stop that you wicked child," said Nicholas scooting towards me with his pants still around his ankles.

"I can't help it! You look so funny," I managed to gasp out as he grabbed his member and tried to get on top of me.

"I'll show you what funny is," he said as he slapped me and tried to insert his small self in my smaller body. It was no use. My laughter had deflated his tiny balloon and he was useless.

"I'll teach you to laugh at your betters," said Nicholas as he rolled off me and pulled up his pants. "You're a witch for sure, Dorcas Good, if you can rob a man of his seed without even touching him. Make yourself ready for your punishment."

"Go ahead you fat pig," I heard myself yell, "I know now that beating me is the only way you can swell that bit of pork." With those words I fell to the side and was once more engulfed in hysterical laughter.

"Reverend Noyes, Reverend Noyes, is that you within?" I heard a voice at the prison door whisper frantically.

"Aye, 'tis Nicholas. Who wants to know?" said Nicholas, looking at me with hatred while he replaced his belt.

"John Ward, sir," said the voice. "Thomas Putnam sent me to find you. You must come quickly. Something's gone wrong on Gallows Hill."

"Wrong?" How could anything be wrong?" said Nicholas as he unlocked the door and let the yeoman in.

"It seems that someone has stolen the bodies of Rebecca Nurse and Sarah Good. Master Putnam says we must find the bodies before someone buries them in hallowed ground. He says that if that happens, the spirits of Good and Nurse will haunt Salem Town forever. He says you must come to the hill right away."

"I'll be there in a minute, yeoman," said Nicholas giving me a long look.

"If you know anything about this, Dorcas Good, you better tell me now or I swear you'll pay with your life."

"Why sir," I said as sweetly as any innocent child might, "what could I know about such things?" You yourself had to tell me about my poor Mama and her sad death. I swear on my honor that I know nothing, nothing at all."

"You'll hang just like your mother if you're lying to me, Dorcas Good," yelled Nicholas as he slammed the door and locked it behind him.

FORTY SIXTH ENTRY

I sat there in the dark smiling. Thank goodness Jack Quelch had taken to the road before they discovered the missing bodies. I could tell by the look on Nicholas Noyes face that anyone charged with stealing the bodies of Rebecca and Mama would be punished unto death. Thomas Preston was a powerful man, well liked by the town, but my Jack had few friends and less power. It would have been upon him that the worst punishment would have fallen. My last thought was of my Mama as I leaned back against the wall and tried to sleep. It brought me contentment to know that she had been buried properly. I soon fell into a deep slumber full of comfort and peace, peopled only with thoughts of a happy Mama and baby Mercy laying in each other's arms. When I awoke the next morning I felt almost like the old Dorcas who had been a child of sunlight and freedom. Somehow having the worst behind me was almost a relief. I felt ready to get on with my life, whatever it might bring.

What it brought was a new prisoner to my cell, a young boy named Barnabas.

"There," said a strange yeoman as he chained the boy to the wall next to me, "let's see if you'll be trying any of your tricks now that ye're safely shackled and shut away."

"These mean nothing to me and you know it!" cried the boy as he rattled his irons at the guard and spit in his face. "I'll soon be shut of you all. 'Twill take more than chains to stop me."

"We'll see about that," said the guard as he wiped the spittle from his face and turned to leave. "The sooner you follow your family to hell, the better Master Papps."

"Better hell with them than in your God-damned puritan heaven!" yelled the boy as the guard hurried out the door.

Young Master Papps was much older than me but still a child. He had coal black hair and sparkling black eyes that shimmered with mischief as he glanced towards me.

"Well, and what are you staring at, brat?" he said as he squirmed about in his chains.

"I'm just looking at you," I said calmly, determined not to let him get the better of me. I was in no mood to share my cell with a bully. My father and Nicholas Noyes had taught me that I mustn't show fear no matter what I felt inside. To show fear was to be beaten before you start.

"And why should you look at me? I'm nothing special," said the boy slumping against the wall and banging his wrists together. The sound that his metal wrist cuffs made echoed through the cell coldly. The hollowness of the sound almost brought tears to my eyes.

"Why are you here?" I asked as I saw the boy's defiant look replaced by one of sad desperation.

"Because I'm a witch," he said sadly, turning his face away from me. "At least that's what everyone thinks."

"Everyone thinks I'm one too," I said.

"You?" Why would anyone think a little baby like you was a witch. Why you're not even out of napkins yet."

"I am too!" I said loudly, thoroughly insulted by the boy. "I'm going to be five in November."

"See, it's just like I said, you're nothing but a baby," said the boy laughing at me. "I'm almost eleven, big enough to do a man's work. Take it from me, anyone 'almost five', is a baby."

"Eleven's not so old," I said. "Why did they stick you in here if you're such a man? The rest of the men are down in the lower cell. This cell is for the women and children. Welcome to the nursery, Master 'what-ever-your-name-is'. My name is Dorcas Good."

"It's Barnabas Papps, if you want to know," said the boy tipping his head against the wall and making the same rocking motions that I had myself just a few short weeks ago.

"Don't do that," I said.

"Do what?" said Barnabas.

"Rock like that. It's a bad habit, one that you'll find you can't stop once you start. It means that your mind is trying to go far away. Mine almost didn't come back. Take it from me, it only makes things worse. You may be a big boy like you say, but I still know more than you about keeping my wits about me in this place."

"That's what you think," said Barnabas with a laugh, "I've got them all thinking that I really am a witch. Did you see the guard? He was afraid of me. They all are. I can do anything I please to them. Everyone's afraid that I'll curse their cattle or give them the pox."

"If they're so afraid of you why did they dare to lock you up?" I said.

"Because my bitch of a grandmother let them in while in while I was sleeping. She said it was to save herself. I was bound and chained before I had a chance to fight back. This is the first time I've been allowed to sit without a gag in a fortnight."

"They gagged you? Why?" I asked staring at the boy in wonder.

"Because when I cursed Magistrate Norwell he fell dead not five minutes later. It wasn't my fault, but no one will believe me. Even my own granny is afraid of me."

"I'm not afraid of you," I said looking at the sad boy's face kindly. "I know what it's like. My Mama was hanged for witchcraft yesterday and everyone thinks that because she was thought to be a witch, I must be one too. I've seen them looking at me when they bring me my food or ask me questions. They can't get away from me soon enough. Everyone, that is, except for Nicholas Noyes."

"I know him," said Barnabas in a bitter tone." He's the one who likes boys. He made me watch while he stuck his fat poker into my cellmates Nate and Eben, but he wouldn't come near me because he was afraid. He's a coward, is old Noyes. Say now, he doesn't come around here does he?"

"Sometimes," I shrugged, feeling reluctant to think about Nicholas Noyes.

"Did he try it with you, or does he just like little boys?" asked Barnabas.

"He tried," I said, "but he went away mad. He looked so funny without his pants that I started to laugh. That made him so tiny that he couldn't do anything. And that made me laugh even harder."

"You made him seem the fool! Why then, little mistress, you've got my respect. Anyone who can laugh at that black dog is a friend of mine."

"I am?" I said happy for any offer of friendship in this dark place.

"Why to be sure," said Barnabas. "I'll even seal my words with a token. Here now, reach out your hand and take this." Barnabas stretched his hand towards me and I saw that it held a gold coin."

"I can't take that," I said shyly. "It wouldn't be right. You might need it. Besides I don't have anything to give to you."

201

"Why sure you do," said Barnabas, looking almost through me. "A girl like you who could laugh at that old lecher must have something hidden away in her pockets."

"Well, I do have something," I said thinking of my Mama's pipe, "but it wouldn't be right to give it away."

"Well then," said Barnabas, "I guess we can't be friends."

"Wait a minute!" I said desperate to keep my new friend, "I do have something." I put my chained hand into my pocket and rattled it furiously. Soon I felt the softness of my little snake, my Osiris, wrapping itself around my finger. I knew that Mama had given the snake to me as a gift, but Mama was gone and I was alone in this dark place. I felt sure that Mama would far rather have me give my snake away to gain a friend than to sit alone with no comfort.

"Here it is," I said as I held my hand up and showed my pet to Barnabas.

"What's that?" he asked, squinting in the dim light.

"'Tis my pet, Osiris. You can have him if you want."

"I can?" said Barnabas as he reached out to pet the snake.

"Yes, you can," I said, sure now that I had made the right choice. The look of happiness on Barnabas' face was enough to tell me that he was even lonelier than I.

Osiris obediently leapt from my fingertips and curled itself around Barnabas' wrist like a bracelet. Then it slithered down Barnabas' arm and slipped into his shirt.

"He tickles," laughed the boy as we watched the moving lump under the his shirt move and settle in a fold near Barnabas' stomach.

"He's really mine to keep then?" said Barnabas patting his shirt gently.

"Forever and ever," I said as I turned the gold coin over in my hand.

"He's better than any old gold." said Barnabas smiling brightly. "I feel like I still owe you something."

"You don't owe me thing," I said, feeling like Queen Mary bestowing a gift upon a loyal subject.

"How about a story?" asked Barnabas. "I know lots of stories and some of them are even real."

"I like stories. Especially real ones. Are you truly a good storyteller?"

"Yes. Granny says that I tell the best stories of anyone she ever heard. Would you let me tell you one to even up the debt? Real friends should never owe each other anything."

"Yes," I said excited for the first time in weeks. "Tell me a story. I'd love to hear one."

"Good," said Barnabas with a far away look in his eyes. "Then I'll tell you a real story. One about my family. It happened many years ago before my family came to this country. Granny says she swears upon her bible that it is true. Her own mother saw it as clear as day. And what's more, Granny says that her mother was about your age when she saw it happen. You see, Granny's mother was accused of being a witch too, and lived to tell the tale."

"Just as my mother told me to do," I said in a whisper as I thought about that other little girl, so long ago, who shared my fate.

"Just so," said Barnabas as he settled into his tale.

FORTY SEVENTH ENTRY

"It was many years ago," began Barnabas, "in a place called Germany. That's where Granny says our family came from. We even had a different name."

"What was it?"

"Something like Pappahimer or Pappenheimer or something, but when we came here we made it sound like everyone else's so we wouldn't be different."

"Now it's Papps!" I said, never having thought about where last names came from at all. My name was so simple and had always sounded like everyone else's. It set me to wondering if my name had always been Good.

"Yes, Papps," said Barnabas, "but back then it was different. Anyway, my family didn't always live safe and snug in a house like now. Granny's grandmother, Anna, wandered from place to place and dug graves. Granny says that when she married Paulus, the privvy cleaner, that she went up in the world. So Anna and Paulus married and wandered around in the next country over, the country of Bavaria. That was where the real trouble began."

"Did they have mean girls like they do here who lie and hurt people?" I asked, fascinated with Barnabas' story.

"I suppose so," he said, "but stop interrupting."

"I was only asking."

"Well can't you wait? Your questions get me confused and make me forget where I am."

"All right," I said, desperately wanting him to go on with the story.

"Now then," continued Barnabas, "there was this bad Duke, named Maximilian, who didn't like people like Paulus and Anna. He thought gravediggers and privy cleaners should be living in Germany and not bothering him in Bavaria. One day the Duke decided to arrest a family for witchcraft. The Duke's priests had been telling him that someone was keeping his wife from having a baby, and maybe it was someone like the Pappenheimer family."

"What's a priest?" I asked quietly.

"Sort of like a reverend, only worse," answered Barnabas knowingly. "So then, this Duke started hunting for witch families because his priests told him to. Once the priests found the witches, the Duke could show his country how powerful he was and get a baby at the same time. So they arrested poor old Anna and Paulus and their three sons. They also took the little girl but they only locked her up. She must have gotten free, because she grew up and had Granny."

"What happened after they were arrested," I asked, becoming confused by Barnabas' change of subject.

"Why," he said, "they were all put into cells just like we are now. But it was different too. They were beaten every day with something called a strappado and tortured awfully."

"I was tortured."

"Not like this you weren't," said Barnabas with a solemn nod. "These Bavarian Germans really could lay it on, according to Granny. They finally made Anna say that she had a demon lover and liked to murder little children. Anna confessed under torture that she made potions from the dead children's hands."

"That's silly," I said thinking of Tituba and her spells. Tituba said it was impossible to do such things.

"I think so too, but the Duke didn't. He decided that the whole Pappenheimer family were witches and they should be made an example of. So, they were taken to a big town called Munich and executed."

"The whole family?"

"The whole family, except for the little girl. I think they forgot about her. Now comes the really great part. They weren't hanged civilized like they do here. The Pappenheimers were tortured and burned."

"Burned!"

"Yes, burned," said Barnabas rubbing his hands together nervously. "They were taken to this big square and the Duke did awful things to Anna, but I don't think I should tell you about what they did."

"Why not?"

"Because you're a little girl and it might make you sick."

"I'm not a little girl and I want to hear."

"All right, but don't say I didn't warn you."

"Just tell me, will you!" I said, frustrated by his manner.

"I'll tell, but don't blame me if you spit up your stomach," said Barnabas. "They took Anna up on this big platform and cut off her breasts. Then they stuck them in her mouth."

"You're lying," I said, sickened despite my brave words.

"I'm not, I swear it," said Barnabas. "And then they stuck her bloody breasts in her son's and husband's mouth. Then they made them get into carts and they paraded them about the town until they came to the stakes. Granny says that Anna bled the whole way. When they got to the burning place they did things to Paulus that I can't tell you no matter how much you say I have to."

"That's all right," I said, sorry now that I had asked for the story. My stomach was churning and lurching violently.

"I'll just say that they dropped heavy wheels on his arms and snapped his bones. Then they stuck a stick into Paulus in a place that would have made fat Nicholas' games look like fun."

"That's disgusting!" I cried.

"Yes, isn't it," said Barnabas sadly. "And to think he was my own ancestor. Poor Paulus."

"And poor Anna," I said thinking of the woman's horrible wounds.

"Then," continued Barnabas, "the Duke had Anna, Paulus and the two older sons tied to some stakes and slowly roasted. Granny says that youngest boy, Hansel, was made to watch. She said he kept yelling, 'my mother is squirming, my mother is squirming', until they finally dragged him away. According to Granny, Hansel was burned three months later."

"How old was he?" I asked with a shiver.

"The same age I am, little mistress," said Barnabas with an odd smile. "He was eleven."

"I don't believe you!" I cried looking at Barnabas in horror. "No one would burn a little boy."

"Well they did, Granny said so and she never lies."

"But she turned you in for a witch," I said bothered greatly by the woman's deed.

"She only did that only because she had to," said Barnabas. "I know now that they would have taken her too if she'd put up a fuss. What's the use of having us both locked away like the Pappenheimers? At least with Granny out there I can get something to eat now and then. Besides, if they locked up Granny they'd take away her house. If I ever get out of here I don't want to be homeless like poor Paulus and Anna. I know now that Granny had no choice."

"Barnabas," I asked, "what do you think is going to happen to us? If they could burn Hansel, they could burn us."

"Don't you worry, Dorcas," said Barnabas, "the worst they could do is hang us. That's the law here you know."

"Yes," I repeated after him, "that's the law."

FORTY EIGHTH ENTRY

The guards brought in our food several hours later. Mine was my usual bowl of milky soup, but Barnabas had a large basket set before him. It was full of fresh bread and meat.

"See, it's just like I told you. Old Granny does her best to keep me alive, bless her soul," said Barnabas as he started to stuff himself.

It almost made me sick to watch him. It had been many months since I had even seen bread or meat. As Barnabas ate the glorious food with his fingers I thought to myself, "I would sell my soul for a bit of that bread."

"Would you like some, Mistress Good?" said Barnabas looking at me suddenly with gleaming eyes.

"Oh, could I? Could I really?" I said fighting back the sudden stream of drool that came to my lips.

"Of course you can," said Barnabas. "We're friends forever, aren't we?"

"Why yes, we are, but food is so precious here, I thought........."

"Think no more. Whatever I have I'm glad to share with you. Besides, everything will even out in the end, won't it? I give you something now and you give me something later."

"But I have nothing to give you later," I said, knowing that I would never part with Mama's pipe, not even if I were starving to death.

"You have more than you know, little Dorcas," said Barnabas as he handed me two slices of bread with a thick slab of roasted venison in between.

Never in my life had I ever tasted anything so wonderful! I bit down on the bread and meat, chewing it slowly. As it slid down my throat I could feel life returning to my body. I tried hard to remember what Mama had always said about eating like a lady, but I soon found myself gobbling the blessed food as fast as I could.

"Slow down," said Barnabas teasingly, "there's more where that came from, I promise you."

"But what if the guards come in and see me. We both know they would take this away and punish you for feeding me."

"Not the guards out there now," said Barnabas. "They're special friends of mine. Granny slips them a piece of gold now and then to be nice to me."

"Your Granny must be very rich," I said as I gulped down the last bit of bread and meat.

"Not really," said Barnabas, "but she makes out well enough for an old one. Years ago she was a pirate's doxie and she still has some of his gold hidden behind the fireplace. She says that if Micah hadn't been hanged we would be living in a palace now. 'Tis a shame she had to turn him in."

"Turn him in? Who, the pirate? Your Granny turned in her pirate? Why?"

"Because the men who run things here abouts hauled her up on a hook and burned the soles of her feet until she told them where Micah Sweet was hiding. They burned her good too. She never has been able to walk proper since that day."

"How awful," I gasped. "She must have felt so sad when they hanged her pirate."

"Well, yes and no," said Barnabas. "He left his gold with her after he died. I was real small then, but I still remember her walling it up behind the stones. She sang as she worked and later that night brought home a bottle of the finest rum she could buy. That was my first taste of the stuff and I must admit that Granny and I share the thirst. In a way that's what I miss most about being down here. Granny and I had some high old times with that rum sitting between us."

"It sounds like your Granny is rich enough to do almost anything," I said.

"Not rich enough to get me out this place," said Barnabas sadly. "Besides, if Granny starts flashing about too much gold they'll be on her quick as a wink. There's many in this town that would love to get their hands on Micah's treasure."

"But it's pirate's gold," I said. "Shouldn't it be returned to the people it belongs too?"

"They're long dead, you darling girl. Micah Sweet saw to that," said Barnabas with a sinister chuckle. "Besides you don't really think that the judges and magistrates give back anything that passes through their fingers, do you?"

"Of course they do. At least some must. There has to be at least one honest man amongst them that wants to do right."

"Just like the right they did your Mama when they strung her up on Gallows Hill. You are such an innocent, Dorcas Good! Take it from me, Barnabas Papps, trust no one and you'll never be disappointed when they stab you in the back."

"Not even you?"

"Not even me, little girl."

FORTY NINTH ENTRY

It was to my sorrow that I learned the truth of Master Papps' words a few days later. From the minute he had given me his meat and bread I had felt uneasy. The stuff churned in my gut and turned into a small knot of pain. Barnabas also made me uneasy. I'm not sure if it was the gleam in his eye or knowing that his own grandmother saw nothing wrong in betraying her kith and kin to save her own ancient hide. I knew that my Mama would have died defending me if she had been given the chance. If Barnabas' grandmother could do such things, then so could he. She had been his only teacher.

I was awakened in the loneliest part of the night and taken to a small stone chamber with two chairs and an old table. The strange guard who had brought Barnabas to my cell sat on one side of the table and I was forced roughly into the chair across from him. To one side stood Barnabas Papps, free of his chains and warming himself by the fire.

"Go ahead, ask her about the snake," he said gleefully as he rubbed his hands over the flames. It must have been a trick of the light, but it seemed to me that he was passing his hands through the flames without being burnt.

"Is it true, Dorcas Good, that you tried to give this boy your familiar?" asked the guard who had removed his outer coat and now displayed a shiny badge on his vest.

"What's a familiar?" I asked, confused and not yet fully awake.

"Your link with the Devil, you little fool," said the guard, coming around to my side of the table and sitting upon it. He hovered over me as he placed his hands on my shoulders and dug his fingers into my flesh.

"I don't know what you're talking about," I said, shaking with fury at Barnabas' betrayal, expected though it was.

"The snake you call Osiris is what I'm talking about, you little witch," said the guard.

213

"I have no snake," I replied quite honestly, knowing that I had given it to Barnabas.

"Then what do you call this!" cried the guard, pulling my snake from his pocket and placing it on the table in front of me.

"Admit that you are a witch and that this snake sucks blood from you at night to gather strength to do you bidding. Admit it and you will go free."

"I don't believe you," I said staring at Barnabas in fury. "Where are the regular guards, where is Matthew Taylor? Why am I here and why are you trying to make me tell lies. I refuse to become a liar like Barnabas Papps."

"My nephew never lies," said the guard as he strode over to the boy and tousled his curls fondly.

"Watch her while I tend to a private matter, Barnabas. Perhaps you can make her see some sense." The guard grabbed his coat and locked the door behind him.

"You traitor," I hissed at Barnabas as he came over to the table and sat across from me.

"Listen to me you little fool. Do you think I want to do this? Do as we say and Uncle Damien may be able to free us both. All he needs for you to do is put your mark on this piece of paper and we can both walk out of here, free to live the lives we should. We're just children and deserve better than a cold death in the dungeons of Salem."

"What piece of paper?" I asked, unsure of what was wanted of me. If Barnabas was telling the truth then maybe he wasn't a traitor, maybe he was my savior.

"This one," he said, taking a piece of fine piece of parchment from one pocket and a carefully wrapped quill pen from the other. The pen had been touched with ink and left a smudge on his hand.

"Sign here and be free, Dorcas Good."

"But what am I signing?" I asked, feeling suddenly dizzy.

"Just a bit of paper, nothing more, sweetheart."

"But what does it say?" I asked, holding my breath. How I wanted to believe Barnabas and grab that piece of paper, but Mama had always said that I must never put my mark to anything without knowing what it said. That was how she had lost Grandfather's money.

"Sign it quickly, Dorcas, before they change their minds," said Barnabas leaning towards me with glowing eyes.

It was then that I saw something that twisted my heart. The black of Master Barnabas Papps eyes had changed to red and the hand that held the paper before me had become a skinny claw.

"Who are you?" I screamed as I jumped up from the chair and started backing away from that hideous claw.

"Your friend, Dorcas Good, come to save you from your own purity," said the Barnabas thing.

"I don't know what you are, but I know you're not my friend," I said backing towards the fire.

"I'm the only friend you have left, little one. Sign this paper, Dorcas, and I promise that you shall know happiness and riches beyond belief."

"You're the Devil," I whispered.

"Aye, that I am sweetheart, and I want you for my handmaiden. Come to me my beautiful child, and I'll show you how to pay back all those who have hurt you so cruelly. Be mine own true love."

"I would rather die than ever be yours," I said to the Devil in a strangled voice. "If I sign your paper I will never see my Mama again. She waits for me in a heavenly place."

"That's just a fairy tale, you foolish child," said the Devil with a cruel laugh. "Do you think there is such a thing as a heaven? Hell is all we have. And for you it is here as well as in the afterlife. Sign my paper and at least live in heaven here on earth. It is the only place it exists. Sign my book and live!"

"No," I cried turning my back on the Devil and getting on my knees before the fire. I closed my eyes and screamed, "help me Mama, please help me!"

FIFTIETH ENTRY

When I opened my eyes, the Barnabas thing was gone and I was back in my cold, moldy cell. Beside me were chained the two women that I have come to think of as my only friends.

"Look Hannibelle, the child is awake," said the smaller of the two women.

"Easy now, Mercy, don't startle the child," answered the tall, gaunt woman who was chained in the very shackles that had held my Mama but a few days before.

"You're not startling me," I said as I pulled myself into an upright position. "After what I've been through, nothing startles me."

"She speaks like you, Hannibelle," said the small woman who had been called Mercy."

"Why, so she does," said Hannibelle.

"I speak like myself," I said feeling oddly irritated by the two women. What right did they have to sit where my Mama and Rebecca Nurse had sat? Whoever they were and whatever the reason they were here did not entitle them to think they had the right to sit there so casually. They were unwelcome in my world of pain.. All I wanted to do was to be left alone with my memories. Didn't they know that I was Dorcas, the child of witch Sarah Good? I deserved some peace and quiet, especially after what I'd been through with the boy devil, Barnabas.

Barnabas! I'd completely forgotten about him! My eyes searched the cell frantically for some sign of him but there was nothing. It was as if he had vanished into thin air.

"Did you see anyone bring me back here?" I asked the two women, trying to keep my voice steady.

"Why no," answered Mercy.

"You were here when they brought us in," replied the calm voice of Hannibelle.

"Are you sure?" I said hearing my voice raise itself into an almost hysterical tone.

"I assure you there was no one, no one at all," said Mercy kindly.

"Oh," I said, not trusting myself to speak further.

"Tell me dear," said Mercy, "why are you here?"

"Because I am my mother's daughter," I said as I turned away from the two women.

"And who is that?" asked Mercy.

Why wouldn't the woman just shut up and leave me alone! I needed to think right now. Couldn't she see that? My mind was still whirling from my encounter with the Barnabas thing and I desperately needed a few minutes peace and quiet to gather my wits about me.

"My mother is, no I mean was, Sarah Good. A few days ago they took her away and they hanged her. And they're going to do the same thing to me. So now that you know that, you can leave me alone."

"That's utter nonsense," said Hannibelle with a snort. "You're nothing but a child. They don't hang children."

"Yes they do," I said nastily.

"No they don't, and don't use that tone with me young lady. I'll be damned if I'm going to spend what time I have left cooped up with an ill-mannered little brat."

"I'm not a brat! And you shouldn't swear!" I yelled back at the thin woman as I turned around and glared at her.

"Stop it you two," said Mercy putting her hands over her ears.

"Then make her stop," I said stubbornly, sticking out my lower lip and thumping my body against the wall.

"I won't take it back," said Hannibelle, as stubbornly as I had. "Whatever you've been through is no excuse for your rude behavior, Dorcas Good. We've both heard of you and your mother, haven't we Mercy."

"Aye, that we have."

"And we know what happened to your mother. Listen to me child. Your mother would want you to."

"How do you know what my mother would want?"

"Because she was a woman of great sense and spoke plain, just the way I do," said Hannibelle.

I could tell by the woman's voice that she was leading up to a speech, much like the ones Mama used to give me. I found that I wanted to hear what she said despite her mean words to me a moment before.

"They can't hang you without a trial, Dorcas," said Hannibelle, "don't you know that? You were examined before they brought you here, but you have never had a real trial like the one they gave your mother and Rebecca Nurse. Think back, Dorcas. Once you were brought here were you ever taken away like they were? Did you ever stand before Cotton Mather, the high judge, and answer his questions? Were you ever sentenced to hang?"

"No."

"Then they can't hang you. You must be sentenced to die before you can die," said Hannibelle. "It's a mystery to me why you haven't been taken to trial before now when all those who were examined with or before you have been tried, but there you are."

"Do you think they've forgotten about me?" I asked not really flattered by the thought, but seeing how being invisible to the adults around me might save my life.

"I think they may have," said Hannibelle nodding her head. "And I can tell you right now that acting the way you were a minute ago is no way to stay forgotten. If you scream at anyone else the way you did at me they might just take you to trial to save themselves the bother of putting up with you."

"Hannibelle!" said Mercy.

"It's true and you know it my friend. Look what happened to us."

"'Twas you that got us into this spot," said Mercy, "but I don't regret your actions, dear friend."

"If you hadn't defended me you might have gone free," said Hannibelle almost lovingly.

"But what good would my freedom have been to me if I hadn't done everything I could to help you. No, dearest Hannibelle, I would much rather face the gallows with you than think I had failed you."

"There you see?" said Hannibelle gruffly as she looked at me. "See what stating your mind gets you. We are both here, sentenced to die. Stay quiet, Dorcas Good, and you may yet get out of here."

"That's what my Mama said!"

219

"And right she was, dear," said Mercy. "Listen to Hannibelle. She's very smart."

I looked at Hannibelle and truly saw her for the first time. Before, all I had seen was a thin, nasty woman who wanted to make me miserable. Now I noticed her fine clear brow and the intelligence burning in her eyes. She looked not at all like my own sweet mother on the outside, but there was something within this angry woman that matched my mother's soul. From that moment on I began a strange journey, trusting in Hannibelle Black the way I have never been able to trust in anyone else. And, I have been richly rewarded. Never has she lied to me, whatever the cost to either of us.

"I'm sorry for what I said, Mistress," I said, truly meaning it.

"And I too, little one," said Hannibelle with what I know now was a rare smile. "Tell me, Dorcas, why did you look so odd when you opened your eyes?"

"I forget," I said avoiding Hannibelle's steady gaze.

"No you don't, child. I can tell when someone is lying."

"It was nothing, really," I said knowing that if I said anymore my new friends would think me mad.

"It was something," said Mercy brightly. "I remember your exact words. You said, 'did you see anyone bring me back here?' I thought it was a funny thing to say because you had been here the whole time, but when you said, 'are you sure,' I felt very confused."

"Yes, Dorcas, why did you say that?" said Hannibelle.

"Because I had a strange dream," I said, hoping the two women would be satisfied with my answer.

"And what was it about?" asked Mercy gently.

"About the Devil," I whispered.

"Was he in the form of a child, Dorcas?" asked Hannibelle.

"Why yes!"

"Then it was no dream. Mercy and I have seen him too."

"Where," I whispered.

"Right here in this cell, dear, while you were asleep," said Mercy.

"How did you know he was the Devil?" I asked, starting to shake.

"Because he offered us gold coins, coins with the head of a ram on them," said Hannibelle. "He must have thought us very simple to think we would accept such a thing from him. Everyone knows that the Devil often appears in the shape of a little boy offering food and gold."

"That's exactly what he did!" I cried, feeling about in my pocket for the gold coin that Barnabas had given me. "See, here it is," I said triumphantly as I drew the coin from my pocket. I held the coin up for Mercy and Hannibelle to see and when I did it started to shimmer and move about between my fingers. Then it cracked into two pieces and fell into a pile of dust between my feet.

"See there," said Hannibelle, "tis the Devil's gold for sure. Tell me child, did you trade him anything for that worthless piece of earth?"

"Yes", I said slowly, thinking of the little snake, the snake that Barnabas had used against me. "I gave him my pet snake."

"And did he do try to do you favors," asked Hannibelle.

"Yes! He gave me food and said I could pay him later if I felt I hadn't given him enough. He was so bad! He told a guard that I was a witch and they took me to this room to question me. Then the guard, who said he was Barnabas' uncle, left us alone and Barnabas turned into the Devil. But he didn't start turning until I refused to sign his piece of paper. He frightened me so that I ran away from him and started praying to my Mama. The next thing I knew I was back here with you."

"Thank heaven," breathed Mercy softly. "If you hadn't done that you would have been tried and hanged for certain. The paper he wanted you to sign was his own Devil's book. Once you had signed it your doom would have been sealed.

"I don't believe it!" I said, still confused by what I had seen with my own eyes. "There is no such thing as the Devil."

"The Devil lives," said Hannibelle, "and he is abroad in Salem. Of that you can be sure. The gold he gave you and the food he tricked you into eating was just the beginning. Soon you would have been knocking at yonder door and screaming to the guards that you wanted to confess. Once you had done that all would be lost. They have ways of making you betray others, child, and once you did that, coupled with the lies you told to save your own life, you would have become a lost soul."

"Like the girls who accused Mama?"

"Yes Dorcas, just like those girls," said Hannibelle. "I have seen that there will come a time when the Devil will stop his work in this place, at least for a time, but his legacy will live on in those he has marked for his own. Beware of them when at last you leave here. The Devil's seed has been sown and he will have many children who will live on and carry out his work here in Salem."

"How do you know that?" I asked.

"By what I feel in my heart and what I have seen with my own eyes. Already there is a great drought upon the town and the crops are beginning to fail. Salem will be made to pay a heavy price for letting the Devil build his temple here."

"And what of the Putnam girl and Rebecca Nurse's family, tell her what you told me," said Mercy.

"I have seen that Ann Putnam will never be happy. She will live out her days in misery trying to recover her soul, but she never will. She will die without issue. As for the descendants of Rebecca Nurse, someday they will number in the thousands and her memory will live on far into the future as an example of all that is virtuous."

"The people in Salem think that anyone who tells the future is a witch," I said, suddenly thinking of the way Barnabas had tried to trick me. What had I done! What if these two women were just another form the Devil took!

"The people in Salem are superstitious fools," said Hannibelle in disgust.

"How do I know you're not the Devil?" I asked, fearful of her answer but tired of walking into danger. If these two women were agents of the Devil then let them show themselves now and be done with it. I was too weary of the game to be cautious any longer.

"I understand how you feel my dear," said Mercy. "You have been through so much and you don't know us. Think. What is something that the Devil can't do that a mortal can?"

"Why," I thought suddenly, "pray. They asked Mama about prayers and wouldn't believe she was innocent even when she said her favorite prayer right in front of them all. They said she was guilty, but I knew that no one who could say her prayers the way Mama could, was a witch."

"Then pray with us, Dorcas Good," said Mercy, "and believe that we are what you are. Innocent souls in a guilty place."

With those words Mercy Phillips put her childlike hands together and began the words that fell upon my heart like gentle rain.

"Our Father, who art in heaven.........."

FIFTY FIRST ENTRY

From all accounts the summer of 1692 was beautiful one, despite the heat and dryness that plagued the town. Goody Phillips, Mistress Black and I watched a steady stream of prisoners live in and then leave our cell. Most were bound for the gallows where Mama had died. Sometimes the place was so crowded that we barely had room to move our feet, much less talk about heaven, hell and the Devil.

There were many good souls among the prisoners, women I had known all my life. It was with great regret that I watched them, one by one, leave our hideous refuge bound for Gallows Hill. It seems strange to me now that they left a child in the cell of the condemned, but perhaps what Mistress Black said was true. It seemed that somehow I had become invisible to my jailers. The only time I was remembered was when they shifted me about the room in an effort to make way for the other prisoners. If not for the kindness of the other prisoners, I would have surely starved. Matthew had long ago disappeared, running for his life after he was accused of witchcraft, and my own father seemed to have decided I was either dead, or needed nothing from him.

They had also forgotten about Mercy and Hannibelle. Week after week they waited for the summons that would take them to Gallows hill, but it never came. Whatever the reason we were ignored, I thanked God for it.

It still brings tears to my eyes when I think of the poor women who passed before me during that summer and early fall. For the most part they lived out their last days with dignity and courage. I only saw one of those women falter and it haunts me to this very day.

Martha Corey had been imprisoned and condemned to hang by the very neighbors she had lived with, side by side, for years. She was a quick tempered woman and often berated her old husband, Giles, for no reason at all. But we also knew that she truly loved the old man and had been sadly grieved when Giles had been tricked into testifying against her.

How joyous she was on the day that she heard that Giles had recanted his testimony and had stood up in court, declaring for all to hear, that Martha was innocent. But the next thing that happened let me know that the warnings that Hannibelle and Mercy had given me were true. Giles Corey was arrested for witchcraft and thrown into jail. At his trial he refused to speak, so the people of the town took him out to his own farm and crushed him to death with his very own stones. How brave he was to stay silent! Old Giles knew that if he said nothing the judges could not take away his land. Giles Corey's death was a triumph over the Devil that had come to Salem. But that was small comfort for Martha as she sat in her cell waiting to die and listening to the song the children of the town chanted outside her cell.

It went like this:

Giles Corey was a wizard strong
A stubborn wretch was he.
And fit was he to hang on high
Upon the locust tree.

So when before the magistrates
For trial he did come,
He would no true confession make
But was completely dumb.

"Giles Corey," said the Magistrate,
"What have thou here to plead
To these who now accuse thy soul
of crimes and horrid deed?"

Giles Corey, he said not a word,
No single word spoke he.
"Giles Corey," said the magistrate,
"We'll press it out of thee."

They got them then a heavy beam,
They laid it on his breast.
They loaded it with heavy stones,
And hard upon him pressed.

"More weight," now said this wretched man,
"More weight," again he cried,
And he did no confession make
But wickedly he died.

I will never forget the tears that ran down Goody Corey's cheeks as they chanted her to Gallows Hill singing those very word. I will also

224

never forget the last verse of the song added after she had breathed her last. The final words were:

Dame Corey lived but three days more,
But three days more lived she.
For she was hanged at Gallows Hill
Upon the locust tree.

There were many more that passed through my cell, but the one that became my friend and I grieved over most sadly was Rebecca Nurse's own dear sister, Mary Easty. Mary had been imprisoned with her sister, Sarah Cloyce, until Mary had been taken to trial. At that point the two had been separated and Mary brought to the Salem dungeon. It was Mary Easty who turned my heart from the bitterness of its thoughts to better things. Day after day she sat near me, blaming no one for her condition. She had tried in many ways, petitions and the like, to free herself, but nothing had worked. In the end she settled on writing the judges a letter that almost broke my heart with its sweetness. The tears ran down my cheeks as she read it to me in her soft, sweet voice.

"Your poor and humble petitioner, being condemned to die, does humbly beg of you that you take into consideration, knowing my own innocence and blessed be the Lord for it, and seeing plainly the wiles of my accusers, cannot help but judge charitably of the others who are condemned with me. I petition your honors not for my own life, for I know I must die at the appointed time, but for theirs.

I know that your honors would not knowingly be guilty of shedding innocent blood, but by my own innocence I know that what you are doing is wrong. The Lord, in his infinite mercy, show his blessed will to you in your great work and let no more innocent blood be spilled. I humbly beg you to examine the poor afflicted girls strictly and keep them away from the confessing witches. I know that some have lied and the truth of this shall be shown in the heaven where I am going.

The Lord above, who is the searcher of all hearts, knows that I know not the least thing of witchcraft and therefore cannot lie and confess. I beg your honors not to deny this humble petition from a poor, dying, innocent person. I question not but the Lord will give a blessing to your endeavors."

Two weeks later Mary died, just as Mama and her sister Rebecca had died before her. There were eight to be hanged that day, sad Martha Corey among them, and I remember listening to the creak of the over-crowded cart as it pulled away from the dungeon. I heard later that

Nicholas Noyes had once again tried to turn the crowd against the poor victims, but this time it didn't work. He waited until all eight bodies were suspended from the hanging tree and then turned towards the crowd.

"What a sad thing it is to see eight firebrands of hell hanging there," is what he said.

Surely the sweet figure of Mary Easty and the sad body of old Martha Corey looked like anything but 'firebrands from hell'! That seemed to be the turning point for the people of Salem because over the next few months they began to wake from the evil spell they had been under.

FIFTY SECOND ENTRY

By early October the silence of my cell became almost maddening. I swear that if it had not been for Mistress Black and Goody Phillips I would have torn the hair from my head and banged it against the wall until the stones were bloody. There were still prisoners in the neighboring cells, but it seemed that not many were being taken for their final trials. Finally, one morning I summoned up the courage to ask the jailer who brought our food about the state of things in the outside world.

"Sir, if you please," I asked in a trembling voice, "are there to be any hangings this week?"

"Why bless you child," said the man in a kinder voice than I had heard in many a month, "don't you know?"

"Know what?"

"About the new rules, child. The 'afflicted' have overstepped their bounds for sure and it's the new rules we now have to live by. It's a wonder the Governor didn't throw all the Putnams in jail after what their girl tried to do."

"Ann, Ann Putnam? Oh, what's happened, please tell me!" I cried throwing away all my caution in my excitement.

"It seems, young miss," said the guard warming to his gossip, "that young Ann accused Lady Phipps, the Governor's wife, of witchcraft!"

"No," said Goody Phillips with a stunned gasp.

"Aye, 'tis true, I swear it," said the guard with a grave nod, "and now all that accuses another has to have some real proof, none of this, 'you killed my cow ten years ago because you looked at it cross-eyed, nonsense."

"Then their reign is almost over," said Hannibelle with the first smile I had seen upon her face in a month.

"That's right, 'tis almost over indeed," agreed the guard. "There'll be no more hangings around here without good reason."

"But what about us and all the others that are in this place and the other jails?" I asked, sensing that freedom might not be to far away.

"That's for the magistrates and judges to decide, missy," said the guard as he spooned out the grain filled gruel that served as our supper. "First they must pardon you, or decide that they don't want to bother with you any more. Then there are the fees that must be paid before you can go free."

"What fees?" I asked, wondering why Hannibelle suddenly looked so sad.

"Why the fees for your food and lodging and such," said the guard. "It must add up to a pretty penny by now, what with those special chains you had made."

"I never had any chains made," I said indignantly, rattling one of my leg irons at him.

"That's not what the judges say. Any who live in this place and eat from our bowls must pay for all they use. The chains, the horses that brought you here, and even that small candle yonder are all upon your shoulders now. You must pay your debt before you can go free, that's the law."

"But I have no money and no friends," I said, knowing that my father would rather leave me in this cell to rot than to spend his rum money on me.

"Then rot you will, young mistress, unless you can find a benefactor."

"How can I do that?" I asked.

"How would I know? said the guard as he closed the door behind him.

What the guard had said was true, and on October 29th, 1692, Sir William Phipps put an end to Cotton Mather's Court of Oyer and Terminer. The 'afflicted' girls still tried to convince the town that there were witches about, but the people of Salem had bigger things to worry them now. While they had spent the spring and summer chasing down witches and hanging innocent souls, their fields had lain fallow and unplowed. There was little food that fall and soon the cruel New England winter would begin. Meanwhile, Hannibelle Black, Mercy Phillips and I waited, and waited, and waited.

It was on my birthday, November thirteenth, that I finally found reason to hope. That morning I received a letter along with my usual bowl of thin mealy soup. I couldn't read a word, so I passed it to Mistress Black after the guard had left.

"Who is it from?" I asked, hardly daring to breath.

"From a Captain Quelch, child," said Hannibelle turning the note over in her hand.

"Jack!" I cried in delighted excitement, "please tell me what it says, please."

"It says that he has traveled far since he saw you last, and that he wishes you well. He says that he has not forgotten his promise and that soon he will find a way to free you of this place. The Captain goes on to say that you must watch for a man in a blue wool cap who will come to take you away."

"How strange," I said. "I wonder why he can't come himself now that most of the trouble is over. Does he say anything about that, Mistress, or about how he became a captain?"

"No child, that is all there is to it, I'm afraid."

"Oh," I said, leaning against the wall and closing my eyes. So he hadn't forgotten after all! I could just picture the fine figure Jack must cut in his captain's gear with a sword by his side. I knew now that soon I would be free of this place and back in the real world. A world without my Mama.

"I'm not sure I remember how to live outside this place," I whispered fearfully to Mercy Phillips. "I'm not the same Dorcas that I was a year ago."

"None of us are the same, child," said Mercy.

"But it's different for you," I said, trying for the first time to imagine myself free of the dark dungeon that had been my home for so many months, "you are older and had a chance to grow up before you were put here. I'm only five, but I feel like I should be a hundred."

"Trouble does that to you," said Hannibelle nodding her head. "Don't think you are the only one who has ever been forced to grow up before your time, Dorcas Good. There are many who have been deprived of home and parents like you have. This new world is a cruel and unforgiving one and leaves many orphans in its wake. Take me for example. I wasn't always the woman you see here today. Many years ago I lost my whole family in the Indian wars up in Maine. If my mother hadn't hidden me in the small haystack near our lean-to I would have had my head bashed in by a rock just like my baby brother. I would never have lived long enough to share this cell with you."

"I didn't know."

"There's a lot you don't know, Dorcas. Never assume that because you have had your heart broken and your childhood stolen, you are alone. The best we can do when that happens to us is go on, that and keep a listening heart out for others who need our help. We are a special sisterhood and must seek the comfort of one another."

"Then what should I do when I get out of here?" I asked, bemused by Hannibelle's words.

"Go slowly at first, Dorcas," said Mercy.

"Yes, do that," said Hannibelle, " and speak to no one about what you have seen and done in this cell. Wait upon your speech until you discover who is your friend and who is your foe. Never forget that what happened here could happen again. Watch, listen and cross no one is my advice to you."

"That all sounds very fine," I said, "but what do I do about me? Who's going to take care of me? Who am I going to live with?"

"It sounds like your Captain Quelch can give you the answer to that, little one," said Mercy. "He sounds like someone who really cares for you and will see that you come to no harm."

"But what about my father? What if he comes for me first. I would rather die than go back to him," I said with a shudder.

"Worry not about things that may never happen, is my advice," said Hannibelle. "From what you've told me of William Good it sounds like there is precious little chance that he will come for you, especially if it costs him money."

"That's true," I said with a lighter heart. "How I will miss the two of you when I go."

"Who says you have to miss us, Dorcas?" said Mercy brightly. "I see no reason why you can't ask your blue hatted friend to help us out too."

"Do you think I dare?"

"Why not," said Hannibelle. "The worst he can say is no. But if your Captain Quelch can help you he might be able to help us too. Think of it Dorcas! The three of us free and together out in the big world again. I don't mean to be overbold, child, but do you think you could try for our freedom as well as your own? Both Goodwife Phillips and I would be happy to work off any debt we owe once we're free of this place."

"Of course I'll try," I said, ashamed of my fears. These two women had been my only comfort and solace for months and here I was hesitating about helping them to freedom. It was true what they had said. We whose hearts were forged together through the misfortunes of the witchcraze must never abandon one another. The world we would face once our feet were set upon free earth would be a hard one beset by many dangers and much coldness. Our only hope of survival was to cling to one another and take our comfort there.

Then I thought of Mama and all the strength my two friends had given me drained from my body. I had never really lived without Mama by my side, listening to my every word and telling me I was her beautiful, bright little Dorcas. I knew now that this cell, this dungeon, was a mere waiting room that held me fast. I had not lived here, merely survived.

"Mama, oh Mama," cried my heart, "I don't want to go back out into the world without you, not with Jack Quelch, or with Hannibelle or Mercy. I just want to die now and spend eternity in your arms just like my little sister!"

Those thoughts brought a fierce jealousy into my heart as I pictured Mama and my little sister in heaven sitting together on a golden cloud. I could see Mama holding the baby and telling her that she was Mama's bright and beautiful little girl now. It was all more than I could bear. I put my head into my arms and began to sob.

"Dorcas, Dorcas Good," whispered a voice in my head, "do you think I have forgotten you? You who are my light and my life on earth?"

I sat up straight and stared ahead. It was the voice of my very own Mama, the sweet voice that I had completely forgotten about during my months of darkness.

"No Mama," I whispered as I turned my face away from my two earthly friends.

"Trust what I say," said Mama, "and be happy. I will always be with you, in the birds that sing and the flowers that grow. Live and let me see the wonders of the earth through your eyes. I promise that I will never leave you. Can you do that for your Mama, my blessed little girl?"

"Yes Mama!" I cried with a heart full of joy.

"Hey now, what's all this noise," said a gruff voice in front of me.

I looked up and out of my golden haze to behold the large figure of Nicholas Noyes before me.

"Someone told me that you are a big girl of five now, Dorcas Good, is that true?"

"Yes sir," I said, still dizzy from Mama's voice.

"Someone also told me that on your birthday you had received a note, a note from someone who was not your father."

"She received nothing, sir, I can swear to that," said Mercy as Hannibelle touched her fingers to her lips and motioned me to be silent.

" I happen to know different," said fat Nicholas as he pulled me to my feet, chains and all.

"I received nothing, nothing at all," I said as he unlocked my chains and gathered me into his arms.

"We'll see about that," said Nicholas Noyes as he carried me from my cell.

FIFTY THIRD ENTRY

"No more, no more," I screamed as Nicholas Noyes came at me with the red hot poker. My legs, arms and buttocks were already covered with fiery red marks where he had laid his iron.

"Then tell me what I wish to hear, wench. Tell me about the letter," said my tormentor as he rubbed a thin line of spittle from his lower lip.

I turned away from Nicholas and cried waterless tears as I thought about Jack Quelch. Somehow I knew that if I told this fiend about my letter any hope I had of living far away from the curse of Salem was gone. Why else would I be in this terrible room, hanging by my chains from a rusty meat hook? It seemed strange that after so many months of being totally forgotten by the rest of the world I was now the object of such fury by old Nicholas. Why was Jack's letter so important?

"I'll ask ye once again, little mistress," said Noyes, approaching me with the freshly heated poker, "tell me what I want to hear or I'll make sure that no one will ever look upon you again with anything but disgust." It was then I saw what he meant to do. Instead of aiming towards my arms or legs, Nicholas Noyes was holding the poker up to my face.

"Spill what ye know, lass, or I'll see to it that you never see the sunlight again." With those words he held the poker close to my cheek. I could feel the heat of the thing burning at my eyelashes and singeing the curls around my brow.

"What do you mean to do?" I asked, trying to buy time. I had to think! Think of a way out of this! The small burns on the rest of my body were horrible, but a horror I could stand. I knew that my wounds would fade in time and leave only small marks upon my flesh, but I could tell by the look on Nicholas' mad face that he meant to do something that would ruin me for life.

"I'm going to burn the lying eyes out of your head unless you tell me the truth, Dorcas Good. Speak now of all you know or I swear that I'll turn you into a monster."

233

"Oh please, no!" I cried, twisting my head away from him in an effort to avoid the hot brand. It grazed my hair and lightly touched my cheek, sending its cruel message to my heart. I knew now that I would do anything to stop Nicholas, even betray Jack Quelch.

"Then speak up girl, this is your last chance."

"All right, I'll tell you," I said as my body hung heavily from the meat hook.

"There's a sweetheart," said Nicholas, rubbing my small thighs with his hands. "Just you tell old Nicholas what you know and I'll make sure that you're right cozy and warm 'till you quit this place."

I opened my mouth and spoke the words that sent what was left of my soul to hell. As I spoke I realized why Mama, Rebecca Nurse and countless others had chosen death over lying and the betrayal of their friends and family. When I was finished I was left with my eyes but empty of anything that had ever been Dorcas Good.

FIFTY FORTH ENTRY

It was a dream Dorcas that now lived in the foul smelling quarters that Nicholas Noyes kept in the belly of the dungeon. I no longer felt anything. When he touched me it was as if he held a doll in his arms and I received many a blow because of it.

"Say something, damn you!" Nicholas would scream at me while he explored every crevice and fold of my body in an effort to find pleasure. But I had none to give. I was a dead doll with nothing left inside.

"If it weren't for the money ye'll soon be bringing me I'd have thrown you to the guards long ago," he said one day as he thrust me from him after trying vainly to take his pleasure. The only thing that ever seemed to give him satisfaction now was when he bound and beat me, and this night even that had failed.

I could tell by the way he was fastening his keys around his waist, that it was time for his nightly rounds. Wearily I rolled over on the old blanket he had thrown on the floor and closed my eyes. Soon I heard Nicholas leave, abandoning me to my velvet blackness. All was velvet blackness now. Not even my old companions, my happy dreams, were left to me. Any hint of that had left me when I had turned into a Judas and betrayed my only friend. I knew that it was now only a matter of time before the man in the blue hat came for me and was punished or killed by Nicholas Noyes for the gold he carried, the gold Jack had given him to purchase my freedom.

"Well then, what of it?" came a small evil voice from within me that sounded strangely like the devil boy, Barnabas. I kept my eyes closed and watched as the black velvet enveloped the voice and returned me to silence. Silence now was my savior and I embraced it as a drunkard would cradle his rum. I sank deep into my silence and dreamed the days away.

At last the moment came. I knew from the way Nicholas was dressed that it was a festival night.

"Put this on, whore," he shouted as he tossed a small red dress to me. I had never seen such a pretty thing. It was all velvet, just like my soft dreams only brighter. That dress was almost bright enough to bring me to some state of wakefulness. I reached for the pretty thing and began pulling it over my other clothes.

"No, you dim witted fool," said Nicholas as he grabbed me roughly and took back the velvet dress.

"Ye must take off your other things first, don't you know that?"

I stared at him and nodded my head, not really knowing what he said, but guessing by his motions that he wanted me naked as he had so many time before. Slowly I took off what was left of my ragged clothes and dropped them on the earth beside me. Then I took the dress he held out to me and put it on. The low cut bodice that laced up the front barely covered my babyish nipples and left me shivering in the cold December night.

"Come on now," he said as he grabbed my arm roughly and dragged me from my place of velvet blackness. Suddenly the torches and lantern that lit the gloomy corridor flashed into my brain and I remembered the poker Nicholas Noyes had held to my face.

"No more, no more," I started screaming as I imagined him holding the burning metal to my cheek.

"What are you talking about, bitch!" cried Nicholas as he hit me across the face and stunned me into silence. "Here I am trying to get you to talk for weeks on end and you pick now to screech like a cat in heat. It's glad I am that I'll be done with you this night. Hurry up now before I cease to care what happens to your worthless hide."

Nicholas and I made our way up through the twists and turns of Salem dungeon until we came to the outer room where the guards took their rest. I had no memory of the place, although I know now that I must have passed through it with Mama when we were returned to Salem for Mama's hanging.

'What's this?" said a bright haired soldier with dirty boots and a scraggly beard. His rough hands grabbed at my skirt.

"'Tis not for the likes of you," said Nicholas as he picked me up in his arms and carried me out the door.

"'Tis only brother Nicholas' baby whore," I heard one of them say with a drunken laugh as Nicholas slammed the door behind him.

The stars that shone overhead were almost too bright for me to bear after my many months in darkness and I gasped as I watched an owl fly across the moon.

"Where are we going?" I asked as Nicholas ran with me towards the platform that held the town stocks.

"Never you mind where you are going, Dorcas Good. Look up and see what happens to all those that defies the King's law."

I saw now that we had stopped directly below the stocks. Nicholas grabbed my chin and thrust my face upward so that I looked directly into the empty eye sockets of a dead man locked inside the wooden manacles. The man's head was covered by a bright blue wool cap. I watched in horror as the form of William Good stepped from behind the stocks and tossed a bag of coins to fat Nicholas.

"Well done, Master Noyes," said my father as he jumped down from the platform and took my hand. "'Tis only right that you should have half of this for the hard work ye've done this night. Come along home now daughter, I have missed you sorely."

I looked up at my father's face but all I could see was the empty eyes of the man in the bright blue cap. It was then that my silence broke into screams.

PART SIX

MASTER JACK

FIFTY FIFTH ENTRY

"Where are you, bitch?" I heard my father yell as he kicked the door open. I was hiding under the bed, hoping that if he were drunk enough Willliam might not take me to the tavern to stand upon the table. But it was no use.

"Come on out, Dorcas Good, or I swear you'll pay and pay dearly."

I slowly crept out from under the old bed where I had once helped my mother give birth and presented myself to my angry father.

"How many times have I told you that a disobedient daughter is an abomination to the Lord?" said my father as he twisted my arm behind my back and pushed me out the door.

"Yes Father," I said breathlessly, knowing that to argue with him would only make things worse.

"Then make haste, girl, before others take your place and your poor father has no money for food."

"Or drink," I thought rebelliously as my own father dragged me towards the Blue Anchor Tavern to whore for my supper and his rum.

Gone were our days in Salem Village. Since the spring of 1704 William Good and I had lived in a shack by the wharf in Salem Town, catering to the sailors who landed there and were hungry for female flesh. My sixteen year old body was the only thing my father had left to sell and sell it he did, night after night to the delight of every disease ridden scurvy that could lift a noggin at the Blue Anchor Tavern. And why not? What other use could anyone have for a dull witted girl who was tainted by witchcraft. My father had told the townsfolk that I was too crazy to know that spreading my legs for men was a sin. It was the only joy left to his poor damaged little girl, he would say, as he held out his hand for the piece of silver that would buy my flesh for a quarter of an hour.

I almost choked from the smell of rotting fish as my father dragged me towards the Blue Anchor Tavern. It always amazed me that I still felt shame at the way my bare legs peeked through the tatters of my ragged skirt. You would think that my father might have taken it into his head to dress his chief commodity, his daughter, in a less disgraceful fashion, but no, William Good was more taken with downing his rum than he was with dressing his daughter smartly. I would often sit by the window by day envying the other whores who had kinder pimps. They would saunter by, tossing their velvet skirts and throwing curses at me. I knew that even though they had fine bright velvets around their knees and real satin ribbons flashing from their curls, that none could match my face and form. It did not take a genius to measure the joy on a young sailor's face as my father handed me over. I also knew that many had turned me down because of my angel's face and sweetly turned figure. There was even one man, a First Mate my father had said, who had told my father to keep the money and buy me something pretty with it. That, after he stated that he couldn't use a girl who looked so much like his own sweet daughter. How my father had laughed at the man after he left. But I had run to the tavern window and watched as his blue and gold coat disappeared from sight. What a lucky girl the First Mate's daughter was! It took not a moment for my father to set me back up on the table and resume the bidding for my favors. No wonder the other whores hated me. I brought more than anyone else on the docks, in season and out.

"Up with you now, my girl," said my father as he lifted me onto the sturdy wooden table that stood in the middle of the Blue Anchor. The place was so crowded that it took a few minutes for the crowd to notice that there was a fresh girl for sale. I looked out over the smoke filled room and saw many faces that were new to me as well as a few regulars who could always be counted on to drive the price up.

"Tis the Brigantine 'Charles' that has put ashore," shouted my father to me as he tried to quiet the crowd.

"What?" I yelled back.

"The 'Charles', daughter, the 'Charles'. Surely ye've heard of it. 'Tis the ship your old friend Quelch took command of after they murdered the real captain."

"Hey now, what's this talk of murder?" asked an old sailor standing next to my father as he ran his callused hand up my leg.

"Why everyone knows that the crew of the 'Charles' took the rightful captain, Captain Plowman, out beyond Marblehead and dumped him in the sea."

"There's no truth to what you say," said the sailor, favoring the hand that my father had slapped away from my leg. "The old captain died fair and square. 'Twas sick he was before we ever left port."

"Then why did the owners rush to Marblehead and try to stop the ship?" asked my father. "I heard that Daniel Plowman wrote them a note saying he feared embezzlement aboard the 'Charles' if they set sail. 'Twas his bad luck that the owners missed the ship by two hours. By the time they made Marblehead dock, Daniel Plowman was sitting at the bottom of the sea."

"Ye've got a foul lying mouth for sure," said the old man backing away from my father and eyeing the door.

"I'm just saying what every child in Salem knows as fact," said my father with a nod. "Why else would the 'Charles' have set sail for South America and sunk all those Portuguese ships? Ye certainly don't believe the tales Jack Quelch has spread about his hundreds of pounds of gold dust do ye? He swears that the gold and his two hundred silver bars came from a Spanish Galleon that he salvaged off a West Indian reef. Some say he stopped and buried the lot on Appeldore Island before making for Salem. Tell me now, is it true? I'll give you the girl for free for as long as you like if you can point the way to some of that buried treasure."

I shuddered as I looked down at the pock marked, toothless pirate. I knew that if my father struck a deal with the old sailor I would have no choice but to let him put his rotting flesh into me. Was it true what he and my father had said? Was Jack Quelch really so near? My heart began to beat wildly at the thought.

"'Tis foolishness you speak," said the man backing towards the door.

"Then I'm a wise fool," muttered my father as he watched the man disappear in the crowd. "Your old father is on to something, girl, mark my word. Before this night is over there'll be a treasure map in my pocket, or my name's not William Good."

"William Good, is it," said a tall man who had appeared at my father's shoulder.

"Aye it is, and who wants to know?" asked my father.

"An old friend, sir. He told me to seek out a Goodman Good, and his daughter, Dorcas."

"That's me," I cried as I jumped down from the table. I was too excited by all the talk of Jack Quelch to remain quiet any longer. Let my father beat me. He had done it so often that I no longer feared him. I knew that he would never really damage his only source of rum money.

"Calm yourself, daughter," said my father patting my hand with mock gentleness. "I know that ye have had no word from your 'Uncle Jack' for many a year, but please remember yourself."

"Tell me sir, is Jack well?" asked my father as he gave me a sly kick.

"Very well, Goodman Good," said the man, looking me up and down and making me feel doubly shamed about my ragged dress. "And he wishes to see the young mistress as soon as he can. Is there someplace in this town where such as the Captain could have a private word with the girl without the likes of Cotton Mather sticking his big nose in their business?"

"Of course, sir, of course," said my father eagerly rubbing his hands together. "But 'twill cost dearly to arrange such a thing, sir. You see how it is, what with the stories and such floating about the place. Mather sits in the upper room of this place as we speak, toasting some of Quelch's crew and gathering bits of speech from them such as might do in their captain."

So, my Jack was in peril! Then why was he even here? It must have occurred to him that it was dangerous to land on Salem's traitorous shores. Of all people, Jack Quelch knew there was no friendly welcome for him here. Could I dare hope that he remembered me and his promise? Had Jack Quelch come at last to save me?

"Please sir," I said, "tell the Captain that I am well and have no need to see him," I said as I avoided a blow from my father's outstretched arm. "You see how it is. I'm not the innocent little girl he knew. I'd be ashamed to have him see me as I am now."

"Hush now, daughter," said my father, catching my ear with his fist.

"The Captain's not like that, Mistress," said the man, taking my hand and drawing me away from my father. "If he says he wants to see ye then see ye he will. What ye have become means little to him. It's what ye are inside that matters to our Captain Jack."

"That's true daughter, so true," said my father as he sidled up to Jack's friend and put his hand on the man's shoulder. "You just bring Captain Jack to Burying Point at the rise of the moon and I'll see to it that the girl is there."

"The Captain will be there too, sir. It's much in your debt I am," said the stranger as he placed a bag of coins in my father's hand. "See that she's on time and there'll be another bit waiting for ye. 'Till the light of the moon then, Goodman Good?"

"Till the light of the moon," said my father as he put his hand over my mouth.

FIFTY SIXTH ENTRY

"What do you mean to do?" I asked my father as he strapped his hunting knife to his leg and lowered his breeches over it.

"What I mean to do is none of your business, girl. Just do as I say and neither of us will ever have to work again. Wouldn't you like to leave this place and be set up fine, like a young lady? Think of it Dorcas, all the folk in some town somewhere, bowing to you and calling you young Mistress Good. Why ye'd be respectable and might even catch yerself a grand husband!"

"Not with the blood of Jack Quelch, I won't," I said sitting on the floor of our cabin, prepared not to move till daylight had safely come. Better to break Jack's heart than to see him hanged or knifed in the back.

I closed my eyes and tried not to think of that long ago time, but it was no use. Try as I might to keep it away, the scarred face of the man with the blue wool cap crept into my mind, just had it had almost every night since that terrible time. My days and nights had blended into one unending nightmare until I was numb from the pain. My numbness was my only comfort. I had become used to it and it was my only friend now.

"Oh Lord," I prayed silently as my father kicked me with his boot, "do something, anything to keep me from going to Burial Point this night. I don't think I could stand it if someone awakened me from my nightmares and made me live this life in the bright sunshine of sanity."

I knew that the whole town thought that I was crazy, and in a way the town was right. I looked at my witlessness with a sane inner eye, the one that I kept hidden from everyone lest they try to draw me out through some misguided charity. It would be no kindness to remind me what I had gone through as a child, or present me with the cold facts of my everyday existence now. I would still be my father's whore, bound by law to do his bidding, and seen as an embarrassment by the town. It was better by far to remain numb to my pain. Let Jack Quelch go back to sea. It was too late to do anything for Dorcas Good.

"Get up now, Dorcas sweetheart," said my father as he kicked me again.

"Why should I?" I said, with uncharacteristic liveliness.

"Because I'll beat you to a pulp until you do."

"Better that than to betray the only friend I ever had!" I screamed, feeling the cold fingers of sanity grip around my mind. "Go back, go back," I thought furiously, terrified at what lay within me. I rolled into a ball on the floor and began to hum a droning tune as I rocked back and forth.

"Now, none of that my girl," said my father in a more kindly tone as he squatted on the floor beside me and began to rub my back.

My only response was to hum louder as the blessed black velvet began to creep over my thoughts. Soon all I could see or feel was my soft black friend enfolding me in its embrace.

"There's a girl," I heard a far off voice say as I was lifted and carried out to my father's wagon. "It don't really matter what you do, Dorcas my sweet, as long as you're there."

I don't know how long after that I awoke tied to the double oak tree that stood at the far end of Burying Point. I do know that the full moon was directly overhead. I looked up and could feel the warmth of its comforting glow filling my body with peace. This was what I liked most, to be filled with half madness but feeling those things that could bring me comfort. The things of the night were friends of my black velvet spirit and always welcome in my halflit world.

My happy silence was suddenly broken by the warble of a bird. How strange I thought, birds don't sing to the moon! I sat up straight and looked about me in terror. The only night birds around Salem were the ones that came disguised as Indians who scalped whole families in the middle of the night. Why, half the townsfolk housed orphaned children who had been left parentless by Indians. I heard the bird again, closer this time, and began to sweat despite the warmth of the late May evening. I felt the terror rising in me until I thought I could stand it no longer. It was then that I truly realized that I had been left alone by father in the graveyard, tied helplessly to a tree. I began to struggle as the song of the bird came closer. Then I began to cry.

"Hush now, lass," said a voice behind me, "I won't hurt you. 'Tis your old friend, Jackie. I've come to take you away."

"Go away!" I cried as I felt his hand upon my shoulder. "It's a trap!"

"Aye, I know that lass. I knew it the minute I first set eyes upon you so charmingly arranged on that tree."

"Then why didn't you run?" I whispered furiously.

"Because I promised years ago that I would come for you, Dorcas Good, and come for you I have. Don't you think that I knew the minute I had my mate find that father of yours I was putting my life in his hands?"

"Then why did you do it?" I said

"Because there was no other way to get to you, lass. They say that he keeps you locked away except when he takes you to the Blue Anchor. So you see, I had no choice. Is it true what they say? Are you really mad?"

"Only at you for being such a fool, Jack Quelch. Untie me now and get out of here. I can make for home and you must make for the safety of the sea."

"Not without you I won't, lass," said Jack as he untied my bonds and lifted me into his arms.

"Put me down, Jack," I cried as I kicked at him with my unshod feet.

"And why should I?" said Jack.

"Because I won't be moved and carried about like some sort of bundle. It's bad enough that my father treats me that way without you joining in on the fun. Do you think I want to trade one idiot for another?"

"There's my girl," said Jack as he set me on my feet. "I knew the little girl I left behind was more that some old drunk's whore."

I'm no one's whore!" I said, feeling my black velvet world turn an angry red.

"Then prove it by leaving this place with me now, Dorcas Good. Prove to me you remember your fine mother and all that she stood for. She would be ashamed of you if you let this chance go by."

"If we were caught you would be hanged for sure and you know it, Jack," I said touching his arm lightly in an attempt to make him see some sense. My fine instinct for survival had been honed and polished in the last ten years until it shone as brightly as a silver buckle. It told me now that we were being watched. Jack's only hope was to disappear into the night, alone and traveling fast.

"And would you care if I were hanged, beautiful lady," said Jack, taking my hand and kissing my fingertips.

"I'm not beautiful, and I'm certainly not a lady," I said, "but I would care if something happened to you, Jack Quelch. You, above all people, should know that I've had enough of hangings to last me through this lifetime and into the next. I don't think I could bear it if something like that should happen to you."

"Thank you my lady," said Jack as he drew me into the shadow of the double oak tree. "Tell me, Dorcas Good, why do you think yourself base and ugly?" he asked with a look that almost burned my soul.

"Look for yourself," I said as I angrily threw his hand from mine. "Can't you see what is real? Why must you torture me with questions that we both know the answer to? Why don't you get out of here and leave me alone."

"Because I love you, little Dorcas, and I always have," said Jack in a voice barely above a whisper.

"How can you love someone you know nothing about?" I asked as I tried to back away. The bark of the old tree caught the rough hem of my skirt and pulled me back.

"I don't know why I love you, wench, I just know I do!" said Jack with an anger that almost matched my own. "Do you think I would have chosen to love anyone if I had a choice? Perhaps it was the way you looked in the courtroom that day, all alone and brave, despite your size. Or maybe it was later when I saw you being taken away by the guards to join your poor Mama in prison. You might as well ask why the trade winds blow. All I know is that the little girl I knew I had to save, has grown into the woman I dreamed of. You are the child of my heart and the woman of my dreams, Dorcas Good, and there is no denying me."

"But what of my life, Jack?" I asked as I managed to free my tangled skirt.

"What of it?" asked Jack with a growl. "Do ye think I've been a saint, little lass? The man who stands beside you now is not the manling that went away so many years ago. I have done terrible things, Dorcas, things that I am truly ashamed of now. The only excuse I have is that I had a heart full of anger and a belly full of rum. When old Ned failed to come back with you that Christmas Eve in 1692, I figured you must be dead. Then I heard, from some mates who had passed through town, that he had been killed and left in the stocks for all to see, while your bastard of a father had dragged you to the tavern and sold you to the highest bidder that very same night. Is it true that old Ned was left up there till the birds pecked out his eyes."

"Not the birds, Jack, my father," I whispered, fighting the vision that flashed through my mind of the man in the blue wool cap."

"What matter now, lass," said Jack with a shrug, "What's done is done. I've a feeling that William Good will someday pay dearly for all his crimes. Remember lass, there is a higher judge than the one that sent your dear mother away. One that we must all face. I certainly wouldn't want to be William Good on judgment day. He's not the repenting sort."

"And what of you, Jack?" I said touching his dear face as he sat in the soft moss that lay under the great oak tree.

"Me? Why I'm done with all that lass, and it's glad I am of it. There's no going back and breathing life into those I took it from, but at least I can tell you there wasn't one in the bunch that didn't deserve it. Still, I'm sorry about it lass, and I intend to beg the forgiveness of the Almighty and do penance for my wrongs. I would do it differently if I had the chance, Dorcas, but we both know that's there's no going back on it once a deed is done. All I can do is pray that being sorry is enough."

"Saint Jack Quelch!" I said as I started to laugh and cry at the same time. "I can just see it now! All those fine folks at the meetinghouse speaking of your noble soul and good deeds in awed voices."

"There now lass, don't go making fun of me," said Jack as he put an arm around me and rested my head on his shoulder.

"But can't you see how funny it is?" I said, trying to stop the giggles that rumbled inside of me. "What makes you think that anyone will ever forgive us our crimes? You're a murdering pirate and I'm a whore tainted by witchcraft. We'll never be left to live in peace."

"And what makes you think I would stay around here one more second than I have to?" said Jack, giving me a squeeze. "Come on now, confess you have some feelings for old Jackie and we'll be on our way, gold and all. 'Tis a fine lady you'll be Dorcas Good, and it's honored I will be to be seen at your side, doing your bidding."

"And you don't mind that I'm a whore?"

"The only whore I saw at the Blue Anchor was that sick son-of-a-bitch that calls himself your father. 'Tis a virgin heart you carry in your breast, Dorcas sweetheart, one that I pray will someday belong to me."

"It already does, Jack," I said as I lifted my lips to his.

FIFTY SEVENTH ENTRY

It must have been the spirits of Burial Hill that protected us that night as we lay in each other's arms under the shadow of the great oak. No one came near us. What wondrous madness it was that filled us both as we found delight in each other and forgot the world around us, and what folly too. It was only when I awoke to see the first warmth of dawn rising over the sea that I realized what we had done.

"Wake up Jack!" I cried softly as I shook him hard.

"What is it lass?" He asked as he put his hand upon his pistol and awoke fully in an instant.

"We must get away from here! Oh how could I have been so foolish!" I said, close to tears. "I knew it was a trap and I let you stay here with me."

"I knew it was a trap too, girl, don't forget that," said Jack as he pulled his great hooded coat around me to protect me from the cool morning air.

"Why didn't they come for us, Jack? I don't understand. We were here all night, alone and helpless. Nary a soul came near us."

"I don't know, lass, but it's the strangest trap I've ever been in," said Jack as he smelled the air about him.

"Do you suppose they've decided to leave us alone?"

"The Governor and Judge Mather? Are ye daft girl? No darlin', they want my gold and that's a fact. 'Tis strange no doubt, but not above believin' that they've got a new plan, one that will net Jack and his gold. Get your gear together and come along now. We've been lucky so far, but let's not chance it any more."

"Where are we going?"

"Why to the 'Anchor', lass."

"On no Jack! We can't go there," I said as I pulled away from him in fright.

"And why not?" said Jack, grabbing my arm and pulling me back.

"Because my father is there!" I said in a panic.

"And did I say anything about going in the front way?"

"No."

"Then stop struggling and come along. Old Jack's got a few things to settle with his mates, Maddie Primer and Anthony Holding, in the upper room at the Blue Anchor. Put that hood over your head and take my arm like the proper woman you are, Mistress Qulech."

"Yes Jack," I said believing that somehow nothing could hurt me as long as Jack stood by my side.

Jack and I took to the woods rather than stroll boldly down the dock to the Blue Anchor Tavern. The branches scratched my face and tore at my dress, but it was a small price to pay for our safety. At last we arrived at the backside of the tavern, hot and tired, but unseen by any who wished us ill. I held my breath as Jack let out a whistle and a thick rope was dropped from the third floor window down to where we waited.

"Up ye go now, lass," said Jack as he motioned for his mates to pull me up.

"I can't do it," I said to Jack as I tried to control the tremors that had taken hold of my body.

"Why of course you can lass. Just grab ahold and my mates will have you up quick as a wink."

"That's not what I mean," I said pointing at the rope in horror. The end of it was tied in a noose, just like the one Nicholas Noyes had used to hang my Mama.

"Oh that," said Jack with a hearty laugh, "think nothing of it lass. I'm sure Maddie just thought it t'would be easier to get a grasp that way."

"Are you sure, Jack?' I asked. I wanted to believe him but felt confused by a strange swarming in my mind.

"I'm sure, darlin'," said Jack as he put my hands inside the loop and tugged on the rope.

At his signal, I was pulled up sharply. I barely had time to think about anything but keeping my feet from banging the walls of the Blue Anchor. A fine thing it would be if we were caught because of the noise my heels made.

At the top, I was pulled into the upper room by two men. One was a regular sailor, complete with striped shirt and grizzled beard. The other could have been mistaken for the captain of a fine vessel if I had not known differently.

"Here now, what's this?" said the sailor as he lifted me over the threshold of the window and set me on my feet. "You're not the captain now, are ye lass?"

"No, he waits below. Please hurry before anyone sees him," I said, not liking the way the other man was looking at me.

"Right you are, my lovely lady," said the sailor as he dropped the rope back over the side. "Come on now Tony," said the sailor with a grunt. "Give us a hand now. I'm sure those soft white hands of yours still remember how to pull a rope."

The man called Tony gave me a disgusted look and quickly joined the sailor at the window.

"It seems all this good livin' has made ye as heavy as a rich man, Captain," said the sailor as Jack appeared in the window.

"I'm as fit as I ever was and ye both know it, Maddie Primer," said Jack, giving the sailor a bear hug. "I thank ye for what ye've done this night past."

"Twas nothin' matey, just a bit of diggin' here and there."

"Nothing!" said the fine man, "we've labored like galley slaves through the night while you were having your fun, Jack Quelch. If I'd known how you would treat me now that we're back home I would have never have volunteered to help."

"Come now Tony, or should I call you Master Anthony Holding now, it's not what you think. This girl is an old friend, one to whom I owe a promise. You wouldn't have me breakin' my promises to a lady, now would you Tony?"

"She doesn't look like a lady to me," said Master Tony as he took a small bit of snuff from a beautiful gold box and pressed it to his nose.

"A lady she is, and I'll have none of your disrespect," said Jack as he suddenly slammed Tony against the wall, getting dirt and sweat all over the dandy's coat.

"Here now, stop it the two of you," said the sailor as he pulled at Jack's sleeve.

"I'll not stop, Maddie, until he apologizes to the lady," said Jack as he put his hands around Tony's neck. "I've had more than enough of you, Tony

Holding, and it's only because you are my mate that I haven't sent you to the bottom of the sea before this. It's your fault we're in this mess and don't forget it."

"All right, I'll apologize to the 'lady' if that's what you want, Jack, but I still think you're a fool to drag a woman into this."

"I'll let you know the next time I care about what you think, Tony," said Jack as he grabbed the man's collar and made him face me. "Say the words now, lad."

"I'm sorry if I offended you, Mistress," said Master Anthony Holding to me between tight lips.

"I took no offense, sir," I answered back politely, despite his obvious dislike of me. The last thing Jack and I needed now was more trouble. I was determined that I would do nothing to ruin our chances.

"There's a lad," said Jack as he slapped Tony on the back, almost sending him into the wall. "I guess it was worth the trouble of pushing the old captain over the side after all. It's a mystery to me why ye've changed your tune, but just remember your mates are your mates 'till the day they plant you."

"Right you are, Jackie," said Tony with a beautiful smile as he adjusted the lace cuffs that peaked out from the sleeves of his coat.

"Tell me now where our treasure is buried so that we can get out of this place. I've no liking for the goings on here abouts. There are too many men in red stationed in this town."

"That's your own fault, Jack," said Tony with a look towards Maddie. "If you had stayed on the Isle of Shoals like I wanted you to, we wouldn't be here now."

"And what fun would that be, matey," said Jack with a laugh. "It's showing what we've got that I'm after. These folk about Salem deserve a bit of torture after what they've done."

"Well, it's an act of stupidity that may cost you your head," said Tony.

"What do you mean, lad?" said Jack in a sober tone.

"What I mean is that your men have been spending their bit all along the coast on rum and whores. How long do you think it is before one of them tells someone that the gold came from Portuguese ships, not a Spanish wreck."

"Mayhaps ye've got a point there, lad," said Jack. "There's many in this town that are lusting for gold, and not a lot of it to go around. I can see now that I didn't think as clearly as I should have."

"Perhaps you were thinkin' of other things, eh Captain," said Maddie with a wink.

"Well," said Jack, "there's no changin' things now. What we have to do is split the map and get out of here as quick as we can."

"I'm afraid that's going to be harder than you think, Jack," said Tony. "Maddie and I can go as we please, but there's talk about that Governor Dudley and his son Paul are lookin' for you. There's a price on your head."

"Where did you hear that?" said Jack.

"From a man downstairs," said Maddie, wiping his sweating brow with an old rag. "It was worth our lives to haul ye up here Jackie, but we couldn't leave ye to be caught."

"Then give me my share of the map and I'll be on my way, lads," said Jack as he stood up and tightened his pistol belt around his waist.

The next instant I was almost crushed by the heavy wooden door as it was forced open. It smashed me in the chest and knocked the wind out of me. I tried to cry out, but it was no use. I know now that the old wooden door saved my life.

"Is that our man?" I heard the all too familiar voice of Nicholas Noyes demand.

"Aye sir, that's him," said Anthony Holding.

"And the treasure, did he tell you where it is?"

"No sir," said Maddie Primer, "he didn't."

FIFTY EIGHTH ENTRY

It was almost dark when I pushed the door forward and looked around the room. I don't remember the time passing, but I knew, by the rosy light that shone through the window, that I had been there far longer than I thought.

"Where have they taken you, Jack Quelch?" I whispered to myself as the tears ran down my face.

What was I going to do? I had to find out about Jack, but I knew that if I asked even one question the folk about Salem would become suspicious. I was the mad Dorcas Good, not some sensible mistress who could gather information as she wished.

The tavern downstairs was quiet, except for the sound of sweeping, so I gathered my thoughts to me and carefully made my way down the stairs.

"Here now, what are you doin' up there," said the maid servant, Abigail Hobbs, as I tried to sneak past her. I just looked at her and laughed crazily.

"Leave her be," said the good natured Goody Burns from the pubside. "Can't you see it's the daft girl. Go along home now, Dorcas, before your father comes looking for ye. It's a beating you'll get for sure if he finds you missing."

I gave Goody Burns a quick curtsy and ran out the door. Now I had my answer! If anyone knew where Jack was it would be that old sot, William Good. He gathered gossip like others gathered gold. Besides, it was my own father who had hoped to catch Jack by tying me to that tree at Burial Point. It all became clear to me as I raced towards home. My father must have known about the reward! Why else would he have tried to capture Jack on his own? But where had my father gone to last night? And why hadn't treacherous Will had us arrested at the Point?

"Because the Governor wants Jack's treasure. Jack's mates must have made a better deal when they promised up the treasure," I said to myself

259

as the shack I called home came into sight. I crept cautiously to the hole, covered with oilskin, that we called a window and peered in. Through the greasy paper I could make out the bloated figure of my father lying on the bed.

"Perfect," I muttered to myself as I slid along the side of the house and opened the door noiselessly. I could tell by his snores that it would be sometime before William Good awoke. As hard as it was to be patient at a time like this, I knew I should wait until he roused himself. Experience had taught me that to rouse my father from a deep stupor would only anger him. And that certainly was not what I needed now. I went to the small box that housed our meager food supply and took out some rye and salt and began to make some bread. I had also learned that sometimes, if my father had not made himself too sick with the rum, old Will awoke with a hunger. The few happy moments I had ever had with him were when he awakened and was able to fill his sagging belly with hot food. It was to my delight that I also discovered a few stray tea leaves at the bottom of the box. Not enough for a real cup of hot tea, but if I brewed it carefully and let it steep overlong it would do. I set about my tasks, almost happy in my plans. Again the worst had happened to me and I was alive with my full wits about me. The black velvet fog that had been my companion for so long was gone. In its place was a desire to live, at least until I had saved Jack.

I settled in the rickety chair by our small fire and waited for the smell of the baking bread to awaken my father. The mending I had in my hands fell into my lap as I stared into the fire. The glow of the red yellow flames seemed to jump from the hearth into my mind and make a merry dance, twisting and turning my thoughts until I could stand it no longer. I closed my eyes in an attempt to make them go away, but the fire demons remained, more alive than ever, threatening to burn my heart out with the pain. In my mind I could see a firebrand, held by Nicholas Noyes, coming closer to me. He was promising to burn out my eyes unless I told him where Jack's treasure was. I could see myself forming the words that denied any knowledge of the treasure, but I could hear no sound. Then Nicholas turned away from me and I could see that he was standing by the lifeless form of a man who was hanging from a noose. Nicholas Noyes was laughing as he turned the corpse around and I saw that the man, face blackened by strangulation, was my own beloved Jack Quelch.

"What's this, Daughter?" I heard as I struggled to escape the flaming heat that filled my body.

"What?" I heard myself cry.

"Why this good bread and tea," said Will, coming over to me and shaking me roughly.

I opened my eyes and gazed into my father's smiling face. What had I seen? Was it only a nightmare, or had my dreams returned after so many years, stronger and more terrifying than before?

"What's wrong, Dorcas? Have ye lost your senses again?" said my father as he sat before the fire with a piece of hot bread in one hand and the cup of tea in the other.

"No Father," I said cautiously, trying not to upset his mood. "I'm just tired is all. I hope you find your food pleasing."

"Excellent Daughter, and quite a surprise too. I take it you don't think ill of me for leaving you out in the chill all night/"

"Why no, I....."

"You see," said my father, stopping me before I could say anything else, "I had it in mind to catch that meddlesome Quelch, but someone got to him before me, blast the luck. I swear I would have come for you, Daughter, if I hadn't spent most of the night in Salem jail answering that fool Noyes' questions. I still can't believe that the idiot thought I knew something about where Quelch's treasure was stashed. Ah well, I suppose he guessed that Quelch might have sought us out, him being so fond of you and all."

"They were almost right, Father," I said, delighted that he was in a talkative mood.

"Aye that they were, and if they had held onto their britches we might all have been rich by now."

"I'm sorry that you lost your chance, Father," I said kindly.

"It's a good girl ye are, Dorcas, despite your strange ways. And a forgivin' one too, I might add. Now tell me, how did you happen to come loose of that tree?"

"I'm not sure," I said knowing that I had been seen in the tavern by Abigail and Mistress Burns. "All I know is that I found myself near the tavern this morning and walked home from there. I must have had one of my spells. I don't remember a thing."

"Not a thing, eh," said my father.

"No Father, not a thing," I said trying my best to sound tired, but sweet.

261

"Well then," said William, "we may yet be able to salvage something if we look smart. Gather your shawl, Daughter, and for God's sake comb that hair. I want you to look pretty when we visit the Captain."

"Visit the Captain!"

"Aye, my sweet. We're off to Boston Town to pay a mercy visit to an old friend, Captain Jack Quelch."

"You know where he is?" I said jumping to my feet.

"Of course I do," said my father proudly. "Noyes told me that when they caught him Quelch would be taken before the Governor's son, Paul Dudley, and then hauled off to Boston jail to cool his heels. Hurry now, we must make for Boston before the Governor's son tortures Master Jack into giving up the treasure. I'll warrant that when our Jack sees the tears in your eyes he'll give up his secrets to only Dorcas Good."

"But how will you get them to let us in?" I asked, suddenly unsure that I would be doing Jack a favor by following my father's plan.

"Don't you worry about that, Daughter, just get in that wagon before we lose anymore time!"

FIFTY NINTH ENTRY

I prayed as the old wagon rattled towards Boston Town. In truth it was the first real prayer I had breathed in years and I was not at all certain that anyone would be listening, but it was all I could think of to do as I tried to drown out my father's voice with my thoughts.

"Thank your stars that it's May and the night is late in coming," said my father as he whipped the old nag that pulled our wagon. "We may just make Boston Town before the highwaymen come out."

"And what would they want with us, Father?"

"Not us, you, Daughter. You're uncommonly pretty despite all your addled head," said my father, giving me the first compliment I had ever heard from his lips.

"I am?" I said.

"You are, Daughter. And it's a lucky thing for us 'tis so. Most that have been used as you are become lined and ugly, or suffer from the French disease by your age. But you look fresh as a daisy and twice as sweet."

"What's the French disease?"

"Never you mind, Dorcas. I'll let you know when you get it. Until then let's work on feathering our nest, eh Daughter."

"Yes Father," I said, wondering what the French disease was. I had heard the term before, but had not really thought it had anything to do with me. Why hadn't I listened to the old women on the wharf when they spoke of it? And then I knew why. Every time something had threatened my fragile existence I had embraced my old friend, my black velvet fog. What had I done to myself? I suddenly felt a great sadness for all the years I had spent living far away from the real world.

"There it is, Daughter," said my father as he pointed to a dusty scene that was loud and seemed terribly confusing. Ahead of us lay Boston Town. The same Boston Town that I had been brought to as a child. It seemed remarkably changed and far more crowded.

"How will we ever find our way here?" I asked as I turned this way and that in wonder.

"Just leave that to me, Daughter," said my father as he whipped our poor old nag forward.

"What do you mean this girl can't see her poor Uncle Jack!" yelled my father standing nose to nose with the guard.

"No one is allowed to see the prisoner, Governor's orders," said the guard as he raised his pike to block my father's way.

"Oh Father," I said trying to make my sobs sound convincing, "we promised my dear mother that we would take care of Uncle Jack, no matter what he did. How could anyone be so cruel as to deny Mama's last wish."

"'Tis not my orders that keeps you away, young mistress," said the guard, "but my major's. If it were up to me I would be glad to let you see the prisoner, even though you are the fourth 'niece' who has tried to see Quelch this day. I must admit you're the first one who has dragged her father along."

"The fourth 'niece'!" I said, looking at my father in confusion.

"Yes, well," stammered my father," you must see that those other girls were just trying to bring comfort to the poor prisoner."

"Comfort!" said the guard, "I'd give a lot for such 'comfort' as has passed before my eyes in the last few hours. Old Quelch must have cut quite a path through the ladies of this town. It's enough to make a man take up the pirating trade."

"Jack's not a pirate!" I said.

"That's what the Governor's son thought too until Quelch's own mates saw to it he was tossed in jail good and proper. It's amazing what a man's mates will do for a full pardon and a bit of gold, Mistress."

"Oh, please tell me what happened," I said.

"Well, Mistress," said the guard, putting his pike aside and settling into his story, "it seems that yon Quelch almost had the Governor's son, Paul Dudley, convinced that he had only collected the gold and took command of the 'Charles' at the order of it's dead captain, Captain Plowman. But the others in the crew said different. That, and the gold they had stuffed their pockets with, convinced Dudley that there was more to Quelch's

264

story. Quelch said that he was comin' to Boston Town to present his Spanish treasure to the owners of the 'Charles', but now the Governor knows the truth. England's at peace with Portugal now and any that has plundered their ships is a pirate. There was no Spanish wreck and the Dudley's know it. Why right now the Governor's got men out scouring Cape Ann for the rest of the treasure."

"What will he do with it when he finds it?" asked Will, barely able to cover his disappointment.

"If he finds it ye might ask," said the guard, "the Governor's right angry with Quelch for not tellin' him straight off where the gold is. And Quelch is a fool. Even I could tell that Quelch could have bought his freedom and gotten a fine commission to boot, if he'd confessed to where the gold was. 'Tis the Governor's favorite game to go treasure hunting on our shores."

"What will the Governor do with the treasure after he finds it?" I asked.

"He says he'll turn it over to the King, all good and honest, but we all know that most of it will find it's way into the Dudley's coffers. Why the Governor's a bigger pirate than yon Quelch, and has probably killed more men too, all for their being hanged legal like."

"How terrible! We must do something to save Jack. Father, please do something!"

"Aye lass, you are different," said the guard as he looked me up and down. "Ye really seem to care about that wretch in there. And ye look like a lady too, despite those rags and that dirty face. What say I let ye slip in for a moment, that is if yer father can make it worth me while."

"What's the point, now that the Governor's on to the treasure," said my father with a grunt."

"What's the point!" I screamed, hitting old Will in the chest with my fist," I swear that if you don't help me, Father, I'll stand on the platform in the middle of Salem Common and tell everyone what you've been doing to me all these years."

"Settle down now, girl," said Will, wiping his brow and looking at me in amazement. "I was only joking. Besides, mayhap Uncle Jack might still have a bit of his gold hidden about that he might tell ye about. I suspect it might even bring him comfort to know that his dear 'niece' would be taken care of when he's gone. What say ye let the girl in, sir, so's we can see what the pirate tells the her?"

"Why t'would only be doin' my Christian duty to bring the lady comfort," said the guard as he winked at my father and motioned us to folow him.

265

SIXTIETH ENTRY

It was all I could do to keep from screaming when the guard slammed the heavy wooden door behind us and began to lead us down the damp corridor that led to the cells. Nothing had changed since that long ago time when I had been carried down this very corridor as a child. The earthen walls still sweated with the moisture of the river nearby and the murmur of the forgotten prisoners moaned through my very bones. I felt the brush of fur and whiskers as a large rat ran across my foot and disappeared into the twilight of the prison below.

"Never you mind about that, Mistress," said the guard as he held his lantern high. "They won't hurt you as long as they have the prisoners to feed on, and we've got plenty of food for the rats what with Quelch and his mates here."

"I don't mind them at all," I said to the guard with a strange smile. How could this man know that I had made pets of many such creatures during my childhood stay in the very prison.

"Why," I whispered to myself, "it's almost like visiting my nursery."

"Eh? What was that, Mistress," asked the guard.

"Oh nothing, nothing at all," I answered, still somewhat bemused by the strange peace that began to fill my soul. For the first time in years I felt at home.

"Here we are," said the guard, as we stopped in front of a sturdy wooden door held together by heavy iron locks. "Take whatever time as you need, Mistress. 'Twill be time well spent if you can get us some gold," said the guard as he pinched me on the cheek.

"To be sure, sir," I said with a curtsey as the man held the door open while I slipped through.

Inside I squinted and looked around for some sign of Jack Quelch. At last my eyes alighted on a dark form curled up in the far corner of the shadowy room.

"Jack, my love," I whispered in his ear as I shook him gently.

"Who goes there?" asked Jack, instantly awake and on guard.

"Tis only your Dorcas, Jack, come to see you."

"Dorcas? Dorcas Good? I don't believe you, " said the voice that sounded like Jack, only older and very tired.

"Yes, your own Dorcas Good," I said as I grasped his hand and drew it to my face. "Don't you know me?"

"It's a wonder I still know my own name," said Jack, as he struggled to sit up. How I wished I could see him more clearly. Now it was my turn to put my hand on his cheek and feel something sticky and warm. It was blood. Prison blood.

"What have they done to you, my love!" I cried as I gathered him into my arms and held him tight.

"Nothing that can't be healed by the touch of your lips, my darlin'" said Jack as he set me on his lap and pressed his lips to mine."

"Jack, my beloved, what are we going to do?"

"Make the most of the time we have left together," he said as he fiercely kissed me again.

"What do you mean, 'the time we have left'!"

"Can't you see it, darlin'" said Jack, "there's no hope for me. Even now Dudley's constables are scouring the taverns of Cape Ann looking for my crew. It seems our fine Master Holding has set a trap for us all. I also heard them whisperin' the name of my mate, John Clifford. He'd just as soon slit yer throat as look at ye, and they'll be no stopping' his yappin' mouth if he's offered a pardon. Damn the luck that Clifford knows that Larimore's Galley is headin' out of Gloucester to the Isle of Shoals to bury the rest of the treasure."

"Then you didn't give it all to Holding and that old sailor, Maddie?"

"Of course not, lass! What do ye take me for, a fool? They only got what was comin' to them plus a bit more for services rendered."

"What services, Jack?"

"Never you mind about that, sweetheart," said Jack with a sigh. "Just believe that whatever ye hear about me after I'm gone may be the truth, but I died mightily sorry for any innocent folk I have harmed. I've been a bad 'un, all right, there's no denying it. Promise me that ye'll pray for my soul in the old way when I'm gone, Dorcas Good."

"Don't say such things, Jack!" I said trying not to cry.

"Listen to me, love," said Jack. "There's no stoppin' what's to happen. Sooner or later Dudley's Major Sewall will find Larimore's Galley, with the treasure aboard. Do ye think that he wants any of us about telling the people of Boston Town that most of the pirates gold will be going for fine lace around the Governor's collar? He may let my men off, but I'm a dead man for sure."

"No, Jack, no!" I cried as I laid my head upon his chest. "This can't be happening. I'll not let them hang you! There must be a way to stop them!"

"Listen to me, girl," said Jack as he shook me hard. "There's little time left to us. It's a bloody miracle you were able to even get into this place. It's too late for me, but not for you. I've a secret for you that you must tell no one. Once you're clear of this place, act the fool and bide yer time until they stop watchin' you. Then make for old Jackie's treasure and use it to free yerself."

"I don't understand, Jack. You said that Larimore had the treasure."

"Not your portion, darlin'. Can't you see that your Jack would never trust what belongs to his sweetheart to another pirate? It's not as much as it should have been, but it's enough to get you out of Salem and make you a fine lady."

"Then tell me where it is Jack, and I'll use it to bribe the guards and free you!" I said, suddenly thinking there was a way out.

"No lass," said Jack as he turned me, making me look him square in the face. "If you do that, ye'll hang beside me down there on Scarlett wharf. The best we can do is have you keep the secret to yourself and live on with my treasure in yer pockets. It's all we have left. 'Twould bring great comfort to me to know that I kept my promise to you, girl. Do this for me and I'll accept my fate with a song upon my lips."

"I can't Jack, I can't. I'm not that strong. Let me die with you. Don't you see that ever since I was put in this same prison, a thousand years ago, my life has been nothing but misery and pain. I should have died then but for fate and it's cruel tricks. When you came back I thought there might be some hope, something left for me, but now I see that it was all a cruel joke. My whole life has been a cruel joke that only death can end."

"Such talk!" said Jack. "That doesn't sound like my brave girl! Never have I known you to run away from anything, Dorcas Good, and I'm not going to let you start now. Don't let me die thinking you a coward."

"I'm not a coward!"

269

"Then prove it by taking your hands from your ears and listening to what I have to tell you, my love. Take what I can give and pray for me, Dorcas Good. If you deny me now, ye'll have let these foul puritans win. Is that what you want?"

"No Jack," I said, realizing that he was right.

"There's my girl," said the pirate, Jack Quelch, as he held me close and spoke to me of treasure and love until the guard came to get me.

SIXTY FIRST ENTRY

"What did he tell you?" hissed my father, shaking me until I thought my arms would snap under his grasp.

"Nothing!" I cried as I looked towards the guard and prayed that he would not take it into his mind to join in.

"Nothing is it?" yelled my father, twisting my arm behind my back and pushing me towards the table that stood in the center of the room. "I'll teach you to lie to your own flesh and blood."

As my head banged against the heavy planks of the rough wood I began to feel the familiar sensation of blackness and comfort fill me. "No, not this time!" I screamed silently as I forced it to retreat. There was no telling what I might say if I gave myself over selfishly to the blessed relief that lay within the numbness of my black fog. This was not the time to seek comfort at Jack Quelch's expense.

"Here now," said the guard as he approached the table, "give the lass a chance to speak. How do we know that Quelch told her anything for sure? She looks not like one who could deceive."

"You don't know her as I do," said my father. "She's the daughter of a witch, born and bred. She spent many a day in this very place for her evil ways. She has a black soul, sir, one that often hides the truth from my eyes. This is Dorcas Good, witch of Salem Village."

"Why," said the guard, "I've heard of you, lass. My own wife told me of your sad tale many a year ago. It was when we were first married and newly come from England. She said there had been a child kept within these walls for the crimes of a witch. But we thought the daughter of Sarah Good had died many a year ago."

"A daughter of Sarah Good's did die here," I said, amazed that anyone had heard my tale outside of Salem, "but it was my little sister, not me."

271

"Ah, now I remember," said the guard, "you're the one that folks say went mad. Tell me lass, have ye now recovered your wits enough to tell us about Pirate Quelch and his treasure?"

"There's nothing to tell," I said, removing myself from under my father's hand and sitting on the table. I had learned long ago to take my friends where I could find them. If this guard was in the mood for cozy chat then so be it."

"Speak, lass," said the guard, "what did he say? Perhaps he spoke in riddles that were beyond you."

"Yes, Daughter," said my father eyeing me suspiciously, "tell us everything Quelch said.

"Well," I said, "at first he was surprised to see me, and then he grabbed me and started to kiss me."

"That's no surprise," said the guard, "Master Jack's known for his way with the ladies and you'll forgive me if I say you're likely lass."

"Thank you, sir," I said hoping that if my smile were bright enough the man might forget about the treasure.

"And then what?" said my father, not fooled by my smiles.

"And then he sat me on his lap and started to tell me about the voyage of the 'Charles' and how he and his crew had come upon a Spanish wreck."

"Come now, Dorcas," said my father, "we all know that Quelch's treasure came from them Portuguese. Who do you think you're fooling'?"

"I'm just telling you what Jack told me, Father," I said trying to look as dim as possible.

"Poor girl," said the guard, "can't you see she's a bit confused. I'm surprised you don't know that, you bein' her father and all. Here now, lass," said the guard sitting beside me on the table and rubbing his leg against mine, "don't be afraid. I tell you what. You give up everything Quelch said to you and I'll see to it that we tour the town this very afternoon for a fine lace bonnet. You'd like that, wouldn't you lass?"

"To be sure, sir," I said as I returned the man's smile.

"Lace bonnet or not, she'll tell us what she knows or be beaten blue for holding her tongue," said my father as he dragged me from the table and began shaking me.

Luckily, we were interrupted by the sound of fists banging on the outer door before my father could do any real harm to me. It was a good thing

272

too. I could tell from the look on his face that I would not have left Boston jail with any teeth left in my head.

"Sergeant, Sergeant," came a voice from outside the door, "open up! The Governor wants the prisoner right away. They've got him dead to rights!"

"Here now, what's this?" said the guard, looking first at my father and then at me with a warning glance. "Act smart now," he whispered, nodding his head in my direction. "And straighten out that petticoat. It would be a fine thing if I found myself sitting' in the stocks for no reason at all."

"What's the trouble, Nathaniel?" said the guard, I now knew was a sergeant, as he opened the door and let in three armed men.

"There's no trouble, sir," said Nathaniel, 'it's just that the Governor is in a frenzy to bring that there Quelch to trial. They thought they'd found most of the crew with nothing but a few grains of gold dust filling' their pockets, but it seems that Major Sewall followed their trail to the Isle of Shoals and captured something special. You see, when they set eyes on the Isle, there lay Thomas Larimore's galley in plain sight with none aboard but Larimore and the cabin boy. Sewall captured the two and boarded Larimore's ship. There they waited until a goodly number of the pirates came aboard carrying sacks of gold. They say it's at least half the fortune the Governor was looking for. And now, a few of the Captain's mates have decided to squeal on Quelch to save their own necks."

"Who are they?" I cried out. I would have said more if my father hadn't put his hand over my mouth and pushed me to ground.

"Say now, what's this?" said Nathaniel, noticing me for the first time.

"Pay no attention to them," said the sergeant, with a wink, "tis just a poor daft girl and her pimp."

"Having a little fun at the Governor's expense, eh Sergeant?" said Nathaniel with a laugh. "Well I can't say that I blame you. She is a pretty bit."

"That's what I thought when I lifted her skirts," said the sergeant, trying his best to look frustrated. "I was just givin' the man his coin when you interrupted us. Here now, take what I give ye out of the goodness of my heart and get out of here."

"Thank you, sir," said my father taking the coin from the sergeant and dragging me out the door. It was not until I heard it slam behind us that I realized what had happened.

"Why did he let us go like that, Father?"

"Didn't you hear what the man said? They've found the treasure and Quelch's mates have turned against him to save their own skins. All the Sergeant could gain from us hangin' around him now is a trip to the galleys for tryin' to sneak the Governor's treasure out from under him."

"But it's Jack's treasure," I said stubbornly as my father dragged me towards the sunlight.

"Treasure belongs to him that can keep it, Daughter," said my father. "Come on now, there's still a bit of time to see what we can make out of this day. What with all the excitement about the town, I'll warrant the streets are filled with fine gentlemen just waiting to sample a new girl."

SIXTY SECOND ENTRY

What I had known of whoring before was nothing when I compare it to my weeks in Boston Town. I was used hard and often, but I seemed to feel almost nothing. Jack had wrapped his love so tightly around my heart that there was no room for anything else. The streets were crowded, day and night, with folks trying to get a glimpse of the evil pirate, Jack Quelch.

Poor Jack, there was no one left in this world who cared anything about him. All the curious wanted to know was where he had hidden the treasure. How amazed they would have been to find out that the little whore they used and beat was the only one in town that could have told them. But I kept my mouth shut and prayed for a chance to run away from my father.

If only I could get in to see the Governor! Day after day I waited until my father drank himself to sleep on the dirty pile of rags we now called home, and slipped out to make my way to the courthouse. And day after day I would return, heartbroken by the fact that I had no hope of getting near the place, what with all the fine folk there before me crowding into Jack's trial like it was some sort of show. It was with terror that I watched May fade into June and the days get longer and longer.

The Governor made much out of being the presiding magistrate who was spending his days in the sweltering summer heat just to make sure justice was done. Some said he was truly saintly, but I knew him for what he was. Governor Dudley was a man who could be purchased for gold. Jack had said so. If only I could get near the Governor to offer him a bribe! Only the Portuguese gold could set my Jack free.

As low as the Governor seemed to me, lower still were Maddie Primer and John Clifford! They stood, day after day, testifying against their mates. In the end they did their work well, seeing to it that fifteen of Jack's mates were shipped off to England to serve on Queen Anne's ships as slaves until they died. The rest, seven in all including my Jack, were condemned to hang for murder and piracy. I knew the moment Jack was sentenced by the wails that came from inside the courthouse. It seemed that Jack's winning smile and brave ways had captured the hearts of the ladies of Boston Town. With my own eyes I had watched as many a finely dressed mistress pulled up in front of the courthouse, handkerchief over her nose and a tear in her eye, asking after my Jack. It would have been enough to make my heart falter if I had not known the true Jack Quelch. These ladies were in love with a dream, not the real man.

"And a lucky thing that is too," I said to myself as I walked back to my father. "If they knew the real man they would have been carrying about a heart as heavy as mine."

"Where have you been?" asked my father as I approached our matted rags.

"Just seeing the town, Father," I said as I lay down wearily.

"Don't lie to me girl. I know where you've been, but I suppose there's no harm in it. Ye've been to Quelch's trial."

"That I have, Father," I said, too tired and heartbroken to lie. "But it's over now and Jack is to hang. There, now that you know you can leave me alone. All I want to do is sleep."

"Sleep! At a time like this?" said my father rubbing his hands together. "Do you realize the fortune that is to made before that wretch hangs, Daughter?"

"It will not be made by me," I said, not caring if he killed me. My black fog had covered my mind since I stumbled away from the courthouse earlier. It was now drifting through my body and bringing me my odd comfort. Hannibelle says that I was in some sort of shock, but I know that it was my blessed dreams protecting me from throwing myself into the nearby river. For that is what I would have done if I had realized the horror of what was to follow.

"Get up now, slut," said my father, tugging at my skirt and kicking me with his foot.

"Didn't you hear me?" I yelled as his boot hit my ribs, "I need rest and I'm taking it. And what's more, I'll do no more whoring for you, William Good. Get away from me or I swear I'll kill you."

"With what, you little bitch?" said my father as he backed away from me.

276

"With anything I can lay my hands on," I said, knowing I was bluffing, but full of a fury so murderous that any who looked upon me would have believed my words.

"Then I'll leave ye for now, Dorcas Good," said my father backing away from me like the coward I knew he was. "But you are my daughter and my property, for all your fine words. Don't think ye've heard the last of me."

"I'm sure I haven't," I said as I turned my back on him and fell fast asleep.

SIXTY THIRD ENTRY

The day of June 30th, 1704, was what my mother used to called a bride's day. I awoke to a softness in the air that wrapped itself around my body and made me tingle with its freshness. I sat up and looked about me. The space under the bridge where Father and I had made our home for the past few weeks was deserted! Where were all the other beggars and whores who shared our shelter? Then I remembered. Today was the day Jack Quelch was to die.

"No!" I screamed as I leapt to my feet. The echo of my voice bounced against the walls of the Charles River bridge like a cannon shot. What had I done! Why had I let myself become wrapped in my mad fog when I should have been throwing myself at the Governor's feet, begging him for Jack Quelch's life.

"There might still be a chance to save him," I said to myself as I bundled up my shawl and kicked the rags I had slept on into the river. I climbed up the embankment of the Charles river and joined the crowd that filled its banks. Never in my life had I seen so many people. They were all headed toward Scarlett wharf.

"Pardon, sir," I said to a passing stranger as I sighted Scarlett wharf, "can you tell me what time they are bringing the prisoners?"

"Why bless you, lass," said the man looking down at me with glee, "where have you been? The whole town knows that Steven Sewall has ordered that the pirates be brought here by three o' the clock. That's the only way they can be hanged between high and low water. Listen now, girl, I think I can hear the piping of the guard."

I pushed the man aside and began to fight my way through the crowd. The madness of my frenzy must have alarmed those around me, for the crowd in front of me parted to let me through. I picked up my skirts and ran towards the sound of the drums.

"Hey there, don't I know you," said a voice as I felt myself grabbed from behind.

"Let me go!" I screamed while I struggled to free myself from the meaty arms that held me.

"Why it's the little whore of Salem, Dorcas Good," said the man as he set me on my feet and turned me around.

"Let me go or I swear I'll kill you!" I said, pounding the man's fat chest with my fist.

"A fine way to treat an old friend, sweetheart," said the man as he laughed and grabbed at my breasts.

I continued to hit and kick at the man until he loosened his grip enough for me to look him full in the face. When he did, Nicholas Noyes received a full wad of spit in his eyes.

"What'd you do that for?" said Nicholas as he wiped his face.

"For the same reason I'm doing this," I said as I bit his hand and fled into the crowd. The drums were louder now as I ran towards the edge of Scarlett wharf. There I saw my beloved Jack surrounded by forty of the Queen's most trusted men. He was being placed in a boat with another man, who was all dressed in all in black.

"Tis a sure bet that Mather wants to save the Captain's soul this day," cackled a woman, "t'would be a feather in Cotton's cap if Quelch repented and was sent to the galleys instead of the noose. Move along dearie so's big Hannah can get a look at the fine 'un that's broke half the hearts of Boston Town," said the woman as she shoved me.

"Where's Cotton Mather?" I asked, suddenly realizing that if I could get to the Reverend and speak to him there might still be a way to save Jack.

"There he is," said Hannah, blocking my way. "He's still a fine looking man for all his piety. I had him in me bed when I was a young and likely lass."

"I'll slit your throat if you don't let me pass," I yelled as I pushed big Hannah down and jumped over her. Only thirty feet and forty Queen's men now stood between me and the boat that held Cotton Mather and Jack Quelch. I ran down the embankment and hurled myself towards the small boat, not caring who I trampled in my way. Now there was only a few feet to the boat. Then, I tripped over a large rock that had been hidden by the grass. I found myself rolling down the embankment and landing near the side of the boat. I stood up, soaked to the skin.

"Reverend Mather, Reverend Mather," I called out, praying the man would heard me.

"Get away from here now," said a guard as he put his hands on my shoulders and began dragging me out of the water.

"Reverend Mather," I screamed, ignoring the guard and looking straight into Cotton Mather's eyes. "Don't you remember me? 'Tis little Dorcas Good, from Salem. I've information for you that might yet get Governor Dudley what he wants."

"What's this?" said Mather, looking up from the prayerbook he had been reading to Jack.

"'Tis nothing but the daft girl from Salem," said Jack, struggling to stand up in the boat, despite his chains.

"And what does she want, Quelch?" said Mather eyeing me suspiciously.

"I want to tell you where the rest of the treasure is so that you can free Jack Quelch," I cried.

"Pay no attention to her, Reverend," said Jack. "Can't you see that she's lost her wits. She's been without them ever since they let her loose of Salem prison over ten years ago."

"But what's this about the treasure?" I heard Mather say as he motioned the guard to bring me to the side of the boat.

"I know where the treasure is, sir," I gasped out, trying to avoid Jack's angry stare. "And if you free Captain Quelch I'll tell you."

"Ah, little girl," said Jack giving a hearty laugh, "didn't ye know that I was just tellin' ye a tale so's we could have a tumble. I'm sad to admit it at such a time, sir," said Jack as he turned his back on me and spoke to Cotton Mather, "but it seems that I'm guilty of tellin' this sweet thing a story so's she would give me her favors. 'Tis not a thing I'm proud of now, but there's no changin' what I did. Go along home now, sweet Dorcas, and be done with it. 'Twas a nice time we had, but it's all finished now what with Jackie's hangin' this day."

"Please," I said as I fell on my knees in the water, "can't you see he's just trying to protect me. Please listen to me Reverend Mather."

"There's nothing to listen to but the sound of this man hanging," said Mather as he motioned for the rower to push away from shore. "Only repenting of his crimes will save your Captain Quelch now."

"Repenting!" laughed Jack as he turned his face away from Mather and looked at me. "The only thing I repent of is not treating that little wench better. Why, if I had a bit more time upon this earth, who's to say that I might not have made her Mistress Quelch and settled down."

"Then pick up your oars, yeoman," said Cotton Mather.

"Come along now," said the guard as he set me back on dry land. "I'll let ye go because Mather said nothing about keepin' ye, but I'd make myself scarce if I were you. There's always a chance he might change his mind."

"Thank you," I whispered through my tears as I watched the second boat, filled with Jack's six mates, push off.

The afternoon was so still that you could hear every word that Cotton Mather said as the hangman fastened the noose around Jack's neck. It was to Mather's credit that he tried, once more, to get Jack to repent and save his life. But it was no use. From over the water I heard the last words of Jack Quelch.

"I am not afraid of death, but I am afraid of what follows. I am condemned only upon circumstances, but all should take care how they bring money into New England, to be hanged for it."

The crowd gave a great cheer as Jack bowed to the crowd and nodded to the hangman. A moment later, the lifeless body of the pirate, Captain Jack Quelch, swung in the soft summer breeze.

SIXTY THIRD ENTRY

That night I stole a boat and rowed out to the small island in Boston Harbor called Nix's Mate. The Governor had ordered that Jack's body was to be gibbeted there, for all to see, as a warning to other pirates. But I was determined that Jack should be buried properly, just as my own sweet mother had been. It may sound strange, but the calmness of rowing in the quiet waters towards the island that held my love, brought me a peace and serenity beyond belief. I felt as if there was nothing left on this earth that could bring me grief. My heart lay elsewhere now, forged forever to those who had already died. As I rowed I thought of my beautiful mother and her sweet prayer.

"Yea though I walk through the valley of the shadow of death" I whispered as a bat flew overhead.

The valley of death was where I was now, and where I would remain until my heart was joined, in death, to my beloved Jack. Long ago my mother had said something to me that I had not understood 'till this moment. I thought of her now as I rowed in the starlight.

"Dorcas," she had said, " never do battle with anyone who has nothing left to lose. Those who have gone on such a journey and returned are the strongest on earth and cannot be defeated, for you see they have no fear of death. They have been burned in the crucible and come out the other side as pure as an angel, the angel of death."

Was that what I was, I wondered? Is that why people look at me so strangely. I knew I was but a young woman in my own eyes, but I also knew that others saw me as the child who had walked through the hell of the Salem dungeon and emerged to live my life in the hell my father gave me. It is true that when I walked through the streets of Salem the folk made way for me, rarely speaking a word or acknowledging my presence. I had always thought it was because they were ashamed of what they had done to me, or perhaps they thought I was beneath them. But was there another reason? Were they a little afraid of what I was because of what I had been through? My madness was, of course, an outer sign of that, but there was something more to it. Others had been mad before me in Salem and they were treated with friendly gentleness. Take Ann Putnam's own mother who wandered about the town, near hysterical, most of the time. Then there was Abigail Hobbs, known to run through the woods at night, singing to the moon. Salem held many secrets that were beyond human understanding and perhaps I was the most terrifying of them.

"But I'll no longer be a secret!" I cried to the moon as I sighted Nix's Mate, the small island off the Winthrop settlement. "I'll not be the 'mad girl of Salem Town' any longer. I'm through with them all forever. As soon as you're buried, Jack Quelch, I'm finding your treasure and taking to the sea. It's off to anywhere I please, the Carolina's or maybe even down to Barbados to look for the place that haunts my dreams. What matter as long as I'm far away from here."

"That's my girl," I heard a voice inside my head laugh as I pulled my small boat onto the banks of Nix's Mate.

"And your girl I'll always be, Jack Quelch," I said with an answering laugh as I approached the body of my love that hung from the gibbet that Cotton Mather's men had erected.

"Jack Quelch, you're more of a man in death than most can hope to be in life," I said as I climbed the gibbet. The knife I held between my teeth had been found in the boat that lay on the banks below. It was as if some dark angel had placed it there for my purpose. Whatever lay behind the luck of my find was beyond my caring. All I knew was that the strength that filled my limbs as I climbed that gibbet was greater than any I had ever had. Was this what Jack felt when boarding a boat or climbing a mast? If that was so then who was to blame him for living his life beyond the prison of New England's shores.

At last I reached the top and swung myself, hand over hand, along the wooden beam that steadied Jack. I held my breath as I reached out and felt for the rope that held him. Sure enough, it was there, strong and sturdy and wrapped tightly about his neck. I took the knife from my lips and began sawing at the thick rope, all the while praying that the arm that held me had enough strength to carry me through. I knew that if I fell there was no hope for me. I would either be killed instantly or lie there injured until I died of my wounds. No one ever set foot on Nix's Mate unless they had to. It was said that the place was haunted.

The quiet of the night was suddenly interrupted by the screeching of an owl. The sound, after the profound silence that had filled me, almost caused me to let go of the wood and fall to my death, but somehow I gathered my strength and tightened my fingers around the beam.

"I hope you appreciate this, you darling fool," I said to my dead Jack as the blade sawed through the last bit of rope and his body fell to the ground below. Mine almost followed it as I recoiled from the shock of the lightened beam. But again I managed to hang on and grab the wood with both hands. Then, I carefully retraced my way down to where Jack lay.

It was at that moment that all my strength left me. I gazed down on his beautiful face and felt everything that I had been refusing to feel during this longest day of my life.

"Oh Jack," I cried as I threw myself atop his body and held him tightly, "how could they do this to you? You who were so fine and brave. I swear that I shall love you all my life and take no one but you into my heart. All else but you are dead to me. How could it be otherwise when everywhere I look I will see your beautiful smile and twinkling eyes. I know now that Mather would have killed you, or put you into the living death of the King's galleys, no matter what you did. It was hopeless to think anything else. Dear love, I can't help but feel the pain of it all. If only you had left me as I was, then perhaps none of this would have happened. Why did you risk it all for me?"

And then, blessedly, I had my answer. Jack had come for me in Salem the same as I had come for him this night. True love is something that cannot be denied, no matter the cost. At least our love was good and pure and something that would belong to us forever. Somehow the thought of our love gave me the strength to do what I knew I must. I took hold of the rope that held Jack and looped it around his body. Then I dragged it towards the boat and slid both Jack and the boat into the water. It was a close thing, but somehow I managed to tip the boat to one side and roll Jack and myself into it. Then I grabbed the oar and made for the open sea. When I had gone out far enough, I stopped rowing. This was the moment I had dreaded most.

"Dear Jack, how can I let you go alone," I said as I freed him from the rope and kissed his lips.

I looked at the rope, and for a moment thought of tying it around both Jack and myself and jumping into the sea with him. What a pleasure it would have been to leave this torturous world behind me and die in the arms of my love. But I knew it was impossible. If the boat were found floating anywhere near this spot, Cotton Mather would dredge the ocean for our bodies. There was little chance of him ever finding us, but even the chance of such a thing stayed my hand. I would not have us displayed for all the world to see. Jack Quelch deserved an honorable death.

I reached over and pulled Jack's body to the side of the boat and tried to tip it enough to let him fall free. Miraculously, my plan worked and he began to fall out. At the last moment I reached towards him and touched the sweet curls that framed his face. Then my love, my Jack, disappeared into the sea forever.

PART SEVEN

THE COMFORT
OF
GALLOWS HILL

SIXTY FORTH ENTRY

"Dorcas Good, you're under arrest!"

"For what?" I yelled above the sound of the waves as I struggled to pull my borrowed boat back onto the rocky embankment where I had found it. If I was to be arrested for taking the boat then so be it, but I was determined that those who blamed me for the theft should see that I had at least tried to return the boat to its rightful owner. I was not by nature a thief and would not be branded as one.

"Never mind for what, young mistress," said the man, dressed as a sergeant-at-arms and surrounded by several other guards. He grabbed me and pushed me away from the boat. "Just come along with us quietly before you add disobedience to the charges against you."

"I'll ask you again, what charges?" I said standing my ground and making myself as large as possible. No more would I go like a docile sheep into the night. I was Dorcas Good, beloved of Captain Jack Quelch, and as fine as the Governor's wife.

"All right," said the man, looking as if he took no pleasure in his task, "if ye must know, your father, William Good, has made a complaint against you and it has been co-signed by the Reverend Nicholas Noyes of Salem. They charge you with disturbing the peace and as a runaway. Now, will you come with me like a good girl or do I have to drag you."

"That complaint is false," I said boldly, trying not to let the man see me tremble. "Nicholas Noyes is no 'reverend'. He stands as deacon and teacher of the Salem Village church, but it's been many a year since anyone called that man 'reverend'."

"Even so, mistress, the warrant is properly signed by your father and you must abide by it."

"And if I don't?"

"Then I'll put you over my shoulder and carry you to jail. Believe me, it will go far easier for you if you just come along."

"How did you know to find me here?" I asked, realizing that any further resistance was useless. Let the man take me to jail, what did I care? The only reason my father had sworn a warrant out against me was to get me back to Salem. Once there, I'm sure he thought I would make his living for him as I always had. Little did he know that I had whored my last for that sot, William Good. It was really no matter whether or not I was arrested this night as long as I would soon be set free. And how else but free could I do my father's bidding? Let them take me, as long as they left my Jack's body rest safely in the sea. The one thing I had to know before I let myself be chained was if any had seen me making for Nix's Mate. The sergeant's answer would tell me that.

"I don't know how they knew you were here, Dorcas Good, I only know that I was told, by the Reverend, that sooner or later you would show up here and that I was to take you in."

"And I'll bet you've a pocket full of silver to show for your trouble now, don't you?" I said to the man with a smile.

"That, lass, is none of your business. Now come along and face what ye must," said the man as he grabbed my arm and hauled me up the embankment.

That sneaking, lying Nicholas Noyes! I knew now what must have happened. He was more than capable of following me through the crowd and watching my sad scene with Cotton Mather. Thank the heavens above that Jack had laughed at my pitiful attempt to free him. I knew that Noyes thought that Mather was God himself and would believe anything Mather said. If old Cotton thought my tale of treasure was false than so did Noyes. But then, why did he follow me to this place and tell my father where I could be found? There must be some reward in it for him. Ah, that was it! For some reason fat Nicholas had always taken pleasure in the misfortunes of others, especially my misfortune. It was reward enough for him to see me belittled and brought back to Salem in chains, especially after the way I had spurned him this very day.

I was much cheered by the thought and banged the sergeant on the back to get his attention.

"Here now, what's this?" said the man, shifting my weight.

"You can let go of me now if you've a mind to," I said sweetly. "I've decided to come along peaceful like."

"Well then," said the man, "that's better. 'Tis a heavy load ye are for all that ye look so light, little Dorcas. Tell me now, just what is it ye've done to make Noyes so angry."

"I won't let him lift my skirts, if you must know," I said with a scornful laugh. "The fat pig disgusts me."

"As well he should," said the sergeant as he looked at me with respect. "Tis rare that I meet a whore with scruples. Tell me now, is this Noyes a friend of your father?"

"Why, there're as thick as thieves," I said, "and always scheming with each other. I guess there's no stopping them or keeping me from going back to Salem, now is there?"

"I suppose not, lass, especially now that the Governor's been petitioned about the trials and all."

"What are you talking about?" I asked, stopping in the middle of the road.

"Why, haven't you heard?" asked the sergeant, warming to his gossip.

"Heard what?"

"It seems that the families of the poor victims in the Salem trials have asked the Governor to repay them for their losses. There's to be a pretty penny in it for any who lost folk or were injured during that witchcraze."

"I see," I said, my thoughts suddenly pulled away from the day's tragedy and thrown back into that long ago time of terror. "And did they say how much the poor 'survivors' would get?"

"'Tis said that each householder stands to reap many pounds sterling for his loss, more if a loved one was hanged. Tell me wench, you bein' so young and all. Do you even remember the trials?"

"Oh yes," I said, feeling the hysterical laughter beginning to swell within me, "I remember them quite well."

SIXTY FIFTH ENTRY

The look of satisfaction on Nicholas Noyes face as they placed me in the heavy wooden stocks was enough to confirm my suspicions. He had turned me in for pure spite and was reaping a greater reward than any he could have hoped for.

My punishment for refusing to whore for my father was to be brought back to Salem and displayed on the Common for all the world to see. Hanging from my neck was a sign that read 'whore' and 'disobedient child.' I suppose I should count myself lucky that my punishment was only to last three days.

But, I was unprepared for the cruel gossip that Nicholas Noyes spread about the town. Before now, despite being looked down upon for my poverty and misfortune, I had always been treated as one of Salem's own. I had been protected from the worst of the jeers that had met many who had gone against the strict rules of the puritans. Now I was being treated as an outcast. Tomatoes and rocks were thrown at me by the children of Salem. I was puzzled by the turn of events until I realized what one woman was saying amid her angry screams and tossed garbage.

"Tis the whore of a pirate ye are and a shame you weren't hanged with him. My Richard was on the 'Charles' and never to this day has he returned. 'Twas your pirate that saw him to his death I'm certain. I hope ye die!"

Was there really such hate against me because of Jack? Yes, I was to learn, there was. Many had lost a loved one through the folly of the "Charles' adventure, either to the galleys or to the hangman, and for some reason the people of Salem had chosen me as their scapegoat. Who else was there with Jack gone? That, along with my already tainted status as a witch's daughter, made me realize that my fate could have been much worse than to be covered with rotting vegetables in the middle of Salem Common. To judge from the mood of the crowd that surrounded me during those three days, they would just as soon see me burned.

293

It was during my time in the stocks that I began to feel the return of the life within my life. It had been only the love of Jack Quelch that had taken me away from my inner mist, and now with him gone, it returned to me in earnest. It was my only strength, my refuge. I suppose that many wondered how I could stand being locked in those stocks for three days, day unto night, without a murmur. I knew the answer. The real Dorcas Good had fled far from the place and was sailing through her gentle mist with a happy smile upon her face. By the third sunrise I was beyond caring about rocks, vegetables or any other offal that was thrown my way.

How pleasant it was inside myself. Why had I ever ventured forth into the real world when all that it held was terror and heartbreak? Not even Jack Quelch had been able to bring me such comfort and love to calm my soul. It was only my beloved mist that took away that horror of the world my body was forced lived in. I felt like a traitor who had sinned and been taken back into the loving fold of forgiveness. I was truly blessed that my mist welcomed me back into it's tender arms with such swiftness.

"Perhaps," I whispered to myself, "it is the people of Salem who are mad and Dorcas Good who is sane."

"Here now, what's that?" asked the constable who was releasing me from the stocks.

"Nothing sir," I said giving him, what I knew the outer world thought, was a sweet smile.

"How easy it was to trick everyone!" I thought as he smiled back and helped me down the ladder. Not even the pain of moving my stiff limbs bothered me through my wonderful, familiar haze.

Then my feet touched the earth, the very earth that my mother and so many others lay under in Salem. I felt a glorious sweetness begin to rise in my body. What was happening to me?

"Take my arm, young Dorcas," said a kindly voice next to me. I turned towards the sound and was amazed to see Goody Mercy Phillips, the lovely woman who had shared my last months in Salem dungeon. Beside her stood the still tall and slender Hannibelle Black. Both were a bit grayer than I remembered from that long ago time, but except for that, unchanged. It seemed as if I began to shrink under Mistress Black's concerned gaze, until I felt once again like the five year old Dorcas Good they had first known.

"How did you know me?" I asked as Hannibelle took my other arm and the two women led me away from the merciless glare of the townsfolk.

"How could I not know you, child," said Mercy, stroking my arm gently. "You are our small friend from those long ago days. Still as sweet and untouched as when we knew you."

"Little do you know of it," I said sadly.

"We know it all, Dorcas Good," said Hannibelle with the small grunt that I remembered was a part of her.

"Yes, Dorcas, we know all, and much more too," said Mercy Phillips as she motioned for me to follow her off the path and into the woods beyond the clearing.

We walked in silence for awhile. I couldn't help but marvel at the way my two friends had known me. But mine had been a strange life and I had the gift of being able to accept almost anything that came before my eyes and cried out as true.

"Here now," said Hannibelle, as she cleared away some brush that concealed an entrance in the rocks hidden beneath, "duck your head as you enter."

The tall woman stooped down and disappeared into the rocks.

"Where are we going?"

"To a place where we can talk without being interrupted," said Goody Phillips as she gave me a little push.

The feeling I had earlier as my feet touched Salem's earth grew stronger as I walked between my two old friends. Where were they taking me? Soon I had my answer. The initial darkness of the cave gave way to an unearthly glow as we journeyed further into the rocks. I could tell, from the angle of the path beneath my feet, that we were going deeper. The glowing rocks imbedded into the side of the cave gave the air around me an almost shimmering quality, not unlike my own blessed mist.

"Isn't it pretty?" said Goody Phillips from behind me.

"Yes," I said in an awed gasp. The curious, yet glorious feeling that had come to me earlier was now singing through my body and mind. I was beyond caring where we were going or who I was with, as long as the fantastic melody filled my soul. It was then that I began to hear the whispers.

"Dorcas, Dorcas Good, are you there?" I heard a woman's voice whisper in my ear. I whirled around and saw no one but the small Goody Phillips.

"What's wrong, my dear?" she asked kindly.

"Nothing," I said, afraid that if I spoke I would lose the strangely painful inner joy that filled me. Then I heard my name spoken again. This time it was sung by a chorus.

"Dorcas, can you hear us?" asked the voices as tone overlaid tone. "We have been waiting so long."

I tried to keep going, but soon found myself unable to take another step. The voices that flooded through me were weighing me down.

"Just a few more steps, dearest, " said Mercy, pushing my unwilling body into an underground clearing.

Everything was forgotten as I glanced up into the sparkling rocky canopy that covered the room. We were under a great hill of perhaps a small mountain. All about me were stones made up of the same shimmering stuff that had lit our way.

"Welcome Daughter," said the voices in my head as I was forced to the ground by the weight of their ecstatic singing.

"What's the matter?" asked Hannibelle, sitting next to me and taking off her shoes.

"Can't you hear them?" I asked.

"Hear what?" said Hannibelle rubbing her toes.

"The voices," I said holding my head and beginning to rock back and forth.

"Oh, she means the others!" said Mercy with a giggle. "Don't let that bother you, Dorcas. You'll get used to it after awhile."

"But what is it? Who are they?" I asked as I battled to make myself heard over the clamor in my mind.

"Just the poor souls trapped within the rocks," said Hannibelle with a sigh. "Listen closely and see if you can recognize a few."

I leaned back against the rocks and felt the all too familiar dampness of cold stone. Then I tried to empty my mind of the voices. It was easier than I thought! The shouts became plain speech and then settled down into a vague rustle as I wrapped my mist around the sounds.

"Now," said Mercy, "let them back in, little by little."

Heeding her words, I lifted the curtain of my mist and felt a single voice fill me.

"More weight, more weight," groaned the voice of a man that I recognized, even after all these years, as that of Giles Corey. I opened my eyes in alarm and stared at Hannibelle Black.

"Close your eyes and try again," she commanded.

I found myself obeying her, despite my terror, and closing my eyes. I turned inward and told my mist to release old Giles and let another spirit enter.

This time it was the kind spirit of Mary Easty, sister to my friend Rebecca Nurse, who spoke.

"The Lord above, who is searcher of all hearts, knows that as I shall answer it at the tribunal seat that I know not the least thing of witchcraft."

How well I remembered those words, written on the eve of the good lady's death! Then, to my everlasting joy, another voice filled me completely, one that I had never hoped to hear again.

"Listen to us daughter, and learn of our fate. We are the condemned of Salem. Beneath this town lies a city of lost souls. We beg you to find your way to us. Only you, Dorcas Good, can bring us comfort. It is for this that you were spared."

"Mama!" I cried as I stretched my empty arms towards the voice without a body. "What can I do?"

"You must make the veil between the world that is yours and the place where we are trapped within these rocks so thin that you can pass through and guide us home. Learn all you can from Mistress Black and Goody Phillips. They can show you the way, but only you, Dorcas Good, have the power to enter."

"But how, Mama, how?" I screamed as her tortured voice left me.

SIXTY SIXTH ENTRY

"There now, sweetheart," said Mercy as she stroked my hair, "there's no need to cry."

I sat up and looked about me, realizing that my hair and my tattered dress were soaked with tears.

"Is she really here?"

"Yes Dorcas," said Hannibelle. "This cave lies beneath Gallows Hill."

"But Mama lies elsewhere! She's buried with my sister on the Nurse homestead," I said, frantic at the pain I had heard in her beloved voice.

"Your mother's spirit is trapped within these stones, as are all who died, condemned, in the witchcraze," said Mercy Phillips.

"That cannot be," I said through chattering teeth. The shock of my mother's agony, combined with the dampness of my dress, made me cold beyond belief.

"Come now," Dorcas Good," said Hannibelle as she gave me a piercing stare. "You know better than to deny your inner voices. This is not the Dorcas I remember from Salem dungeon. That Dorcas would have embraced what has happened here."

"Well," I said standing up, "I'm not that Dorcas Good any longer. Can't you see that? The child you knew was innocent, despite her father's pawing and the abuses put upon me by the people of Salem. That was little compared to having my body grow slowly numb from too much use and my soul die when my beloved was hanged on Scarlett wharf. Look now and see what I have become. This Dorcas Good, the real one, is an empty shell. There is nothing I have left to give anyone. I am one of the walking dead."

"That should make you yearn to help those trapped in the stones of this town all the more," said Goody Phillips.

"What do you mean?

"Look into your heart, little Dorcas, and you'll see what I mean," said Mercy, gently. "Only one who has been shaped by the very trials that took the lives of the innocents beneath these stones could hope to understand the true depth of their agony. Think on it, child. What have they done to suffer in death as well as in life? I remember you saying that the greatest comfort you had, in those dark days in the dungeon, was the comfort of knowing that at least your mother's soul was at rest. You, above all, should wish to deliver your mother from her endless agony and release her spirit."

"But how?" I asked.

"By following Sarah Good's wishes. Tell me, Dorcas, what exactly did she say to you?" asked Hannibelle.

"She said that I must make the veil between the world that is mine and the place where she is trapped so thin that I can pass through and guide her, and the others, home. She also said that I must learn all I can from you and Goody Phillips. Mama said that you could show me the way, but only I had the power to pass through the veil."

"That's true," said Hannibelle. "Mercy and I have tried for many a year to do what your mother asks of you. Once, during a night when the stars fell from the sky like rain, I thought we were going to make it, but at the last moment something blocked our way. If your mother says that you are the key and have the power then she must be right."

"How can we reach her?" I asked. The thought of my Mama trapped in some dark limbo was too much to bear, even if it meant pulling me back into the real world filled with the agony of living.

"By forming a bridge between your world and the unseen world of the spirits," said Mercy. "It's really quite simple if you have the power. It just takes time to fill your soul with the energy you'll need for the journey."

"And how do I do that?" I asked, confused by her strange words.

"By coming here every night and letting your soul become as theirs, until there is almost no difference between the living and the dead," said Hannibelle.

"But that's impossible! I'm watched day and night by my father. It's only by some miracle that I'm here with you now. Surely you must know that he sells me as a whore so that he can live in comfort!"

"Then you must change that," said Hannibelle with glowing eyes. "You must become someone that no man would want! Think, Dorcas, there must be a way!"

"I have it!" said Mercy. "I've heard it said about town that after you were freed from the dungeon you became dull witted and seemed to keep your infant's mind long after you should have. What about doing that again? Surely no one would want to bed a girl who appears to be but a small child?"

"You don't know how evil men can be." I said sadly. "There are some about this town who would think taking a woman with a child's mind all the more fun."

"Then become repulsive, too," said Hannibelle. "Spread it about town that you have the French disease. Let them know that any who touch you would be risking agony and death. I guarantee that from the moment you let that be known, coupled with a sudden fit that leaves you dull witted, you shall be as free as an angel."

"The angel of death," said Mercy Phillips, gathering her skirts about her and doing a little jig.

"Then what are we waiting for!" I cried, feeling my heart soar. "Let's get to it! The sooner we begin, the sooner we can deliver the innocents of Salem to eternal rest."

SIXTY SEVENTH ENTRY

Hannibelle's plan worked like a charm and I soon found myself with the run of Salem Town. How strange it felt to be able to wander the streets alone and unburdened. True, most people backed away from me when they saw me coming, but it was a small price to pay for my freedom. How fortunate it was that I lived in Salem, home to many who had been devastated by the events of 1692. There were more than enough sad stories to go around, and soon the folk of the town lost interest in mad Dorcas Good. They were too busy apologizing to one another, and trying to regain the property lost to the judges and magistrates, to pay much attention to me.

Even those who had gained by the witchcraze had found that gold could not relieve their guilt. I almost felt sorry for haggard Ann Putnam. Both her parents had died in 1699, leaving 'sweet' Ann to bring up her many younger brothers and sisters alone. She was unmarried and almost mad with worry and overwork. To add to that, she was weighed down with guilt. I feel a bit evil to say this, but one of my greatest pleasures during the next few years was tormenting Ann Putnam. It was the least she deserved for her part in more than twenty deaths and the misery she had caused the survivors. I would take an almost hideous glee in passing closely by her on the street and moaning out for my dead mother. My soft cries, combined with the limp I affected to show that the French disease was slowly eating away at my body, were enough to bring a look of true madness to Ann's face. I know now that what I did was wrong, but I still find it hard to feel badly about it because I think my actions may have been what caused Ann to make her great confession.

I shall never forget that day, in 1706, when Ann had Reverend Joseph Green read her formal apology to the victims of Salem. Her words cut through to the very heart of the terror that had enslaved us all in its madness and began the real healing. I remember every word as if she were standing before me.

"I desire to be humbled before God," Ann Putnam said, " for the sad and humbling providence that befell my father's family in the year about '92; that I, then being in my childhood, should, by such providence of God, be made an instrument for the accusing of several persons of a grievous crime, whereby their lives were taken away from them, whom now I have just grounds and good reason to believe they were innocent persons; and that it was a great delusion of Satan that deceived me in that sad time, whereby I justly fear I have been instrumental, with others, though ignorantly and unwittingly, to bring upon myself and this land the guilt of innocent blood; though what was said or done by me against any person I can truly and uprightly say, before God and man, I did it not out of anger, malice, or ill-will to any person, for I had no such thing against one of them; but what I did was ignorantly, being deluded by Satan. And particularly, as I was chief instrument of accusing Goodwife Nurse and her two sisters, I desire to lie in the dust, and to be humbled for it, in that I was the cause, with others, of so sad a calamity to them and their families; for which I desire to lie in the dust, and earnestly beg forgiveness of God, and from all those unto whom I have given just cause of sorrow and offense, whose relations were taken away or accused."

In a way, Ann Punam's words gave birth to the mysteries that began to unfold in my own life. I remember running to the Gallows Hill cave and sharing what Ann had said with Hannibelle and Mercy. After I had finished, I looked at them both and began to laugh until the tears ran down my face.

"Stop that right now," I remember Hannibelle saying as she shook me harshly."

"Stop what?" I cried merrily, breaking into a fresh burst of laughter.

"That insane cackle," said Hannibelle.

"I can't help it, Mistress Black. It was such a funny sight watching Ann cowering beside Joseph Green as he spoke the words she was too much of a coward to speak for herself. Can't you see how ridiculous she is?"

"I don't see that at all," said Mercy sadly. "It seems that she is more to be pitied than laughed at, Dorcas. Look at her. She is but a shadow of what she should have been. All the money and lands that the Putnams received through the blood of the innocent lie upon her soul and bring her no pleasure. She lives in a hell far worse than your mother's."

"Than let her!" I said, "'tis fitting punishment."

"If you go on like this you'll never be able to help your mother, Dorcas," said Hannibelle with a withering look in my direction.

"What do you mean?"

"What I mean is that a heart filled with bitterness and revenge has no room left in it for the power of the spirits. I see now why our progress has been slow and you have been an unwilling pupil. Admit it now, Dorcas, your heart has been filled with blackness despite all your fine words of duty and sacrifice."

"'Tis true," I said with a sigh, angry at her words and yet knowing that the truth could not be denied, "but I don't know what to do about it. This town seems to echo with the pain and hurt of what we have all been through. How can I free myself of it?"

"By going back to the beginning and remembering it all," said Hannibelle.

"How do I do that?"

"I don't know," said Hannibelle.

"But I do," said Mercy jumping up and down like a young girl despite her graying curls. "We could write it all down, every bit of it, and journey through Dorcas' life together. It would be such fun!"

"But I can't write," I said, horrified by the idea of reliving the hell that had been my life.

"But I can," said Hannibelle. "Tomorrow night we begin your diary, Dorcas Good."

"And if I refuse?"

"Then we will write it for you and make up the parts that we don't know about," said Mercy as she put her arms around me. "Do this for us and your Mama, Dorcas. But most of all, do it for yourself. Can't you see that you will never be truly free until you let go of the past. There is no future for you unless you do as we say."

"All right," I said, giving the little woman a hug, "I'll do it."

SIXTY EIGHTH ENTRY

And so that is how you came to be, Little Book, and glad I am for it. If not for you I would have spent the rest of my days drowning in bitterness and filled with the blackness of my hate. From the moment Hannibelle wrote the first words, on paper stolen from Reverend Green's study, my heart began to open to the spirit world. The physical world that my body existed in retreated to the shadows and I only really lived when I made my way to the Gallows Hill cave. My father had long since given up trying to talk to me and let me do as I pleased as long as I bothered no one and ate little. I'm sure that he would have turned me away from his door if he could have, but the law said that I was his chattel. He was responsible for my keep and would be held accountable if I starved.

The town thought me mad, indeed, as I made my way between William Good's shack to my cave, night after night, but it was a quiet madness that harmed no one. Little did they know that I was sane beyond belief and being filled with knowledge they could never hope to gain.

I watched and waited during those silent years that were crowded with the loving spirit of my mother and the other victims of the Salem witch trials. The town about me kept churning and moving with its own concerns but it had no power to touch me.

Many involved with the trials had left, and those that remained were busily trying to forget anything had ever happened or even more busily trying to reap some reward from their losses. Reverend Parris and his family moved away after his wife died. I heard that little Betty had grown into a fine young woman and married. Of the other 'afflicted' girls I knew little except to hear that Mary Walcott and Mercy Lewis had also wed after leaving Salem. Mercy Lewis had the shame of bearing her baby first and then finding a husband. To my surprise I learned that Abigail Williams went as mad as people thought me.

As for me, I lived on, doing as Hannibelle Black and Mercy Phillips told me. I spoke my story to them as Hannibelle set it on paper. My great task was to learn how to open my mind and body to the visions from the otherworld. I found the Goddess that had long ago haunted my dreams and felt her soothing healing fill my soul as I stretched my thoughts toward her. Once or twice I questioned Hannibelle about the rightnesss of adding a Goddess to my own Christian beliefs and was told that my Goddess/Friend had always worked together with the God I knew from my childhood. I found Hannibelle's answer confusing, but accepted her words. How could I deny the miracle that filled me each sunset?

So the years passed, and I watched as William Good sank deeper and deeper into his cups, barely knowing me somedays, and remembering me only as a small child on others. I forget exactly when it was, but sometime around the fall of 1709 I asked Hannibelle to move in with us. I was beginning to be afraid of father's violent moods and terrified he might take me to his bed despite my continued pretense of having the French disease. It was becoming very hard to keep up my farce because by now I should have been disfigured or become blind. I covered my face as I walked through town, but it was impossible to hide my continued wholeness from William. Both Hannibelle and Mercy had warned me that there would come a day when my disguise would no longer be believed by my father. I knew that sooner or later I would have to leave Salem if I wanted to remain free of William's evil hand. I found myself praying that he would die first, but Mercy said that I had to stop such thoughts because they kept the Goddess from me. The faster we made an end to the horror on Gallows Hill the sooner I could escape Salem.

By the winter of 1710 I knew we were close. The diary was almost finished and now my mind traveled with ease between my world and my mother's. It was with an empty sadness that I realized that soon my body would follow my mind to pass through the veil and lead the lost souls of Salem to freedom. The lost souls had been my only companions, save for Mercy and Hannibelle, and I would be lost without them if we were parted after they became free. I lived in dread of the day I would find myself standing alone outside my cave, free of obligation, but also free of the task that had given my life its meaning for so long.

It was on the morning of January 21st, 1711, that Hannibelle woke me. A strange light filled her eyes and her dress was torn. I could see that there were bruises on her arms. She was speaking to me, but her words were hard to understand.

"We must make plans to leave this very night," she said, trying to form her words though split lips.

It was then that I understood what had happened. For the past several weeks father had been coming home and beating me, but this was the first time he had ever attacked Hannibelle. Up to now we had believed that he was afraid of her, but from the look of my friend his lust had overcome his fear.

"Do you think we can finish our work?" I said as I shook the sleep from me.

"I'm sure we can," said Hannibelle. She moved stiffly to the place were we kept a small sack filled with dried meat and warm clothing. Ever since father's drinking had become worse we had talked about having to leave quickly.

It was then that we heard the hoofs of my father's horse and knew that our immediate escape would have to wait. I watched with fear as my father entered our small home and threw a heavy bag on the table.

"See now, Dorcas Good, what a little work will bring ye?" he said as he gleefully poured a mound of silver on the table. "Eighteen years I've waited for this and now it's mine!"

"What do you mean?" I asked as I watched him run his hands though the shimmering metal.

"What I mean is that worthless mother of yours has finally been of some use to me," said William with a cruel laugh. "Tis a pity you weren't hanged too, daughter. It makes me sick to think of what you might have brought me, you being a child and all. I tried to get something for your madness and your dead sister, but the judge said that only dead witches brought silver."

"I don't understand," I said, stung by his words despite myself.

"Of course you don't," said William, "you being half daft and all. This here money is my reward for having lost your bitch of a mother to Gallows Hill. It's what I've been waiting for these many years. This very morning the Deacon, Benjamin Putnam, came to me at the tavern as respectful as you please, and told me to put my mark to the paper that would give me my due. 'Tis a fine gentlemen he is and a smart one too. He'll be comin' by any moment now to enjoy you while I'm off to the tavern, Daughter."

"What!" I cried, staring at William with hate.

"Aye, 'tis true you little liar. You've no more the French disease that I have, Dorcas Good, and since ye didn't die and bring me thirty pounds silver like your mother, I'll have to get it another way."

"I'll not do it!" I screamed as I flung myself at him.

"Aye you will," said William, drawing a rope from his waist and knocking me to the floor. Hannibelle, who had been standing in the corner, tried her best to stop him, but William was still a powerful man and we soon found ourselves bound together. The knock at the door told me that it was to late to run.

"Welcome, Brother Putnam," said my father as he opened the door and ushered in the deacon.

"Take your pleasure as ye may," said my father. "I'm off to Ingersolls to celebrate. Do as you're bid Dorcas Good, and mayhaps I'll not bloody ye too much for being such a lair," said my father as he slammed the door behind him.

SIXTY NINTH ENTRY

The sickness of Deacon Putnam's touch was beyond belief. He left me bleeding from every delicate part of my body and crying into the dark for my long dead Mama. Dear Hannibelle tried to soothe me when we were once again tied to each other and left in the dark, but nothing she could say could heal my wounded body and soul. That was something that only my beloved mother's touch could have done.

We waited in terror and pain for my father to return. And return he did, so drunk that he almost seemed happy. I suppose I can count it a blessing that he was in a kinder mood than when he left. I held my breath as he stooped down and merrily untied the ropes that held us.

"There now, you see how sweet your father can be?" he said. "Just bide with me as I take my rest and everything will be as it was before, Daughter."

"It will?" I said as I tried to move my legs.

"Aye, that it will," said William falling upon the bed. "The night's too cold for you to run and where would you go, half dressed as you are, if you did. You may be dull-witted, Dorcas, but even you know better than to take your chances out in such a storm."

I got to my feet and said nothing as I watched, for what seemed an eternity, while William sank into a drunken stupor. Then I motioned for Hannibelle to open the door while I got our warm clothes and food from their hiding place. At the last moment I remembered Mama's pipe, took it from its hiding place behind the hearth, and slipped it into my pocket.

William was right about one thing. The night was an evil one and Hannibelle reached for my hand as we stepped out into the merciless wind. It was not until we had reached the fence that marked the end of the small homestead that Hannibelle and I stopped to wrap our warm shawls about us.

"I hate to leave without saying farewell to Mercy," I said as I fought to make my way through the thickening snow.

"Perhaps she will be at Gallows Hill waiting for us, dear," said Hannibelle. "Mercy often guesses what comes next."

"How true," I said as I prayed for the strength to reach our cave alive.

The night was dark and we found it hard going as we stumbled along. The streets that my feet had trod all my life were buried beneath the heavy white snow and looked unfamiliar to me.

"I'm afraid we're lost," I cried to Hannibelle above the wind."

"No we're not," she screamed back. "Look ahead, Dorcas. I see the lights shining from Judge Corwin's window!"

Sure enough, Hannibelle was right. Directly ahead of us was the large brown structure that housed the Corwin family. We used the blessed light that shone from the windows to guide us towards the path that would take us to Gallows Hill. It occurred to me as we struggled on towards our destination that Hannibelle and I were following the same path Mama had taken to her death so many years ago. The thought filled my heart with hate as I looked back at the Corwin house. Suddenly I halted as the anger welled up inside of me. I narrowed my eyes and spat in the direction of the Corwin house. The only reward I received for my action was a face full of spit. I could hear Hannibelle laughing and turned on her in fury.

"What's so funny!"

"You are," said Hannibelle. "Here we are fighting for our lives in this blizzard and you take the time to do such a thing. From the look on your face I can tell that you've learned the only reward you get from revenge is a dirty face."

"And a friend who thinks its funny when you get a face full of spit," I said.

"Hurry now," said Hannibelle taking my hand. "Its only a little bit further!"

The last part of our journey was the hardest as we left the path and began to climb through the wooded thickets and stony incline that led to the cave beneath Gallows Hill.

"Hello there!" I heard a voice call as I fell against a large tree a few feet from the cave entrance, "I thought you had changed your mind."

It was to my heart's delight that I saw the small round figure of Mercy Phillips beckoning us onward. Hannibelle and I gathered our skirts and lightly crossed the last bit of snowy ground that remained between us and the cave.

"Welcome home, my dears," said Mercy as she held her lantern high and led the way towards our secret room.

Never before had I felt such joy as that night when I walked towards our secret room. The silvery stones that lined the walls shimmered as we passed and filled me with a peace not of this world. I could tell by the way the light flickered around Mercy and Hannibelle that they were feeling something of what was filling me. I tried to keep my thoughts on the task that lay ahead of me, but found my mind wandering back to its earliest days of sunshine and Mama's smile. It was only when I entered the great chamber of the cave that I realized where I truly was.

"Now," said Mercy Phillips as she set the lantern down, "are we ready?"

"I think so," I said, suddenly filled with fear. It had been easy to come to this place night after night and imagine this moment, but now that it was finally here I doubted if I had the strength or power to do what Mama had asked of me. How I longed to run back down the underground path and flee into the cruel night. A gentle death in the white snow would be easy compared to what lay ahead for Dorcas Good.

"Oh Mama," I cried as I fell to my knees, "please don't make me do this. What you ask of me is impossible. Can't you see that I'm only one small person, alone and afraid."

"You're wrong, my daughter," came my mother's voice from the air around me. "You have never been alone. Both on this earth and in the otherworld you have sisters and brothers beyond number. Look to your two companions, the faithful ones who have been your only friends through your journey, and tell me what you really see."

"I see Mercy Phillips and Hannibelle Black," I said, "my heart and my mind. Without them I would have been a lifeless soul wandering about this earth in a meaningless body."

"And there is your answer, my dearest daughter. Close your eyes and beckon them to come closer, closer than they have ever been before. Beseech them to make you whole as you once were."

"You know what she asks?" I said, looking first at Hannibelle and then at Mercy.

313

"Yes, Dorcas," said Hannibelle with a sigh. "Mercy and I have always known that the day would come when you realized we were but a part of you and nothing unto ourselves."

"Oh Dorcas," said Mercy, stretching her arms towards me, "can't you see that it was for this that we were made. Do you think Hannibelle and I have been truly happy wandering about by ourselves, never complete. Do as your mother wishes and let us be as we always should have been, the mind, and heart of Dorcas Good."

"But what if I fail?"

"Then you fail," said Hannibelle, ever the practical one. "But you must know that you will not have really lost anything. You must know, Dorcas, that Mercy and I never existed anywhere but in your own mind. Think back to the day we appeared in your cell when you were but a small child."

"My Mama had just died and Nicholas Noyes had brought me pain beyond belief," I said, trying to see the fading forms of my dearest companions through the fog that now encircled them.

"And what else," said Mercy in a whispery voice almost beyond hearing.

"The devil had come to me in the form of the boy, Barnabas. I remember that I fainted in an outer chamber of the jail and when I came to, you were there!"

"And we stayed with you until you left the jail," said Hannibelle.

"Yes, I remember," I said, "and then you disappeared, not to be seen again until that day I was taken from the stocks."

"We have come and gone only at your bidding, Dorcas Good," said Hannibelle, "and now it is time to say good-bye. Keep 'The Diary of Dorcas Good' in remembrance of us and guard it closely. There may come a time when you wish someone to find it and tell your story. Through it you have been made whole and may help others to do the same. For now, you must become real, Dorcas, joined in mind, soul, and heart into one body. We will always be with you, a part of you, but now it is time for us to go."

"Then you were never real?" I asked, realizing that somehow I had always known the answer to my own question.

"No darling, we were never real," said Mercy as she disappeared into the fog, "but we always loved you."

"Good-bye, Dorcas Good," said Hannibelle as she turned and followed her companion into the unknown.

SEVENTIETH ENTRY

I stood there in the dark for what seemed an eternity and then faced
the wall that my friends had passed through. I knew now what Mama had
been trying to tell me. The strength I thought had belonged to
Hannibelle Black and Mercy Phillips had always belonged to me and me
alone. I was Dorcas Good, daughter of Sarah Good and beloved of
Captain Jack Quelch, but beyond that I was Dorcas Good, survivor of the
Salem witch trials. I had passed through fire and come out the other side,
stronger and more powerful than anyone could imagine. The trials I had
been through at the hands of mankind had only served to refine the gold
that lay within me until I was ready to take on the great task that I was
made for, the freeing of the lost souls of Salem.

"I'm ready now," I said as I closed my eyes and thought of that long ago
green-blue sea two small girls had played upon. It was with joy that I felt
the salty warmth of the waves crashing against me and felt my body being
lifted and hurled into its seductive fury. I gasped as the air left my body
and then cried out in ecstasy as I was filled with something more wonderful than human breath, the caress of my mother's hands as she welcomed
me into her otherworld.

"Wake now daughter and see what you have left behind," she said as
she gently touched my eyes.

I opened my eyes and found that I could see through the veil of the
otherworld back into the cave where I had left my body. To my horror, I
watched the stones that formed the shimmering inner cave begin to crack
and then to fall upon my poor abandoned body, crushing the earthly
Dorcas Good and her Diary beneath the weight of the rocks of Gallows
Hill.

"Let go of your body, my daughter," said my mother as she took my
hand and calmly began to lead me away from the darkening veil. "What
good has it ever been to you?"

315

"None," I said as I felt her calmness flooding my body. "But Mama, what of my Diary? Hannibelle said that it might be found someday, a day when it might do some good."

"And perhaps it will, Dorcas, but that is far in the future. As for now, there is much to be done.

"Much to be done, Mama? I thought that when I passed through the veil our souls would be freed of this place."

"And that they are, Daughter, that they are," said my mother smiling as she guided me through the solid rock and onto the summit of Gallows Hill.

"Look below you, Dorcas Good. There lies Salem. From this night forward you and I shall wander through its streets, calling home to our bosoms all who have harmed us."

"And that would bring you joy, Mama?"

"Great joy and glorious freedom, my beloved daughter."

"Then so be it," I said as I looked out over the town and thought of Nicholas Noyes and William Good.

BIBLIOGRAPHY

Barstow, Anne Llewellyn. *Witchcraze*. London, 1994.

Bonfanti, Leo. *The Witchcraft Hysteria of 1692*. Wakefield, MA, 1971.

Suter, John Wallace (Cust.) The Book of Common Prayer. Greenwich, CT, 1953.

Boston Public Library. Department of Rare Books and Manuscripts. Boston, MA, 1939.

Boyer, Paul and Stephen Nissenbaum. *Salem Possessed: The Origins of Witchcraft*. Cambridge, MA, 1974.

Cahill, Robert Ellis. *Horrors of Salem's Witch Dungeon, Collectible Classics, #9*. Peabody, MA, 1987.

Campbell, Joseph. *The Hero With a Thousand Faces*. New York, NY, 1949.

Campbell, Joseph. *The Power of Myth*. New York, NY, 1988.

Campbell, Joseph. *Transformations of Myth Through Time*. New York, NY, 1990.

Cooper, Somes F.F. Jr. and Kenneth Minkema. *The Sermon Notebook of Samuel Parris, 1689-1694*. Boston, MA, 1993.

Daley, Donald R. *The Tryal of Sarah Good*. Salem, MA.

Lawson, Deodat. *A Brief and True Narrative*. Boston, MA, 1692.

Essex County Court Archives. *Salem Witchcraft Papers*. Salem, MA.

Fleming, Sanford. *Children and Puritanism*. New Haven, CT, 1933.

Frost, Archie N. *The Salem Witchcraft Papers*. New York, NY, 1986.

Hill, Francis. *A Delusion of Satan*. New York, NY, 1995.

Irons, Gregory and Harry Knill. *Pirates*. Santa Barbara, CA, 1985.

Jackson, Shirley. *The Witchcraft of Salem Village*. New York, NY, 1956.

Kences, James E. *Some Unexplained Relationships of Essex County Witchcraft to the Indian Wars of 1675*. Peabody-Essex Institute Historical Collections, Vol. 120. Salem, MA, 1984.

Levin, David. *What Happened in Salem*. New York, NY, 1960.

Peabody-Essex Institute. *The Salem Witchcraft Papers, Fowler Collection*. Salem., MA.

Pepper, Elizabeth and John Wilcock. *The Witches Almanac*. Santa Barbara, CA, 1996.

Perley, Sidney. *The History of Salem Massachusetts, 3 Vols.*, Salem, MA.

Phillips, James Duncan. *Salem in the Seventeenth Century*. Cambridge, MA, 1933.

Robinson, Enders A. *The Devil Discovered: Salem Witchcraft of 1692*. New York, NY, 1970.

The Salem Witchcraft Papers: Verbatim Transcripts of the Legal Documents of the Salem Witchcraft Outbreak of 1692. New York, NY, 1972.

Trask, Richard B. The Devil Hath Been Raised. West Kennebunk, ME, 1992.

Ulrich, Laurel Thatcher. *Good Wives: Image and Reality in the Lives of Women in Northern New England, 1650-1750*. New York, NY, 1980.

Wendell, Barrett. *Cotton Mather*. New York, NY, 1980.